CBB1987

DATE DUE

KILL THE SHOGUN

KILL THE SHOGUN

DALE FURUTANI

A SAMURAI MYSTERY

WILLIAM MORROW
An Imprint of HarperCollinsPublishers

HarperCollins books may be purchased for educational, business, or sales promotional use. For information please write: Special Markets Department, HarperCollins Publishers Inc., 10 East 53rd Street, New York, NY 10022.

FIRST EDITION

Designed by Ann Gold

Printed on acid-free paper

Library of Congress Cataloging-in-Publication Data

Furutani, Dale.
    Kill the shogun : a samurai mystery / Dale Furutani.—1st ed.
        p. cm.
    ISBN 0-688-15819-6 (alk. paper)
    1. Tokugawa, Ieyasu, 1543–1616—Assassination attempts—Fiction.
    2. Matsuyama Kaze (Fictitious character)—Fiction. 3. Samurai—Japan—
Tokyo—Fiction. 4. Shoguns—Assassination attempts—Fiction.
    5. Tokyo (Japan)—Fiction. 6. Japan—History—Tokugawa period,
1600–1868—Fiction. I. Title.

PS3556.U778 K55 2000
813'.54—dc21

                                                            00-022438

00   01   02   03   04   RRD   10   9   8   7   6   5   4   3   2   1

I was adopted. The man who adopted me was not blessed with great intellectual gifts. I can remember him telling me when I was young, with great embarrassment, that he had an IQ of only 75. Even as a child, I knew his shame over this number was unfair and uncalled for.

He was a merchant seaman, and in those days there really wasn't much to do at sea except read. He grew to love reading, even though it was a struggle for him. I can remember him sitting at the kitchen table at home in the evening, with a book or magazine in front of him and a dictionary, written for junior high school students, so he could look up words he didn't know.

Because he worked so hard at it, I got the notion that reading, and by extension writing, must be pretty important. This book, and every book I write, is a result of his love of reading, which prompted my love of writing.

MAJOR CHARACTERS

In this book, names follow the Japanese convention, in which the family name is listed first, then the given name. Therefore, in "Matsuyama Kaze" (Mat-sue-yah-mah Kah-zay), Matsuyama is the family name and Kaze the given name.

Boss Akinari, a gambling boss
Goro, a peasant
Hanzo, a peasant
Hideyoshi, the former ruler of Japan
Honda, a *daimyo* and *hatamoto* of Ieyasu's
Inatomi Gaiki (also called Inatomi-sensei), a master gunsmith
Jitotenno, a brothel owner
Kiku-chan, a young girl
Matsuyama Kaze, a *ronin*
Momoko, a would-be Kabuki actress
Nakamura, a *daimyo*
Niiya, a vassal of Yoshida's
Nobu, a gambler
Okubo, a *daimyo* and enemy of Kaze's
Tokugawa Ieyasu, the new Shogun
Toyama, a *daimyo*
Yoshida, a *daimyo*

EDO (OLD TOKYO), 1603

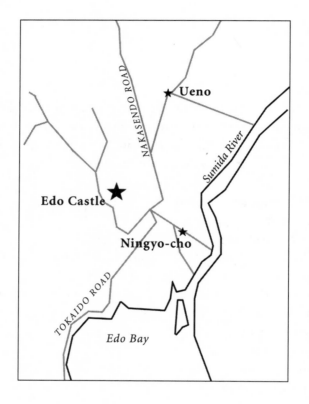

KILL THE SHOGUN

CHAPTER 1

Delicate feathers,
speed, grace, style, and elegance.
Death in an instant.

Japan, the year of the Rabbit, 1603

She looked for something to kill. When she was taken from hooded darkness, it was because something was supposed to die. Her sharp eyes scanned the sky, looking for movement or a patch of dark against either the blue sky or the billowing white and gray clouds.

It was the month of No Gods, and soon it would be the month of White Frost, so the day was not hot. Still, even on a cool day, the sun heated up patches of rock and earth, forming weak thermals that made invisible pillars in the air. Her delicate feathers sought these thermals like sensitive instruments, instinct telling her to use the columns of rising air to loiter in the sky as she sought out her prey. She encountered the buffeting of rising air and banked her wings to spiral into the thermal, constantly sweeping the sky with her bright eyes.

She gave two flaps of her powerful wings, the column of air not being strong enough on a cool day to keep her aloft without effort. Below, the steep hills were densely covered with trees. The fall colors were just beginning to tinge the landscape like the delicate strokes of a kimono painter, touching brush to silk and watching the rich hues spread across the tightly woven, shimmering cloth.

A movement invaded the periphery of one eye and the majestic bird cocked its head to track it. A dove, flying across the treetops. The hawk curled its wing feathers and made a tight bank. With a few beats of its wings, the hunter increased its speed to catch up to the hunted.

The dove was still unaware that mortality was approaching. It was intent on reaching the rice paddies on the horizon, where its own prey, grubs and worms, would be in abundance. The hawk increased its speed as it trimmed back its wings to plummet down on the dove.

At the last moment, the dove heard the rustle of wind in wings, then the needle-sharp talons of the hawk punctured its body.

With a few slow beats of its wings, the hawk rose higher into the sky, still clutching its dying prey. It made a wide semicircle until it spotted the group of men on horseback, and it started making its way back. One of the men held up a leather-covered arm to the bird, inviting it to return to the perch where it would get a tasty morsel to reward it for its successful hunt.

As the hawk approached the hunting party, its sharp eyes noticed another group of men. This group was hiding in the rocks near the men on horseback. Like the hawk, they were also hunters seeking their prey.

The two men had cloths tied around their heads, covering the bottom of their faces. One slowly raised his head above the rocks so he could get a clear view of the hunting party. The man next to him also rose and held out three fingers with his hand. Then he pointed to the right.

The first man counted three figures from the right and stared intently at the face of his intended victim. Even at this distance, it was easy to make out the features of the man he would eventually kill. He found it interesting that this man, secure in his power and lofty position, was actually a dead man. He simply didn't know it yet.

Tokugawa Ieyasu, the newly named Shogun and ruler of all Japan, felt the familiar weight of the hawk settle on his arm. He cooed at the bird and gently stroked its head with one finger. A servant went to pick up the dead dove where the hawk had dropped it and ran over to show it to the Shogun. Ieyasu nodded and turned his attention back to the hawk. He was pleased with the efficiency of the bird's kill. Ieyasu was a man who valued efficiency.

The servant took out a knife and cut a strip of flesh from the dove's body. He handed it to Ieyasu.

"Here, my pretty one," Ieyasu said, feeding the piece of meat to the hawk. "See, Honda, how she enjoys the treat! She is an extremely intelligent hawk."

Honda, renowned for his gruffness, growled, "If the bird were smart, it would keep the entire kill for itself."

Ieyasu looked at his other companion and said, "What do you think, Nakamura-san? Is it proper that the bird only gets a portion of that which she killed? Is she a dumb beast for not flying away and taking it all?"

"No, my Lord, it is not improper. *Takagari*, hawk hunting, goes back to the Emperor Nintoku, over twelve hundred years ago. It is a noble sport and one that follows natural principles. Everyone can see that there is a hierarchy in nature, so it is reasonable that this bird should have a master, just as men do. You are this hawk's master. You have worked with her and trained her to do your bidding. Each time you hunt with her, you stand the chance of losing her. But you have not lost her. She accepts that you are her master. She has returned to you and is quite content to eat whatever you choose to give her. It was her choice not to seek freedom and the ability to eat the entire dove."

"For goodness' sake, Nakamura, you make everything sound like a lesson from a priest. It's a dumb beast. You make it sound like a vassal!" Honda snapped.

"Well," Nakamura said, "in a way it is a vassal. It tenders its services to Ieyasu-sama and in return it's very happy to accept any rewards the Shogun chooses to give it. So it is with the men who fight for Ieyasu-sama."

"I fight because I am a *Mikawa bushi,* a warrior of Mikawa!" Honda shouted. "Next you'll be claiming that this beast understands *bushido!*"

Totally unconcerned about Honda's rising anger and red face, Nakamura said, "Well, you bring up an interesting point. I wonder if there is such a thing as bird bushido? Maybe we should make a study of it?"

Before Honda exploded, Ieyasu stepped in. "Next you'll be talking about rabbit judges and badger physicians," he said. "While it's true that animals can have many human traits, you go too far when you say that animals have a sense of bushido, Nakamura-san."

Nakamura dipped his head and said, "I'm sorry, Ieyasu-sama. You must excuse the ramblings of a man who now has too much time on his hands."

Ieyasu was used to keeping his own counsel and masking his thoughts from appearing on his face. Despite the rebuke he had just given Nakamura, he was quite amused by the notion of bird bushido. But Honda was taking Nakamura's musings much too seriously, and it was easier to rebuke the scholarly Nakamura than it was to calm the volatile Honda.

In his response, however, Ieyasu noted that Nakamura had returned a subtle rebuke of his own. Nakamura was scholarly but also ambitious. He wanted a larger role in the new order for Japan that Ieyasu was creating, and claiming he had too much time on his hands was his way of calling this to the Shogun's attention. Ieyasu was glad that understanding such a subtle response was beyond Honda's abilities, or perhaps there would be a clash between these two vassals that would extend beyond words. Taming men was sometimes like taming hawks. Although Nakamura was scholarly, he was also brave, and Ieyasu had seen him in the heat of battle, calmly discussing Chinese poetry, stopping only to give orders to his troops.

Honda, on the other hand, was of the old school of warrior. A rough country *bushi* who was given to earthy humor and bursts of temper. Subtlety was beyond him. Honda had been with Ieyasu from the beginning, when the young Tokugawa had recovered his fief of Mikawa and labored to restore his clan to a point of respectability. It had taken decades, and many battles, but now the Tokugawas were preeminent in Japan and anyone who could claim to be a Mikawa bushi, a warrior from Ieyasu's original fief of Mikawa, did so proudly.

Ieyasu wondered how many of his old guard, his original Mikawa bushi, ever thought they would go from obscurity to the rulership of Japan. It helped that Ieyasu had his health and a long life, but it also helped that Ieyasu had always harbored an ambition to be Shogun. Sometimes the vagaries of life's twists and turns could be nudged in the right direction if you knew what your eventual goal was.

Time had linked Honda and Ieyasu together like nothing else can. They had seen many battles and defeated many enemies, one by one. Ieyasu trusted Honda implicitly, and he felt most comfortable when he was among rough warriors like Honda. But he knew the qualities that made Honda a valuable general in ruthless battle were not the qualities that would lead him to his eventual goal, establishing a dynasty. It would be the cultured warriors, the men like Nakamura, who would be critical to building a government that would outlast his lifetime. //

Nakamura was a member of the group of nobles who had joined Ieyasu's camp after Sekigahara, the *tozama*. Honda was a member of the *fudai,* the loyal retainers who had, over the years, helped Ieyasu reach the pinnacle of power. The tozama would always be a little suspect, especially ones like Nakamura, who were a bit too intellectual. Too much thinking by a vassal could be a dangerous thing to the person in power.

Still, despite his misgivings, Ieyasu knew he had to draw on men like Nakamura and similar types, such as Okubo, Toyama, and Yoshida, to set up a stable government. So far, Ieyasu had rewarded the tozama much more lavishly than the fudai. While a fudai vassal would get a fief of 30,000 to 50,000 *koku,* a koku being the amount of rice needed to feed a warrior for a year, a tozama vassal might get a fief five to ten times that size. This caused dissatisfaction amongst the fudai, but Ieyasu simply expected the fudai to be loyal. He felt he must buy the loyalty of the tozama and watch them closely in the bargain, too.

The previous two rulers of Japan, Nobunaga and Hideyoshi, did not have their dynasty last past their own lives. As with the dove, mortality intruded while they had their eyes set on the horizon. Ieyasu intended to have his dynasty live long past him, and he prayed to the Gods that he would have just a few more years to establish a firm foundation for the Tokugawa Shogunate.

Ieyasu was in his early sixties, but his age was a little misleading. He was born in the year of the Dragon, just five days before the change to the year of the Snake. Being born in the year of the

Dragon was a most auspicious sign for a samurai, although his family was not then powerful. When he was born, Ieyasu was considered to be one year old. Every baby existed for almost a year in the mother's womb, and, besides, Japanese logic dictated that no one could be zero years old. Just six days later, on New Year's Day, Ieyasu, and everyone else in Japan, was considered one year older. Therefore, Ieyasu was only out of his mother's womb six days, but he was considered two years old.

Ieyasu looked about the small meadow his party was in and said, "Let's try our luck in that direction." He pointed to the direction of the horse, due south. He handed the hawk to one of the falconers and set off in the direction he indicated.

When the hawking party was safely out of sight, the men hiding in the rocks came out.

"I know who now, but tell me when."

"Tomorrow, Ieyasu-sama will make a formal inspection of how the work on the new castle in Edo is progressing. It's a large, open site, with many buildings around its periphery. There will be a large entourage with Ieyasu-sama, all the key *daimyo,* and probably a large crowd will gather to get a glimpse of the new Shogun. You can do it then."

"All right," the first man said. "Consider it accomplished."

CHAPTER 2

Balancing on a
narrow edge of shiny steel.
How confined is life.

The bright faces of children watched the battle intently.

"Give back the treasure!" the brave samurai said.

"I'll never give it back!" the hairy ogre replied.

"All right, I've warned you! I shall take my sword 'Ogre Killer' and thrash you!"

"Owww! Owww! Owww! *Itai!* It hurts!" the ogre shouted.

And the children laughed.

The children were gathered around a *kami-shibai,* a paper play, and they were watching a new world unfold for them within the confines of a wooden box. The box was mounted on spindly wooden legs and it formed a miniature stage. A sheet of painted paper formed the backdrop, setting the scene for the battle in a fantastic forest of gnarled trees with brooding branches. Dark, painted shadows splayed out from the brown tree trunks, giving the appearance of a sinister spiderweb. The actors were two painted paper cutouts, pasted on bamboo skewers. The kami-shibai man manipulated the skewers as he spun his tales of warriors, myths, and monsters.

The children watched with rapt attention, chewing on cheap

senbei, rice crackers, the purchase of which was the price of admission to the show. Near the edges of the crowd, a few ragamuffins stole pleasure by watching the show without purchasing a cracker, but today the kami-shibai man wasn't concerned. Business was brisk because the crowd was in a festive mood, and the mood had infected all the food sellers and street entertainers who had converged to feed off the gathering.

The entire city of Edo had a boomtown feeling to it as the Tokugawas built their new capital. It actually helped that the entire city almost burned to the ground the year before, because it allowed the Tokugawas to think on a grand scale, laying out vast tracks of land for the mansions of dignitaries and building a new castle. After the fire, the lumber, tile, and stone merchants saw wealth pouring in as material was purchased to rebuild. The only ones who didn't prosper were the thatchers, for the Tokugawas decreed that the roofs of the new Edo were to be made of wood or tile, but not straw, because a thatched roof was too combustible.

The Tokugawa victory at Sekigahara three years before cemented the primacy of their clan in Japan, and it allowed Ieyasu to claim the title of Shogun. A vast flood of humanity started flowing into Edo after Sekigahara, as the Tokugawas recruited skilled stonemasons, carpenters, and artisans of all types to help rebuild Edo on a scale suitable for the new rulers of Japan. The growth of highly paid merchant and artisan classes drew food vendors, prostitutes, street entertainers, gamblers, and thieves, all intent on profiting from the wealth that was in Edo.

From a sleepy fishing village, Edo was being transformed into the new capital of Japan. Now an *Edokko,* a child of Edo, was expected to have a free-spending view of life, with a love of luxury and pleasure. It didn't matter if the person was not born in Edo, because being an Edokko was a state of mind, and within months most new citizens of Edo were caught up in the ebullient spirit that seemed to pervade the very air.

Ieyasu was known for his parsimony and considered waste an affront to heaven. He even had his ladies put their soiled *tabi* socks in a box. When the box was full, he would personally go through it, deciding which socks should be passed on to serving girls and which socks should be retired for rags. For a man of such character, the free-spending ways of his capital were troublesome. He made halfhearted efforts to suppress the profligate spirit of Edo, but nothing could stop the rising tide of optimism that fueled the Edokko's spending.

Given the Edokko's natural predilection to celebrate, almost any occasion was an excuse for a festival. This included the big and important occasions, such as New Year's or O-bon, but it also included anything novel that brought people together. Today the occasion was a formal inspection of the work on Edo-jo, Edo Castle, the Shogun's new stronghold, and a good crowd had gathered to observe the inspection, albeit from a distance.

Tokugawa Ieyasu had been ruler of the Kanto, the rich plain around the Edo area, for only thirteen years. He had been Shogun for less than a year. Many in the crowd had never seen the new ruler of Japan, and this public inspection was an occasion to gaze on the mighty. As people gathered, street entertainers and vendors gathered too, feeding off the press of people and their need to keep amused while waiting for the daimyo and Shogun.

A captain of the guards and four men patrolled the crowd. The captain stopped for a few moments, looking at the kami-shibai puppet play. The dancing figures at the end of the skewers brought back fond memories from the captain's childhood.

The captain looked over the crowd gathered at the edge of the Edo-jo construction site. Before them was the wide ditch that would eventually be filled with water to form a moat. The moat was turning into a benefit of another type, because the soil excavated from it was being used to fill in the marshy land surrounding Edo, providing more room for expansion. The moat spiraled out from the castle, cutting through the city and giving it future opportunities for the creation of additional canals and water-borne commerce. Across the now dry ditch was the stone block wall that would form the outer rampart of the castle. Each block of stone was transported by boat on the Sumida River and brought to the construction site, where skilled stonecutters dressed the large blocks so they would fit together in a cunning puzzle designed to thwart attack.

Behind the crowd, houses and shops formed a thick wall of their own. In crowded Edo, each scrap of land was precious, and the town sprang up wherever the land was not claimed by the Shogun, a daimyo, or a temple. The wooden and paper structures were prone to fire, and sections of Edo caught fire constantly. The only method for fighting the fires was to tear down structures in their path, a task done lustily by the volunteer firemen, who were mostly carpenters and roofers, and who would soon prosper as the structures were rebuilt. Sometimes the authorities had problems restraining the firefighters from tearing down structures that weren't threatened by the fire.

If conditions were right, fires could get out of control and destroy vast sections of the city. Fire towers, called *yagura*, dotted the city, where lookouts were stationed to watch for the first wisps of smoke that could lead to disaster.

Because of the size of Edo Castle, the captain knew the inspection would take most of the day. Eventually, however, the new Shogun would want to inspect this section of wall, so the captain wanted to make sure that order was maintained in the crowd. So far, the crowd seemed to be quiet and in a festive mood. The captain had caught a thief earlier, but he knew the law would ensure that the thief would die within the week, so there would be one less villain on the streets of Edo.

The captain and his men left the children at the puppet play and went to see what another crowd was looking at. A gasp came from the crowd, and the captain motioned for his men to clear a path for him, so he could see what was so interesting. As the crowd became aware that samurai were at its edge, people moved out of the way, bowing politely, so the officer and his men could see.

In the center of the crowd was a free space with a lone man. He was of average height, but muscular. He didn't have the shaved pate of the samurai, and his hair was pulled back into a topknot, but there was something about his bearing that made the captain think he was a military man. With fifty thousand samurai left defeated and unemployed after the Tokugawa victory at Sekigahara, it was not unusual to find ex-samurai trying to make a living at all sorts of enterprises. Many had become farmers, some had become robbers and brigands, some had become merchants, very few had found employment with some lord or daimyo, and many were still wandering Japan, living by their wits and trying to find employment for their blades. This last group were *ronin*—literally, "wave men."

This man had the look of a ronin, but it was hard for the captain to imagine that a real samurai would sink so low as to become a street entertainer.

The man took a large child's wooden top, as wide as the span of his hand, and tightly wound a hemp cord around it. Throwing it with a snap of his wrist while still holding the end of the cord, the man set the top spinning. From a scabbard lying at his feet, the man withdrew a sword. Then, with a quick sweep of the sword, the man picked up the spinning top on the flat of the blade.

The man held the blade steady for a few moments, then he tilted the blade slightly and guided the top down the length of the shiny ribbon of steel. The captain was struck by the quality of the blade. Like all men of his class, he had been trained to judge a sword since he was a child, and this was an exceptionally fine blade. Either the ronin had fallen a great distance from his former station, or he had been extremely lucky at scavenging some forgotten battlefield.

When the top reached the hilt of the sword, the man tilted the blade in the opposite direction and moved the top back to the sword's tip, stopping it there. Then with a smart flip of the blade, he tossed the top in the air and caught it with the opposite side of the sword. He again guided the top down the length of the blade and back to the tip. The captain marveled at the man's control of the sword and the steadiness of his hand. The man was so sure of himself that he even had time to look at the faces of the fascinated children sprinkled throughout the crowd around him. In fact, he almost seemed to be searching for someone.

When the top returned to the tip of the sword, the man gave another flip, but this time he caught the top on the narrow back of the sword blade. The crowd gave another gasp, and this time the captain joined them. With total nonchalance, the man guided the top down the narrow back of the sword up to the sword *tsuba*, or hilt, and back to the tip again. The crowd applauded wildly.

The man kept the top on the sword until it started to lose momentum and wobble, and he tossed it high in the air and caught it with one hand. The crowd gave him generous applause, and a few threw coins into a cloth spread at the man's feet. The man dipped his head to acknowledge the applause, then he looked directly at the captain and smiled.

The captain was surprised that a street entertainer, even one who might have once been a samurai, would be so bold. He was used to townspeople bowing, then keeping their heads down and their eyes averted. He wondered if he should say something to the man, but something in the back of his mind kept nagging at him. He looked at the man's face and knew he was not someone he had met formally, but there was something so familiar about him . . . the captain just couldn't place him. He was turning this puzzle over and over in his mind when someone in the crowd shouted, "There's Ieyasu-sama!"

Snapping to attention, the captain yelled, "Everybody down!"

The crowd fell to their knees, most putting their hands in front of them on the dirt in a proper kowtow. A few mothers called over to their children, gathering them to their sides and showing them the proper, respectful position to assume when in the presence of the Shogun. The captain nodded with approval, and took a look around to make sure that all of the crowd was showing proper respect. He saw, to his surprise, that the man with the tops had vanished.

Taking a quick glance to see if he could spot the man somewhere in the crowd, the captain then joined his men in kneeling, one knee on the ground in a proper military salute to a high superior. The man with the tops still bothered him, but he knew that if he thought about it long enough, he would eventually remember who the man was.

Ieyasu was surrounded by the chief architects of the castle and several daimyo, including Honda, Nakamura, Okubo, Toyama, and Yoshida. He was marching vigorously along the wall. The others trailed him, although Okubo, who had a limp, struggled in his efforts to keep up.

Ieyasu was generally pleased with how the castle was progressing, but didn't let the pleasure show on his face. He had cultivated an image of stoicism and was very conscious of the role he believed he had to play in public.

They had been walking all morning. Ieyasu was famous for his potbelly, but he was also a strict believer in military training and discipline, and was known for his ability to walk, ride, and shoot a musket, all things he practiced diligently. He said that hawking was his favorite sport because it emulated some of the rigors of a military campaign. He was not tired by the inspection tour, but the architects were sweating. Of course, it was more than physical fatigue that had the architects sweating.

"As you can see, Ieyasu-sama, the progress on this part of the wall has been considerable," the chief architect said.

Ieyasu made no comment and just stared at the man. The architect started sweating more profusely. The new Shogun demanded the best quality with all things military, including his new castle. He also demanded frugality. This was a combination difficult to achieve, and throughout the tour the Shogun had found fault with either quality or cost at almost every stop. As the absolute ruler of Japan, with the ability to put to death anyone he wished to, the Shogun was not a man the architect wanted to displease.

"What do you think, Okubo-san?" Ieyasu asked. He picked Okubo to comment first because he was still judging this man and wanted to hear his opinion before he had a chance to see how the other daimyo felt.

"I think only you, Ieyasu-sama, can be the judge of how pleased or displeased you are with the progress of this section of the castle."

Ieyasu made no comment but noted that Okubo's reply revealed nothing about his thoughts or feelings. That kind of reply could be a virtue, and it could also be something else. "And you, Honda?"

Honda looked at the walls on both sides of him and said gruffly, "It's fine. Why do you make the poor architects sweat? Every castle costs too much and has problems."

"And you, Nakamura-san?"

"I suppose one would have to compare the progress and cost of this part of the castle with the rest of the castle," Nakamura began. "Then one sees if the relative progress here was better than the rest of the project. However—"

"Thank you, Nakamura-san," Ieyasu broke in. "And what do you think, Yoshida-san?"

"I agree with Honda-san. The progress here is fine."

Ieyasu secretly agreed, and he was pleased that Yoshida was so direct. Yoshida combined the intelligence of the new daimyo with the directness of Ieyasu's Mikawa bushi, like Honda. Ieyasu liked him.

"And you, Toyama-san?"

"I believe—"

A sharp crack rang out. The daimyo, all experienced warriors, knew immediately it was the sound of a musket. Nakamura grabbed his chest and spun around, falling off the edge of the wall and tumbling like a rag doll down the sloping stone wall of the castle into the dry moat. Ieyasu looked down at Nakamura's body and could tell from the way he landed that Nakamura was dead before he hit the earth.

"Protect the Shogun!" Yoshida shouted, and he followed his words with actions, stepping in front of Ieyasu to shield him. Seeing Yoshida's example, Honda joined him in shielding Ieyasu as the other daimyo took Ieyasu behind the shelter of the wall. The Shogun shrugged off their urging hands and stalked off the wall at his own speed.

CHAPTER 3

The mighty make plans
as if they were immortal.
Worms still gnaw their bones.

It was a sign from heaven," Toyama said. "The divine hand of the Gods, sparing Ieyasu-sama like that."

"Ha! It was just a bad shot. If it was a sign from heaven, heaven was a bit hard on Nakamura-san," Honda said.

Ieyasu entered the teahouse that had been constructed especially for this inspection tour. It was designed to allow the Shogun to rest and take some refreshments. He looked as phlegmatic as ever, although now he had a guard around him that waited at the door. Honda, Toyama, and Okubo were already in the teahouse, but, unlike the Shogun, they were still agitated by the incident.

"Are you all right, Ieyasu-sama?" Toyama asked.

"Of course," Ieyasu said. Toyama's excitement reminded Ieyasu that Toyama had relatively little battle experience. Ieyasu had been in over ninety battles and had survived several assassination plots.

Yoshida entered the teahouse and knelt on one knee in salute.

"Well?" Ieyasu said.

"I mobilized my men," Yoshida said. "They're already starting a search for the assassin."

"Is Nakamura-san dead?"

"I'm sorry, Ieyasu-sama, but Nakamura-san has gone to the void. But we will find the assassins. My men are already talking to the soldiers who were guarding that portion of the crowd."

"I appreciate your efficiency, Yoshida-san," Ieyasu said.

Toyama said, "It must have been someone in the crowd. Surely they must have caught him. It was at least eighty paces from where we were to the edge of the crowd."

"I shoot three shots with a musket every day for practice," Ieyasu observed. "I agree an ordinary gun would not carry much beyond eighty paces, but I have killed a crane at one hundred twenty paces using a gun made by Inatomi Gaiki. If the assassin used such a gun, he could hide on the roof of the houses or the yagura. Have someone check this."

Honda, who had been disturbed by Yoshida's willingness to take charge, jumped in and said, "Of course, Ieyasu-sama. I'll have my men look into this."

Ieyasu noticed Honda's willingness to be of help, but he said, "Yoshida-san's men are already investigating. It would be best to let them finish the investigation, instead of having two groups do it."

Clearly displeased, Honda said, "Yes, Ieyasu-sama."

"I appreciate your standing in front of me to block any additional bullets," Ieyasu said to Honda. "You and Yoshida-san acted quickly to shield me. It is the duty of every retainer to die to protect the life of his lord, but you two had presence of mind and acted quickly." This was a rebuke to Toyama and Okubo, and Ieyasu could see their faces turn red.

"But Ieyasu-sama—" Toyama started.

"I don't want to discuss it now." Ieyasu said this in a calm voice, but Toyama was stopped in mid-sentence by the Shogun's tone. Ieyasu noted with satisfaction that Okubo had enough sense to keep his mouth shut.

Yoshida excused himself to check on the housetops, and Ieyasu said, "Call the chief architect in to see me."

The architect was hurriedly summoned. When he arrived, Ieyasu said, "I've decided we should expand the size of the castle. We should also publish decrees that no building or tower may be constructed which looks down into the castle."

The architect was surprised that Ieyasu could be so calm after an assassination attempt and so interested in discussing military matters. Ieyasu was famous for always mulling over political and military matters. Once, during a dramatic moment in a Noh performance, an art Ieyasu was enough interested in to actually participate in performances, he leaned over to a daimyo and remarked, "I've been thinking, it's just about time to cut the bamboo for military banners."

"How much bigger do you want the castle?" the architect stammered.

"I think fourteen thousand paces for the outer wall will do."

"Fourteen thousand! Ieyasu-sama, that is many times bigger than the current plans!"

"I think today's events justify changing the plans," Ieyasu said coldly.

"Yes, Ieyasu-sama," the architect stammered.

"When you get the new plans done, tell me. I'll have to alert the daimyo that they will be contributing to this project."

Ieyasu dismissed him with a wave of his hand; then he ordered tea and relaxed, as if totally oblivious to the attempt on his life and the death of one of his chief counselors.

I have news," Yoshida reported.

Ieyasu raised an eyebrow, but said nothing, waiting for Yoshida's report. Ieyasu had an undistinguished face, with jowly cheeks and a thin mustache. His eyes were close-set but intense, and his pate was shaved in the standard samurai fashion. His hair was now mostly gray, with only a few stray strands of black.

"We found the fire observer killed in the yagura across from the wall. His throat was slit. So the assassin must have been waiting in the fire watchtower. It's around one hundred and forty paces from the watchtower to the wall, so you were correct that no ordinary gun was used. More importantly, we know who the assassin is."

Ieyasu sat impassively, waiting for Yoshida to finish, but the other daimyo in the teahouse couldn't keep excitement and surprise off their faces.

"One of the guard captains was patrolling the crowd when he saw a street entertainer. The entertainer looked familiar to him, but he couldn't place his face. Then we appeared on the wall and the guard was busy making sure everyone in the crowd was showing proper obeisance.

"After the shot was fired, there was pandemonium in the crowd. The common people were very concerned about your safety, Ieyasu-sama. The guard said he started a search immediately, because, like us, he thought the shot must have come from the crowd. The excited crowd made such a search difficult, but the guard captain swears the street entertainer who caught his eye was no longer in the crowd. Obviously, he had left the crowd to go to the yagura to try to assassinate you, Ieyasu-sama."

"For goodness' sake! Who was this entertainer?" the blunt Honda broke in. Years of friendship made Ieyasu indulge his companion's lack of proper protocol.

Yoshida said a name. "He's still on the list of men we are looking for after Sekigahara," Yoshida added. Ieyasu took a quick glance at Okubo, and he saw the tall daimyo's thin, scarred face cloud over with hate. Interesting.

"Who is that?" asked Toyama. Ieyasu had already decided that

Toyama was a fool and that he would be sending him to a new, remote fief in Shikoku or Kyushu to get rid of him. Although Ieyasu hoped to ensure peace, Toyama's ignorance of military matters was still unacceptable.

"He's the one who won the sword contest Hideyoshi-sama had many years ago," Honda said. "Okubo-san has reason to know him!" Honda's braying laughter filled the small teahouse.

Even Toyama understood this reference. Okubo was crippled because he was a finalist in Hideyoshi's sword contest. Although they used wooden swords for the contest, one samurai was killed because every man tried his utmost to win. In the final match, Okubo was defeated by the overall winner. In the course of this match, the winner had maimed Okubo for life, putting a scar on his face and damaging his left leg.

Okubo tightened his jaw but controlled his anger, something Ieyasu saw and approved of. Many times in his life, Ieyasu had controlled his anger and every other emotion, when he found it beneficial.

"I have some information about that man," Okubo said tightly. "He no longer goes by that name. He now calls himself Matsu-yama Kaze, Wind on Pine Mountain."

"What a weird name," Honda said. "How do you know this?"

"After Sekigahara, that man made trouble for me; then he disappeared," Okubo said. "I thought he had taken the honorable way and killed himself, but recently my men spotted him in Kamakura. They couldn't capture him, but they made inquiries in the town and were able to learn his new name. Unfortunately, they weren't able to locate him before he slaughtered a prominent merchant and his entire household. He's obviously become an outlaw of the worst order and now he's dared to try and kill the Shogun! He must be hunted down like a dog and killed."

"Okubo-san, Honda-san, why don't you both try to find this 'Wind on Pine Mountain' for me," Ieyasu said.

"*Hai!* Yes, Ieyasu-sama," both lords said.

"Good. Yoshida-san will be joining you in this search. In fact, I want him to lead the search." Both daimyo showed considerably less enthusiasm when Ieyasu mentioned Yoshida. With Nakamura gone, perhaps Yoshida would make a good substitute. He dismissed the daimyo with a motion of his hand. They left the teahouse, making the proper bows to the ruler of Japan. Trading on his friendship and status as a *hatamoto,* a direct vassal of the Shogun, Honda lingered after the rest had left.

"You know, I don't think I can be killed with a musket ball," Ieyasu mused.

Honda looked at him with surprise. "Why do you say that?"

Honda counted on his long relationship with Ieyasu to leave off Ieyasu's title, not addressing him as "Ieyasu-sama" when they were together.

"Well, in one battle I was shot twice by musket balls," Ieyasu said. "Both times, the musket balls lodged themselves in my armor and didn't kill me or even wound me. Now I've been shot at again, but this time the ball hit Nakamura-san by mistake, killing him and leaving me totally untouched."

"It's all well and good to believe in your own destiny," Honda said. "But destiny or no, a man is dead if a musket ball hits him in the right spot."

Ieyasu laughed, looking fondly at his old camp companion and fellow warrior. "It's a shame that my new responsibilities take me away from talking to you and my other generals," Ieyasu said. "But my life is changing, and I must take care to establish my rule and my family's rule, and that takes time. I miss the old days, when we would share the warmth of a campfire, talking frankly about any topic that comes up."

Honda looked at Ieyasu, thinking that Ieyasu's words paralleled his own feelings and thoughts. He hated the way life was turning and much preferred the path of war, where he understood the rules. The new age they were moving into disturbed Honda and made him feel like an outsider whose skills were no longer needed.

Ieyasu picked up a cup of tea and took a sip. "So, Honda, what have you been up to?"

Honda looked at Ieyasu and almost blushed. Sitting with his old lord, swapping opinions just as they would do on military campaigns, Honda almost weakened and was ready to confess to Ieyasu what he was doing. But Honda knew that his customary bluntness was not always beneficial.

"I'll be spending my time looking for your would-be assassin, so that we don't have to put to the test your theory that you can't be killed with a musket ball," Honda said. "What do you think? Is this ronin, Matsuyama Kaze, the man who tried to shoot you today?"

Ieyasu, who rarely told people what he thought, answered Honda's question with some questions of his own.

"Do you think this Matsuyama Kaze is a true samurai?"

Honda thought a minute. "He's a dangerous man. That's why he's still on our list of men we want captured. Still, he had a reputation for courage and honor before the war, so I suppose he is probably a true samurai."

"And what are the weapons of the true samurai?"

"The sword and the bow," Honda said without hesitation.

"Exactly," Ieyasu answered.

CHAPTER 4

The bottom of a
deep well on a moonless night.
Darker still a heart.

Toyama put one hand on his sword. It was scary dealing with
these people, and now that he saw the meeting place, his appre-
hensions unfolded like the petals of the night-blooming lotus.

The small abandoned temple was in a grove of bamboo. The
roof sagged from rot and neglect, and the tall weeds grew in profusion right up to the door. A light breeze blew, lifting dried leaves
and idly tossing them against the decaying walls. In the light of
the half-moon, the temple looked deserted and empty, and Toyama briefly wondered if he could have gotten confused on the
directions and somehow ended up at the wrong place.

Toyama lifted the reed basket covering his head to get a better
look. He was disguised as a *komuso*, an adherent to the strange
Fuke sect of Buddhism. These men wandered the countryside,
wearing an inverted basket with eyeholes to mask their identity.
They played the *shakuhachi*, the bamboo flute, as their way of
asking for alms. Increasingly, samurai and ronin were converting
to this sect as they sought escape from defeat and shelter in the
sect's temples. They were becoming a familiar sight on the streets
of Edo, and their unusual headgear formed a perfect disguise.

Since so many samurai were komuso, the disguise had the advantage of letting Toyama wear his swords as he masked his face.

Toyama was quite proud of his selection of disguise, and he was convinced that no one knew where he had gone. The guards by the side gate of his villa were surprised when he left without an entourage, and they asked him if he wanted them to accompany him. He told them no and put the hat of the komuso on. The guards exchanged sly smiles at their master's secrecy, convinced that he was out on an amorous adventure, perhaps to visit the wife of another man.

Even with the impediment of the basket out of the way, Toyama saw no signs of life. Returning the basket to his shoulders, he carefully walked toward the temple. In his hand he carried a lantern. The flickering yellow light, smoothed by the thin paper that surrounded the lantern, allowed him to pick his way between the weeds.

He hesitated a moment at the temple door, holding the lantern out before him so the weak light could penetrate the gloom.

"Come in," a voice said from out of the darkness. Toyama gave a start. He expected someone to be here to meet him, but he could not see where the owner of the voice was standing.

"Your light will let others know we are here." The voice was neutral in its intonation, but the speaker was actually quite annoyed by Toyama's hesitancy. He had seen Toyama's face when the Lord had lifted the komuso's hat, so he was sure who his visitor was. Even without this stupid blunder, the man waiting in the gloom of the temple would know that this man was a daimyo and not a true priest. Toyama had adopted the basketlike hat of the komuso and had even stuck a bamboo flute in his sash, but no komuso could have a silk kimono or lacquered *geta* sandals as fine and expensive as the ones this man wore.

At last, Toyama stepped into the temple. The air in the temple was musty and old and full of dead smells. The inside had a dirt floor and the walls were stripped bare, so Toyama could not tell what God had been worshiped there. The feeble light of the lantern made a weak circle in the center of the floor but didn't penetrate into the gloom beyond.

The man saw Toyama kept his hand on his sword, as if this would protect him, and he smiled. If he wanted, the man could kill Toyama in a hundred ways, most of them not involving weapons. The man stepped out of the dark corner and into the light of the lantern. Toyama took a step backward.

"You wanted to speak to us," the man said. He was dressed all in black, with tied pants and a short jacket held by a sash. Black tabi socks covered his feet, and even the hemp ties of his sandals were rubbed with ink to help them blend into shadows. A short Chinese-style sword was strapped across his back, with the hilt protruding over one shoulder where the man could reach back to draw it out. A piece of black cloth was wound around his head and face, masking his identity.

"Are you the one who gave me instructions?" Toyama asked.

The man was disgusted with this Lord's hesitancy and stupidity, but hid his impatience. "I am the one who was sent to talk to you," he answered.

"I . . . ah . . . I understand that you can be hired to do . . . ah . . . certain jobs . . ." Toyama let the sentence trail off, in a characteristic Japanese way that invited comment from the other party.

"That depends on the job."

"I want a man killed."

"That depends on the man."

Toyama took a piece of paper from his sleeve and handed it to the man in black. The paper was folded into a strip and tied into a loose knot.

The man took the paper and unfolded it, shaking it open and tilting it slightly to catch the light of the lantern. He was surprised when he read what was on the paper, but a lifetime of training allowed him to hide his reaction. Through habit, he kept his eyes on the paper, because a highly trained adversary could sometimes learn much from the expression in a man's eyes. It was unlikely that Toyama was so trained, but it could be his ineptness was simply a well-honed act.

"We know this man," he said. "When do you want this done?"

"As soon as possible, but you must tell me first, so I'll know in advance it's about to happen."

"We never tell that. We either fulfill our contract or die in the attempt. If we broadcast our intentions, it would be too easy to trap us."

"But I want to know, so I can make preparations."

"Then you should always be prepared, because we will not make such an announcement."

"What is the price then?" Toyama said petulantly.

The man quoted a figure.

Toyama spluttered. "That's outrageous!"

"As you wish." The man started to blend back into the darkness.

"Wait!"

The man stopped.

Toyama made a counteroffer.

The man shook his head. "No. I have given you the price for this man. It will take several of us to kill him, and even then we may not be successful. The price you were given is the value of our lives if we fail. This man is an expensive one to kill."

Frustrated, Toyama said, "Fine. If that's the price, then I will pay it. I want this man dead. I'll pay you when you are done."

"No. In advance."

"But how am I to know if you will complete your part of the bargain?"

"Do you know who we are?"

"Yes."

"Then you know we have never failed to either complete a mission or to die trying. There is no bargaining. Those are the terms. You may take them or leave them, as you choose."

"All right! But I didn't bring that much money with me."

"Have someone bring it to this temple tomorrow night. In gold. Place the gold in a cloth and leave the bundle on the temple floor. Then leave."

"All right."

The man looked at the sheet of paper once more. "Is this all you know about him?"

"I can describe him."

"I said we know him. You do not have to describe him. Do you know where he is now?"

"No."

"Then this will be a difficult job. It may take us some time. But we will not quit until we have completed the task."

"Tell me," Toyama said, "am I dealing with the Kogas?"

Now the man was extremely annoyed by this silly daimyo's curiosity and lack of knowledge of how these transactions were accomplished and which questions were questions not asked. "No," the man said, "you are dealing with me."

"But . . ."

Before Toyama could complete his thought, the man had quickly merged with the shadows of the temple. Toyama lifted his lantern and let its feeble light illuminate the edges and corners of the room. The man was gone, and Toyama could see no obvious escape route. Outside, the crickets made their lonely lament. Toyama felt a chill pass through him, because he could not fathom how and where the man had disappeared to.

Maybe ninja could turn themselves to smoke or make themselves invisible, as legends said, Toyama thought. He found some comfort in the fact that such men were hunting on his instructions, and not hunting him.

.   .   .

Honda went to the back gate of his villa. He was staying in what would eventually be the guest house when the new main structure was completed. His wife and retainers insisted that he build a bigger house, and he had acquiesced. It was a financial strain because of Ieyasu's policy of giving the fudai small estates, while the tozama became wealthy. Despite Honda's famous temper, his wife had berated him about this injustice. Honda had simply told her *yakamashii,* shut up, and refused to respond. He didn't trust himself to respond. He secretly agreed with her. The Tokugawas had a newfound position as the ruling clan of Japan, but he felt his own position was precarious, and that peace was as great a threat to him as the most desperate battle.

Honda knew he was a rough country samurai. He had a certain blunt cunning honed by a lifetime of warfare, but also he knew that the winds of a shifting nation demanded new skills, skills he neither had nor valued. Honda's skill was killing. This was an invaluable skill when there was a country to be won, and this skill kept him at Ieyasu's side through countless battles. Now that the last great battle was over, the battle at Sekigahara, he could see Ieyasu's mind turning to strategies for establishing a lasting dynasty. Undoubtedly there would be some killing involved in maintaining this dynasty, but other skills, more subtle skills, would be necessary if the Tokugawas and their descendents were to rule without having a state of constant warfare.

These were skills that other, more clever, men, like Yoshida, Okubo and Toyama, had. Nakamura, despite his pompous lecturing, also had a talent for creating stable administrations. Yoshida and Okubo were warriors, but the fact that Ieyasu had allowed men like Toyama and Nakamura into his inner circle showed that the balance was already shifting from the bushi to the bureaucrats.

Honda, as did most samurai, had a fatalistic view of life and death. He attributed Ieyasu's escape from death to simple luck. If the musket ball had been just a few inches to the right, the assassination would have been successful and it would be Ieyasu lying dead, not Nakamura.

Still, Ieyasu had been lucky. He had always been lucky. His primary stroke of luck was simply outliving most of his rivals. The other contenders for the rulership of Japan had died violent deaths or, like Hideyoshi, passed away from old age. Ieyasu simply waited for his time. Ieyasu had also been lucky that, although he had been defeated in battle, none of these defeats turned out to be devastating. Through good fortune and the stupidity of his enemies, he had always survived to fight another day. Looking at Ieyasu's entire life, where he spent his childhood as a hostage to ensure the good behavior of his clan, it was amazing that he had risen so far. He had no special skills, but the ordinary skills of a military leader and daimyo were honed in him to an unusually high degree, and these ordinary skills had proven triumphant in the end.

Still, the luck to conquer the country was not a guarantee that his house would rule the country beyond his lifetime. Hideyoshi had thought his young son would rule the country after him, but after the defeat of the forces loyal to him at Sekigahara, all the child and his mother ruled was Osaka Castle. Ieyasu ruled the country.

Transforming this rule into a dynasty was another matter altogether. Years before, Ieyasu had his first wife killed for plotting against him with another daimyo, and he forced his firstborn son and heir to commit suicide for suspected involvement in the same plot. Recently, he had almost executed his second son and current heir, Hidetada, for arriving late at the battle of Sekigahara.

Honda and others had intervened to protect this tardy son from his father's wrath, saving his life. With such a turbulent and unstable house surrounding his Lord, how could Honda rest assured that his own house would prosper in the future?

Now, because of these unsettling times, Honda was doing something he was embarrassed about. The blunt warrior was uncertain if he was doing the right thing, and even used the back gate of his villa so that his comings and goings would attract the least attention possible.

Yoshida sat on the floor, leaning against a movable wooden armrest that was used to provide comfort in a culture without chairs. He was in the reception room of the temple he had commandeered as a residence while his villa was being built. The priests at the temple were not happy about their enforced guest, but they gave him and his men the expected courtesy, which was all Yoshida required.

He was talking to guard captains, trying to ascertain the status of their search.

"Surely you must have some idea where he is?" Yoshida said.

"Edo is a difficult town to police," one captain said. "Before Sekigahara, it was growing, but still manageable. Now it is completely out of control. Peasants, ronin, merchants, artisans, and scoundrels are pouring into the city, and it's impossible to track them all."

"I'm not asking you to track them all," Yoshida said with some irritation. "I'm asking you to track the man who tried to assassinate Ieyasu-sama. Go back to your men and redouble your efforts. This Matsuyama Kaze must be found before he tries to kill again!"

CHAPTER 5

A bustling city.
Crowded streets can murder peace
in a troubled heart.

Kaze made his way through the bustling streets of Edo. Unlike
people in the country villages and castle towns he was used to, the
Edokko pushed back the night by flooding the streets with the
cheery glow of paper lanterns. Shops stayed open and peddlers
with small stands occupied likely corners, selling various tidbits of
food or cheap sakè to the rushing people. Adults and children of
all ages still crowded the streets.

As he walked, he constantly scanned the faces of the young
children. After three years, it was a habit with him.

This night the crowd was especially active, as news of the assassination attempt spread through the city like the shocks from
one of the periodic earthquakes. Groups of people clumped together to share rumors and news, breaking apart and re-forming
in new combinations to take the same stories and circulate them
in endless permutations.

Everyone knew that Ieyasu-sama had escaped death by the
smallest of margins. Lord Nakamura, who was standing right be-
side him, had been killed instead. The shot was fired from a great
distance, from the nearest yagura fire watchtower, and the lookout

had been found in the tower with his throat cut. To these basic facts, countless flourishes were added.

One man claimed the blood had been drained from the yagura watchman and probably drunk by the assassins. Another claimed that a flash of divine light had been seen, illuminating Ieyasu just seconds before the shot was fired. This showed it was the Gods who diverted the musket ball and saved Ieyasu's life. Still another claimed that he was a former musketeer, and that the distance between the tower and the unfinished wall was too great for a musket shot, proving that the shot actually came from within the unfinished castle, not from without. He hinted darkly that this was evidence of a conspiracy among Ieyasu's own bodyguards. Numerous other variations on the facts were heard as the Edokko hashed and rehashed the incident.

In a city consumed by the attempted assassination, Kaze was perhaps the inhabitant with the least interest. He had gone to the inspection to see Lord Okubo, the man he hated above all others in this life. Okubo and Kaze had been boyhood rivals. As young men, Kaze had bested Okubo and had given him the limp he still carried. Later, Okubo had used treachery to destroy Kaze's Lord, kill and dishonor his Lady, and kidnap the child Kaze sought.

Mingling with the crowd at the inspection site, pretending to be a street entertainer, Kaze had noticed a spark of recognition in the eyes of the guard officer maintaining control of the crowd. He had left before the shot was fired. He had spent the day on business of his own, searching the area to the west of the castle, but he heard of the failed assassination attempt from excited citizens almost immediately. He was surprised at how fast the news of the attempt had rolled through the city.

A self-contained man by nature, he found that for some reason he actually enjoyed the bustle of this city. There was something infectious about the Edokko's energy, curiosity, and general optimism that, after years of solitary dedication to an arduous task, was a tonic that Kaze didn't know he needed.

For almost three years, Kaze had searched for the daughter of his former Lord and Lady. The child would be nine years old now, and Kaze knew that she had been sent from Kamakura to Edo. Kaze even knew where she had been sent. Edo Yukaku Kobanaya, "Little Flower Whorehouse Edo."

The implications of her destination were not lost on Kaze. Prostitutes were usually initiated into their trade at fourteen or fifteen. Marriages were sometimes arranged at this age, and a girl was considered a woman. Perhaps at nine the child he was looking for would be used as a servant in the house, helping with the cleaning and cooking until she could be initiated into the house's business. But Kaze also knew there were men, unnatural men, who took pleasure in despoiling children. From the name of the house, Kaze was afraid the Little Flower Whorehouse would be a place that catered to such appetites.

Knowing the place he was looking for and finding it were two different things. Edo was a large city, with new streets and businesses appearing daily. There was no directory of the city. Perhaps the guard captains in each district would know the businesses in their section, but, as a wanted man, Kaze could not go to them. Instead, he had taken a disguise that would allow him to wander any street in the city, so he could visit each district and find out if any resident knew of the Little Flower Whorehouse.

His choice of what kind of entertainment to provide was easy. He had played with tops as a boy, and it was no great trick to combine a few tops with his skill at handling a sword. Thus he became a street entertainer, with sword and tops tucked into a deep hemp bag that he carried over his shoulder.

Edo was full of entertainers. They filled every busy thoroughfare and also wandered the side streets. They did juggling, puppet shows for children, acrobatics, or spun tales and stories. Even in the part of the city occupied by the great nobles near the new castle of Edo, street entertainers could be found plying their trade to the servants and household workers of the great Lords.

His particular choice also had an added advantage. He could carry a sword as part of his paraphernalia, but not reveal he was a samurai. As a wanted man, the authorities were looking for him in the guise of a samurai. In Edo he was in the heart of his enemy's stronghold, so he had to be as discreet as possible. To a samurai, all *heimin*, commoners, were to some extent invisible, so Kaze wanted to be mistaken for a heimin.

Kaze had even cultivated a normal walk, instead of a samurai's walk, as part of his disguise. As a samurai, he strode down the street, almost marching. As an expert swordsman, Kaze's normal walk also had an additional element, which was a peculiar ability to maintain his center of gravity and balance at all times, instantly ready to move to the attack or defense if unexpectedly assaulted. Kaze knew that he could look up a street and instantly tell which samurai had been vigorously trained in the sword and which had not, just by their walk. Kaze didn't want to have his own walk make it easy for the authorities to spot that he was a samurai.

He was glad that he had successfully evaded capture in the capital city of his enemies. Although he was on a general list of men wanted by the Tokugawas after the battle of Sekigahara, he was happy with the thought that the Tokugawa authorities did not know he was in Edo and that they were not specifically looking for him.

Kaze made his way to the house that had his tiny room. Edo was in the midst of an acute housing shortage, and lodgings were at a premium. Even the daimyo, who were used to being offered accommodations in private houses or large temples, often found themselves squeezed out of their lodgings as higher-ranking daimyo appeared in the capital. The more ambitious daimyo, like Yoshida and Okubo, had received tracts of land from Ieyasu and they were already building large mansions in Edo.

The common people, as they always did, made do with the best they could after the samurai and nobles took what they wanted.

The housing shortage affected everyone. It was not uncommon for an Edokko to find some stranger sleeping in his privy or tucked in the space between houses. The Edokko would simply wake the person up, and the intruder would usually wander away sleepily, often mumbling apologies and making a vague excuse about being drunk or tired.

Kaze knew he was lucky to find a small room tucked upstairs in the eaves of a vegetable merchant's house. He also knew it made his job of remaining invisible harder. It was easier to fool samurai into thinking he was a heimin than it was to fool the commoners themselves. This was made clear to him the first night he spent at the vegetable merchant's house.

In addition to his room, his arrangement was to take a morning and evening meal with the household. Kaze didn't shave his pate like a samurai and his clothes were the traveling clothes worn by commoners of all types, so there was nothing in his outward appearance that made him stand out. Kaze knew his words might betray him, so he was economical with his language around the merchant and his household. What he didn't initially realize was that his intensive training as a samurai made him stand out in something as simple as eating.

The first night he ate with the household, Kaze noticed the merchant held his soup bowl by placing a hand on its bottom. Kaze grasped his bowl with his thumb and forefinger along the side of the bowl. The merchant took his chopsticks, his *hashi*, and put the food straight into his mouth. Kaze used the hashi by placing them to the side of his mouth. Kaze's way of eating was a samurai's way.

Because the merchant held the bowl cupped in his hand, someone could hit the bottom of the hand and splash hot soup into his face, temporarily leaving him vulnerable to attack. The same was true about the hashi. If he put them directly into his mouth, someone could suddenly hit the ends, driving them down his throat and making him vulnerable. Kaze's way of eating avoided both possibilities and maintained *zanshin,* the state of mental alertness that left the samurai instantly ready for a sudden attack.

Kaze realized he was the only one eating like a samurai. He didn't know if the rest of the household saw these differences, but he resolved to minimize his contact with the household. He thought he could fool samurai into thinking he was a heimin, at least for a little while, but he was sure he could not fool heimin into thinking he was one of them, especially if he lived with them. As a result, he kept himself in isolation at the vegetable merchant's house, taking his meals alone and keeping contact and conversation to a minimum.

As he entered the merchant's shop, the merchant's wife and the woman who helped in the shop were taking in the flat wooden trays used to display the vegetables.

"*Konbanwa,* good evening," the wife of the merchant said.

"Konbanwa," Kaze answered.

"Will you be taking your meal in your room again, or will you join us for dinner?"

"In my room, if it is not too much trouble," Kaze answered, starting up the steep stairs to his room. "Just tell me when it's ready and I'll come down and get it."

"All right," the wife responded.

Kaze saw both women looking at him with an intensity that made him uncomfortable. He was sure they knew he had once been a samurai and that they pitied him for having tumbled so low, falling even from the precarious status of a ronin to that of a street entertainer. His samurai pride was repelled by the thought of pity, but his duty of finding the girl kept his pride in check. He finished climbing the stairs and went into the small room he had rented.

I'd like to follow him up those stairs," the merchant's wife said as she watched Kaze ascend to his room.

"You'd have to make room on the *futon* for a third, because I'll be right behind you," the servant said.

Both women laughed. The wife said, "If my husband knew I had such thoughts, he'd kill me! Still," she said, looking up the stairs where Kaze had departed, "that is one handsome man. So good-looking, and with such muscles in his arms and shoulders."

"I'm more interested in another muscle of his," the servant said.

The wife laughed and slapped the servant's arm. "You're bad!"

"I don't have a husband to worry about. I've been sending him signals ever since he showed up here, but he seems so preoccupied that I don't think he notices."

"He is very intense," the wife said. "I also think there's a sadness to him. I don't know why."

"He obviously wasn't always a street entertainer. Such polite manners; you don't learn such things on the street."

"Maybe he's fallen from some higher station in life," the wife said.

"Maybe it's some tragic love affair," the servant said romantically. "He's probably trying to forget some woman."

"I'd like to help him forget! My worthless husband has been spending all his time and money on trying to get rich through gambling."

The servant knew better than to agree about the worthlessness of the master. It was quite all right for a Japanese to criticize a spouse or child, but quite something else for a stranger to do the same thing, especially if he was a servant in the house.

Kaze knew there were people in the house long before he heard their voices. He slept with his hand on his sword, so he saw no need to act, or even move from the warm comfort of the futon, until he understood what was happening. Finally, one of the talkers raised his voice.

"Where is that worm?" A strange man's voice.

"I don't know. I suppose he's out gambling." The vegetable merchant's wife.

"What! He's gambling somewhere else? He owes my boss money. We want it! How dare he gamble somewhere else, after we've given him credit!"

"My husband says your boss doesn't run an honest game. He says—"

A sharp slap, followed by a yelp of surprise and pain. Kaze quickly got up and shrugged into his kimono. They weren't killing her, so there was no need to rush down the stairs dressed in just his loincloth and a sword.

"Please don't hit my mistress!" The servant.

"Keep out of this or you'll get the same." A second man's voice. So there were at least two of them.

"Hey, maybe we should give them both something, just so that bastard understands we're serious!" A third voice.

"What do you mean?" The second voice again, so perhaps there were only three of them. Kaze, his kimono on, started down the steep stairs.

"Well, they're no beauties, but they aren't bad looking. Maybe we should . . . say, who are you?" The speaker spotted Kaze descending the stairs.

There were three of them. Two had swords, indicating they were ronin. One was the man talking to Kaze. The third man was not carrying a sword, but he towered over the others by a good head and his body was at least twice as wide, and very muscular. He could easily be a wrestler, like the kind who wrestled at the shrines during religious holidays.

"I'm your etiquette teacher," Kaze announced.

"Etiquette teacher? What kind of stupid thing is that to say?"

Kaze sighed. "See why I'm needed? First you slap *okusama*, the honorable wife of this house, and now you are rude to me." He shook his head. As he did so, he was gauging the manner of men he was facing. If he used his sword, he would have a relatively easy task, but he didn't want to unsheathe his blade. The men had not yet done something that warranted death, and the inconvenience of three bodies would surely draw the attention of the authorities to this house. Kaze preferred to stay anonymous to the Tokugawa guards.

"I suppose I'll have a lot of work to do," Kaze said. "After all, *rui o motte atsumaru*, the same kind always gathers together. All three of you are probably badly in need of a lesson in proper manners."

"A lesson! Why you—"

Kaze attacked.

Like all samurai, Kaze knew the value of surprise in a fight. In ancient times, samurai would formally introduce themselves before starting a fight. They would recite their lineage and the great deeds of their ancestors. If they had been in notable battles, they would tell their opponent of that, too. Then, after all the lengthy formalities were completed, the fight would finally begin.

Such stilted battle etiquette was long since forgotten, and for good reason. The warlord Nobunaga had defeated an army twelve times larger than his own with a surprise attack, and every warrior understood that striking first was usually a huge advantage. Kaze used this advantage to his benefit.

Keeping his sword in its scabbard, he brought it down on the head of the man he was talking to. With a surprised look, the ronin crumpled to the floor. His companion drew his sword and took a side cut at Kaze's head. Kaze ducked under the swinging blade and used his scabbard to hit the swordsman right behind the knee, collapsing him on his unconscious companion.

The wrestler had charged as soon as Kaze started his attack. In the cramped confines of the vegetable seller's house, Kaze didn't have the room to avoid the man's charge. The huge body hit his with a bone-jarring shock, lifting him off his feet and driving him against an outside wall. The wrestler put one large hand against Kaze's chest, pinning him in place. He drew back his other fist and punched at Kaze's face. Despite having the wind knocked out of him, Kaze remained alert enough to bob his head at the last moment. He felt the wrestler's fist graze his ear and heard it smash into the wooden wall, splintering the boards as the wrestler punched his fist through the wall. The wrestler tried to draw his fist out, but the splintered wood acted like a cruel trap, jabbing into his wrist and causing him to wince as he fought to extricate his hand.

The tiny pause was all that Kaze needed. He brought his sword scabbard up between the wrestler's legs. The huge man gave a grunt of pain, and Kaze saw tears filling the man's eyes. Kaze repeated the maneuver, bringing his scabbard up between the man's legs with all the strength he could muster. The man's eyes squinted in pain and the hand that had pinned Kaze to the wall dropped to his groin.

Kaze twisted free of the giant and brought his scabbard down on the back of the wrestler's head. The wrestler fell heavily to his knees, his trapped hand preventing him from falling all the way to the floor.

Kaze looked at the two ronin and saw that the one he had clipped behind the knee was struggling to get up on one leg, using his drawn sword as a cane. In two quick steps Kaze was next to him. He swept away the man's sword and used his scabbard to hasten the man's journey to the floor, clipping him across the neck and shoulder. The man lay in a heap, moaning.

Puffing heavily, trying to get his breath back after the wrestler's charge, Kaze surveyed his three opponents. One was unconscious and the other two were stunned and in pain. The two women viewed the scene open-mouthed. The merchant's wife still had a hand to her cheek, where she had been slapped.

Getting his breath back, Kaze said, "If . . . we . . . have . . . to have . . . more etiquette . . . lessons, we will . . . do it outside. Teaching etiquette can be . . . hard on . . . the walls of a house."

L ater that night the vegetable merchant came back to his house. The dice had not been kind to him, and he was fretting about how he would ever find the money to pay his mounting gambling debts, now owed to two different gambling bosses in Edo. The late hours for gambling were not compatible with his early rising to buy vegetables, and he wondered if the problem was that he was just showing poor judgment in his bets, instead of a run of bad luck.

His house was on a main street of the district, well situated for its dual role as abode and shop. Earlier, the street had been illuminated by lanterns helping customers find drinking establishments and shops that stayed open late, but except for a single drinking place on the corner, the entire street was now dark, with light coming only from his own house.

The merchant couldn't imagine his wife staying up late for him. Disgusted with his gambling, she had long since stopped waiting up for him like a dutiful wife, keeping the food and rice warm, to serve him upon his arrival.

As he approached his house, he noticed that some of the light was spilling out from a newly formed hole in the wall. Concerned, he quickened his steps to see what was going on.

"*Tadaima!* I'm home," he announced as he slid back the sliding door of his house. He entered the small dirt entryway. The rest of the house was built on a wooden platform, above the ground, and the entry was a place to sit on the platform and take off his hemp sandals. Several heads spun around to look at him as he entered. The only person who didn't react to his entry was the street entertainer he recently rented the upstairs room to. He sat serenely by a clay hibachi, sipping tea. Next to him was the merchant's wife and his servant, apparently serving him. The merchant would have been upset by this special favor to the renter, if it wasn't for the three others in the room.

The three sat with their legs splayed out in front of them in the space the merchant used as his shop when the weather was too bad to display the vegetables outside. They sat in a rough triangle, with their backs together. A length of sturdy hemp rope was wrapped and tied around them, securely keeping them in place.

He recognized them immediately. They were Boss Akinari's men. Even with them tied securely, the merchant started to quake, and he sat at the edge of the house platform in weakness, temporarily too shaky to take off his sandals.

"How . . . how . . . ?" he stammered.

The renter looked up from his tea. "How what?" he asked, in a tone that made it seem like it was unusual for the merchant to be stupefied by three men tied up in his house.

"What . . . what . . . ?"

The renter sighed. "You really must complete a question if you expect us to answer it," he said.

The merchant sucked in his breath through his teeth, a characteristic gesture when some Japanese are nervous. He said, "What are these men doing here?"

"They came to see you," the renter said. He put down his teacup and stood up, holding his sword in one hand.

"Where are you going?" the merchant said quickly, a touch of fear in his voice.

"I'm going back to bed. These men came to see you. Now you are here. I suggest you talk to them, because they seem to be here on serious business." Kaze turned and took a few steps up the stairs. He stopped. "Oh, I suggest you keep them tied until you have completed your discussions with them. You had better make sure that they're happy with the result of your discussions, because they can play rough."

"Hey! Samurai!" The big wrestler was addressing Kaze. Kaze thought briefly of denying he was a samurai and decided it would be a rather foolish denial after what he had done to the three toughs.

"What is it?" Kaze asked mildly.

"What's your name?"

Kaze thought before answering that question, and decided to give the name he had used with the family.

"I'm Matsuyama Kaze."

"I'm Nobu," the wrestler said. "I work for Boss Akinari, the biggest gambling boss in this part of town. If you want a job fighting, come talk to me. We can use a man like you. A real fighter, not like these worthless ronin." The big man gave a shake that moved the two ronin tied to him like dolls.

Because of his size, Kaze had assumed that the wrestler was the muscle for the two ronin. Now he understood that the big man was in charge. He reminded himself of the danger of assumptions, especially ones based on the appearance of people. It could kill you. He smiled. "I'll keep that in mind," he said.

Almost as if it were an explanation of why he had offered Kaze a job, Nobu said, "I've never been bested in a fight before."

Kaze nodded, continuing his ascent of the stairs and leaving the merchant to work out an accommodation with the three men tied up on his floor.

In his room, Kaze allowed himself the indulgence of rubbing his ear. It was still hot from the blood rushing to it when the wrestler's fist grazed it. Kaze had misjudged how much to move because the wrestler had such large hands.

When Kaze was young, he went into the mountains near his home and sought out a renowned Sensei, a teacher, to learn the ways of the sword. During his first lesson on how to avoid blows from the sword, Kaze had nimbly jumped to one side as the Sensei brought the *bokken,* the wooden practice sword, down in an overhead cut.

Kaze was proud of his ability to dodge the blow, but his Sensei scowled. The teacher held up the wooden sword so the edge was facing Kaze. "How wide is this sword?" he asked.

Kaze showed the width of the bokken by moving his thumb and forefinger a short distance apart.

"That's right," the Sensei said. "How far did you jump?"

Kaze put his two hands apart to show the distance.

The Sensei said no more, but Kaze understood the lesson. Economy of movement and judgment were as important as agility. Rubbing his ear, Kaze reflected that while swords were of a consistent width, he must remember that men's fists were not.

CHAPTER 6

Plans woven like the
silk threads in a kimono.
Snags can rend the cloth.

Tokugawa Ieyasu thought he had been chosen to lead by the will of the Gods, and there was little in his life to make him change that opinion. This did not mean that his life was without hardship. In fact, the exact opposite was true. But Ieyasu was fond of saying, "Persuade yourself that imperfection and inconvenience is the natural lot of mortals, and there will be no room for discontent or despair."

This belief in his divine selection must have come later in his life, because his early years were not auspicious. He was born the son of a country daimyo who ruled the province of Mikawa. When he was four, he was sent as a hostage to an ally to guarantee his father's good behavior. Unfortunately, during his journey, he was captured by his father's bitter enemy and made a hostage under conditions that were both harsh and precarious. His captor even threatened to kill him if his father didn't do what the captor demanded. But Ieyasu's father risked the life of his son and ignored the threat. Ironically, the daimyo who had captured him was Oda Nobuhide, the father of Oda Nobunaga, a man Ieyasu was later to become strongly allied to. Two years later, Ieyasu was sent to his original destination, where he remained a hostage of the ally for an additional eleven years.

During his absence, the samurai of Mikawa had not fared much better than their young master, suffering many hardships that forced many of them to return to the soil, to work as farmers, just to survive. Thus, when Ieyasu finally returned to Mikawa, it was with a great deal of surprise that he learned that one of his retainers had preserved the bulk of the Mikawa treasury, because he knew the young Lord would need money to equip and outfit troops. Ieyasu was moved to tears by this gesture of loyalty. Because of the sacrifice that this hoarding of money represented, he adopted a maxim that waste was an affront to heaven.

His frugality did not extend to things military, however. Ieyasu's men were always well equipped, and although their commissary was not lavish, when they were on a campaign they were always supplied with adequate food.

This willingness to spend money on military matters did not always guarantee victory. In fact, there were military defeats and at least one occasion when Ieyasu was preparing to kill himself rather than be captured. But circumstances, bold action on his part, and the hesitancy of his enemies kept Ieyasu alive. And as his long life progressed, he expanded his influence, power, and authority until he was able to seize control of all of Japan. To do this, he bided his time, first allying himself with Oda Nobunaga in his rise to power, then shifting his loyalties to Toyotomi Hideyoshi, Nobunaga's successor.

Hideyoshi was a peasant, and started his military career as an *ashigaru,* a common foot soldier, before advancing to the rulership of Japan. Ieyasu was amused that the people were already making up legends about Hideyoshi, even though he had been dead only a few years. He laughed out loud when someone told him of the talk of lightning flashes and divine signs when Hideyoshi was born. He knew that The Monkey, the derogatory nickname given to Hideyoshi by Nobunaga, had had a totally unremarkable birth in a peasant village.

That was what had made him so unusual and frightening.

In an age when birth was often destiny, Hideyoshi was a man who made his own destiny. Hideyoshi once told Ieyasu that it was important for Ieyasu to become his vassal, because Hideyoshi's common birth meant a lack of respect from other daimyo. If Ieyasu acknowledged a commoner like Hideyoshi as his Lord, then the other daimyo would fall into line, following Ieyasu's example. As with most things Hideyoshi planned, the results of Ieyasu acknowledging Hideyoshi were exactly as he foresaw. Ieyasu was determined to create a Japan where the elite would not be threatened by a freakish political and military prodigy like Hideyoshi.

When Hideyoshi died, Ieyasu gathered his forces and gambled everything on one climactic battle at Sekigahara. He had prevailed, and now was in a struggle to gather the reins of power into his hands. Hideyoshi's son and widow still lived in the formidable fortress at Osaka, and the loyalty of numerous daimyo was still in question. Ieyasu saw the danger and irony of dying at this moment, when he had achieved the pinnacle of personal power for himself with the title of Shogun but had not yet ensured that his clan and family would remain in power long after he had departed to the void.

That's what made a man like Nakamura so valuable, and Ieyasu would miss him. Nakamura had had a genius for bureaucracy. Although his manner had been as irritating as that of one of those pedantic scholars of Dutch or Chinese learning, his ideas for structuring the new government had been inspired. He had proposed an idea for controlling the daimyo that was both brilliant and simple.

The standard way to ensure the loyalty of a shaky ally was to take hostages, just as Ieyasu had been a hostage for his entire youth. If the ally did something to displease you, you simply killed the hostages. If the ally was ruthless enough or under pressure in other ways, the hostages could be sacrificed and the supposed ally could turn treacherous. Nakamura had suggested a variation on this scheme that would make treachery much harder.

Every other year, half the daimyo would have to live in Edo to "advise" and serve the Shogun. After the year's residence in Edo, the daimyo would return to his home fief, but his family would remain in Edo as hostages. After a year's residence in their fief, the pattern would be repeated. This made it much harder for the daimyo to consolidate power in their fiefs, and with only half the daimyo in Edo at any one time, the potential for collusion was considerably reduced. Even when the daimyo weren't in Edo, their entire immediate families remained as hostages.

It was a brilliant scheme, and one that Ieyasu intended to implement as soon as he was in a position to do so. It was too bad Nakamura wouldn't be alive to handle the details.

Still, Nakamura's death hadn't been a complete loss. It had allowed Ieyasu to see the worth of Yoshida in a tight situation. Yoshida also had a flair for government, but he combined it with the spirit of a bushi.

This will be like a military campaign," Yoshida said to the guard captains of Edo. "We have an enemy and we must track him down and destroy him."

Several of the captains exchanged glances, a fact not unnoticed by Yoshida. "I know it is but one man," Yoshida said, using a tone like the one he would use talking to exceptionally stupid children, "but this one man almost killed the Shogun. In that act, he is more dangerous than an entire army. The Shogunate can withstand an army. If we are defeated on the field of battle, we can raise another army and fight another day. If Ieyasu-sama is killed, then where will we find another?" Yoshida glared at the guard captains, who hung their heads in shame.

"Good," Yoshida said. "We understand each other. Now, each of you is responsible for keeping order in a section of the city. All except for you"—Yoshida indicated one guard captain, who had recently been promoted—"you should be familiar with that section." He was replacing the captain who had been in charge of the section where the assassination attempt had occurred. That man had committed ritual suicide, *seppuku,* to apologize for the attempt occurring while he was in command.

"I want you to ask the heimin most likely to know if there are strangers in their neighborhoods: tea shop owners, gamblers, whorehouse owners, and merchants. We are looking for a ronin called Matsuyama Kaze. It's a weird name, so he should be easy to find. I am told he is of normal height and a bit more handsome than average. He walks like a swordsman, and he is more muscular than a normal samurai. He has extreme skill with the *katana.* When you find him, you will report to me."

Yoshida stopped and looked at the face of each man in the room. "Do you understand that last order?"

"Hai! Yes!" the captains said.

"Good. If you try to capture him alone or with just a few men, I am told that you will likely fail. He is an unusually dangerous man with a sword. When you report back to me, I will devise a plan that ensures that we will kill this Matsuyama Kaze."

Toyama paced nervously in his villa. He wondered if he had done the right thing but realized it was too late to change things now. His chief retainer had taken the required gold and left it in the temple. The retainer reported that he was sure the temple was empty when he walked into it, and he placed the cloth with the gold in it in the middle of the floor. He walked out and gave a glance backward, to have one last look at the gold. The retainer swore the gold was gone, silently taken in just the few seconds it took him to walk out of the temple.

The tale sent chills up Toyama's back. He was sure there were many ways to make the gold disappear, such as using a line and hook or something as simple as a man who was fast on his feet and silent. Yet, the rumors and legends about the ninja becoming invisible intruded into his mind once more, and he felt his palms sweating from the thought of becoming involved with such people.

He cursed himself for using the Koga ninja, the same ninja the Tokugawas used. Although they kept their identities secret, they all came from the village of Koga. They were born into *ninjutsu*, the art of the ninja, and only left it when they left this life. Still, Toyama initially had no idea how to contact a ninja clan, and it was one of Tokugawa's own retainers who helped him make the contact. It was only natural it would be the Koga, instead of one of the other ninja groups.

He rubbed his palms against his kimono. He was desperate to kill that man. It was obvious that Ieyasu-sama was not pleased with him, and something drastic had to be done to change the situation. Ieyasu-sama had already reduced, changed, or totally eliminated fiefs for other daimyo. Most of these were men who supported Hideyoshi's heir, but some were part of the Tokugawa camp. They were men Ieyasu-sama didn't trust or was displeased with. With the bulk of his army still intact after Sekigahara, it was unwise to defy the orders of the new Shogun.

"Damn!" Toyama said. "I want that man dead. It is the only way!"

CHAPTER 7

An evil nature
can reside in a small space.
An atrocious child.

One of Okubo's earliest memories was of seeing a man boiled alive. His father had a special fondness for this type of punishment, and he prescribed it often for miscreants of all types. Okubo couldn't remember the crime of the first man he saw boiled, but he did remember the event.

In the center of the courtyard of the Okubo villa, a large iron pot was placed. This kind of pot was normally used for cooking vegetable stew for large numbers of troops, but it served admirably for the purposes of Okubo's father.

On the wooden veranda that encircled three sides of the courtyard, new *tatami* mats were placed. Okubo's father sat on one of these mats, with his young son at his side. Okubo's mother pronounced the proceedings "gruesome" and refused to attend the execution.

Okubo remembered that his father, who was a tall, normally phlegmatic man, was very animated and excited about the boiling. He was constantly leaping up to inspect or supervise some aspect of the execution. He directed his vassals as to how to arrange the logs around the pot and where to put the kindling. Then he sat on the tatami eating pickled radishes as he waited impatiently for the servants to bring bucket after bucket of water to fill up the pot.

When the condemned man was brought into the courtyard, Okubo's father personally supervised tying him up before placing him in the pot. The prisoner was crying, and Okubo clearly remembered his father slapping the prisoner and telling him to be a man.

When he returned to the tatami, Okubo's father explained to him some of the fine points of how the man was tied. Tying up prisoners was one of the skills learned by samurai, but these ties were meant to immobilize a prisoner, not keep him trussed up in a pot. Okubo especially remembered his father telling him not to loop a length of rope around the prisoner's neck, because he might be able to use it to strangle himself and thereby cut short his misery.

Finally, when all was ready, Okubo's father ordered the fire lit.

At first the man was relatively stoic, crying softly as the logs surrounding the pot gradually heated up the water within. By the end, the man was screaming for mercy and begging Okubo's father to end his agony.

At the very end, one of the guards broke ranks and stepped forward with a spear, ready to thrust it into the prisoner to end his suffering. Angrily, Okubo's father ordered the guard arrested before he could deliver the thrust of mercy. Okubo couldn't remember what happened to that guard, but he supposed that the guard was himself boiled at a later date. What he did remember was that his father quite enjoyed himself, laughing out loud while the other witnesses to the execution all turned away.

Okubo's father kept the man in the pot until his flesh started boiling off his bones. Young Okubo and his father sat on the veranda for the entire time this took. Then, when it was all over,

Okubo's father asked his heir if he enjoyed the spectacle. The young Okubo answered, "Hai! Yes!"

When Okubo was around nine, his father conducted a series of disastrous campaigns against his neighboring daimyo. Although he was outnumbered, the neighbor was just too good a general to be beaten by the Okubo clan, and Okubo's father was forced to settle for peace under humiliating circumstances. Part of the peace agreement required the young heir to go to the enemy's castle as a hostage for three years, to guarantee the Okubo clan's good behavior.

So the young Okubo, then ten, was sent to the next fief. He took with him several servants and retainers so he could continue to live in spoiled comfort. He was officially an honored guest, but his entire clan knew his life would be forfeit if his father started another ill-fated adventure within three years.

What only he knew was that, on the night before he left, his father came to him in his room.

"I hate those people!" his father declared. "They think they're more virtuous than us, even though our rank in the Imperial Court is much higher than theirs! I want you to know that since you are my heir, I will try to restrain myself, but someday the Okubos will have a chance to bring that family to ruin! If that day comes sometime within the next three years, I intend to act. I can always father another boy." Then Okubo's father left without a further word. The next morning, as Okubo and his entourage left for the next fief, his father did not appear to say farewell.

Despite his precarious position, the neighboring daimyo turned out to be quite kind and solicitous of Okubo's welfare. Instead of responding to this kindness, the young Okubo felt bile in his soul, and for some reason his hatred and contempt of the neighboring clan grew to exceed even the hatred expressed by his father.

The neighboring fief seemed to be run more efficiently than

Okubo's own, even though the daimyo seemed so weak that he didn't grind his vassals into the dirt. Instead, he treated them with respect, and they responded with loyalty and maximum efforts in peace or in war. Instead of embracing this model, the example only hardened the heart of the young Okubo. It made him want to embrace the autocratic ways of his father all the more.

One thing the young son missed was executions by boiling. When execution was required, the neighboring daimyo had it done swiftly, with a single stroke of a sword. Missing one of his favorite recreations, the young Okubo decided to rectify this.

He had three of his retainers find him a stray dog. They trussed up the poor animal, taking special care to tie up its muzzle. Then, behind the villa of the daimyo, Okubo had firewood and a pot of water brought. The dog was in a panic when Okubo had his retainers place the animal in the water. The dog thrashed about, causing the water to fly. Okubo himself lit the fire; then he stepped back to see the fun.

"What are you doing?"

Okubo looked over his shoulder to see the person who now called himself Matsuyama Kaze looking at him. Okubo's body was shielding Kaze's view of what was in the pot. The three Okubo retainers had stepped away when the young Okubo lit the fire, and none of them made a move to intercept the young Kaze.

Kaze was nine then, and in his youthful hands he held a paper kite and twine. Okubo ignored him. Kaze was the son of a mid-level samurai at the castle, and should not have even been addressing an heir and future daimyo like Okubo.

"I asked, what are you doing?"

Okubo was not used to being addressed in such a tone of voice, and he said irritably, "This is none of your business. Go off and play your stupid games!"

Kaze stepped to one side to see the contents of the pot that was sitting in the midst of the newly lit fire. When he saw the pot's contents, he dropped his kite and twine to the earth.

"Let that poor creature go!" Kaze's voice was sharp and low. Although he was a full head taller than Kaze, Okubo somehow felt threatened.

"Take care of that brat," Okubo ordered his retainers. Incredibly, they made no move to comply. Instead, they stood there immobile and mute.

"I said, let that creature go!" Kaze had advanced on Okubo, his hands now in two tight fists.

Okubo looked at his retainers, still not understanding why they hadn't moved to follow his orders. When he looked back at Kaze, his face was filled with a fist flying toward it.

The fight was not an elegant one. It was a schoolboy scuffle. Okubo was taller and stronger than Kaze, but Kaze had the strength of will and rapid reflexes that rained a shower of blows on Okubo. The fight ended with Kaze sitting on Okubo's chest, pummeling his head, while the older boy tried to protect himself by placing his hands over his face. The three Okubo retainers simply looked on.

Convinced he had thrashed the older boy, Kaze got off Okubo and ran to the fire. He kicked the pot over and the spilling water doused half the flame, sending up a cloud of white steam. Kaze took the struggling dog out of the pot and untied it, first making sure the water had not yet gotten hot enough to harm the animal. As soon as Kaze released the dog from its bonds, the animal leapt up and ran with all speed out of the area.

Okubo complained about the beating. Since he was the son of a daimyo, the Lord who was holding him hostage called Kaze and his father to explain themselves.

As they sat outside the Lord's reception room, Kaze could see his father was irritated by the trouble Kaze had caused. Kaze knew the Lord had power of life and death over his father and everyone in the fief. From the fact that his father was irritated but not concerned, Kaze guessed the situation wasn't as serious as that. Still, he felt acute embarrassment for causing trouble.

He sat waiting, trying to wash all thoughts from his mind and concentrating on his breathing. Breath was life and Kaze had already been taught the breathing exercises that samurai students were drilled in. It calmed him and also steeled him to go through his first direct contact with his daimyo. He wanted to greet the daimyo as a warrior and not a child.

The Lord finally called them in.

As they entered, the daimyo and his son, who was a few years older than Kaze, were sitting on a dais at the end of the room. Kaze and his father marched to the daimyo, stopping a respectful distance away. They both gracefully sank to their knees, put their hands on the floor before them, and gave a deep, formal bow, almost touching their heads to the floor. Then they both sat up, sitting on their legs, with calm faces and rigid backs.

The daimyo was impressed. The young boy had been well schooled in proper etiquette, but any child likely to have contact with daimyo and other high officials of the clan would be so schooled. What impressed the daimyo was the calm of the boy. Most children would be nervous or even crying when summoned to see the Lord of the fief after beating the son of another daimyo. The daimyo glanced at his son, to see if he had also noted the young boy's presence. In the normal course of things, this young boy would someday serve the daimyo's son, just as the father served the daimyo.

"Young Okubo complained about your beating him," the daimyo said without preliminaries. The young boy sat calmly, not denying the charge or rushing to offer an excuse.

"I did beat him, great Lord," the boy said.

After waiting to see if the boy would say more, the daimyo continued. His respect for this youth increased because he maintained an impressive composure, and he started looking at him as a precocious young man, and not a child. "Why did you beat him?" he asked.

"Young Lord Okubo had a dog tied up in a pot of water and he seemed intent on boiling it alive."

"So he was torturing your dog?"

"It was not my dog, great Lord."

Surprised, the daimyo asked, "It was not your dog?"

"No, Lord. I think it was a stray dog."

"Then why did you rush to protect it? Are you aware that some daimyo hunt dogs, shooting them from horseback with a bow and arrow?"

"Yes, great Lord."

"And would you beat up the son of a daimyo if he was doing that?"

"Probably not, great Lord."

"Why not?"

"Because that is not cruelty for cruelty's sake. I was taught that all creatures must die, including human beings. Death is inevitable, by one means or another. The manner of death, however, is important. Being boiled alive to give another pleasure is not a good death, even for a dog. I have never seen this type of cruelty exhibited before by our clan. Young Lord Okubo is a future daimyo, but he is also a guest of our clan. He should abide by the customs of our clan. That includes not inflicting pain for callous reasons, even to a dog."

Kaze's father opened his mouth as if to say something, but then closed it. His son was acquitting himself like a man. He didn't know from what depths the young boy was pulling up the answers he was giving. He wanted to turn his head and look at his son, but protocol prevented him from doing so in this type of formal interview. He had to keep his face toward his daimyo.

The daimyo raised his eyebrows at Kaze's answer, surprised at the response.

"Undoubtedly there are other customs in Okubo's own clan," the daimyo said diplomatically. "Why do you think Okubo complained to me about the beating you gave him?"

"To get me in trouble because he was defeated and . . ." For the first time in the interview, Kaze looked his age as youthful embarrassment flitted across his face. He stopped talking.

"Finish your thought," the daimyo commanded.

"Yes, great Lord. I believe young Lord Okubo complained to you because he has not been properly trained in bushido, the way of the warrior. A true warrior would never complain about such a trivial matter."

The daimyo placed his hand to his face to hide his smile, but his son, who was not as experienced in maintaining his composure, laughed out loud.

After a moment, the daimyo said, "All right. I'm not going to punish you this time, but please try to restrain yourself from beating up the sons of daimyo, even if they're engaged in what you think is cruelty."

Kaze and his father gave another deep, formal bow and left the room. As they left, Kaze's father looked at his son as if he were seeing him for the first time.

When the father and son were gone, the daimyo looked at his own son and said, "Someday that young man will become your right arm."

Okubo was assured that proper punishment had been given to Kaze, but he continued to hate the young boy. He also hated the retainers who did not defend him, and when he returned to his own fief, he had the three retainers put to death.

Later, Kaze and Okubo met again during the finals of Hideyoshi's great sword tournament. There, Okubo's clan tried to bribe Kaze, which made him want to destroy Okubo, not just defeat him.

CHAPTER 8

Poor pay, much hardship,
and the joy of the moment.
Welcome, show business!

Kaze balanced the top on his blade and walked it toward the tip. Although he kept the top balanced on the sword, his attention was not on the spinning orb of painted wood. Instead, he was studying a building across the street from him.

It was a discreet building of dark wood and white plaster outer walls. It might have been an upper-class residence, except for the blue half-curtain hanging from the top of the door. The curtain had the *kanji* for "Little Flower" on it.

The building had no windows facing the street, and in the twenty minutes Kaze took to do his act with the tops, no one entered or left. It was midmorning, and the street was bustling with people conducting their shopping or business. After years of a solitary existence on the road, the swirl of people that made up a typical Edo street was strange to Kaze, but he willed away the distractions and focused his attention on the brothel.

Kaze was in Ningyo-cho, a compact community of Edo, not too far from the construction site of Edo-jo, tucked in the angle of the Sumida River and the Nihonbashi. It was filled with brothels, drinking places, theaters, and other entertainment establishments of various sorts. It also had a great number of the shops that gave the district its name: Doll Town. These dolls were the kind made of porcelain and cloth, and Kaze noted the irony of putting a brothel that apparently specialized in young children in a district where the parents of other, more fortunate, children purchased treasured dolls.

In theory, girls were to be left alone until they were considered women, and they could not be kept in sexual slavery at any age. In fact, there was no organization to see to the welfare of children. If an enterprise like the Little Flower Whorehouse remained low-key and didn't cause problems for the authorities, it was allowed to function.

Kaze watched the Little Flower for almost an hour. It remained quiet, but that was no surprise because it was a business that operated primarily at night. He didn't see any tradesmen entering to deliver food and drink, nor did he see anyone leave. Dressed as a street entertainer, he couldn't just walk into the Little Flower to see if the Lady's daughter was inside, so he decided to circle the block to see if there was an alley or side street that led to a back entrance.

As he made his way around the block of buildings, he entered a few narrow passages, but they turned out to be private alleys leading to particular businesses and not to the Little Flower. He decided to circle the block once more. Like most of Edo, Ningyo-cho had been hastily reconstructed after the great fire, so it was a confusing jumble of makeshift buildings and permanent structures. Kaze was confident of his ability to detect something as slight as the passage of a rabbit on a forest trail, but he wasn't as certain of his ability to see all the possible crannies in and around city businesses, one of which could turn into a back entrance for the Little Flower.

When he was on the far side of the block, a man walked out

of one of the businesses and stopped, looking at Kaze with surprise.

"Samurai-san!" the man exclaimed.

It was Goro, one of two peasants Kaze had met recently. The two men had helped Kaze transport a load of gold for a merchant to Kamakura. At the end of the journey, Kaze had given Goro, and his partner Hanzo, four gold coins, a magnificent reward.

"What are you doing here?" Kaze asked.

Goro puffed out his chest. "I am the proprietor of this business," he said proudly.

Kaze looked at the curtain above the doorway. All it had was the word "Kabuki." It was a word Kaze wasn't familiar with. It seemed to be made up of three kanji: *ka,* which meant song; *bu,* which meant dance; and *ki,* which means skills. Song-dance-skills. It was peculiar.

"And what kind of business is this?" Kaze asked.

"It's something totally new! You samurai have had Noh plays forever, but Kabuki was just started in Kyoto by Okuni. She was a shrine maiden who used to dance in a riverbed to great crowds. It's going to really catch on here in Edo. Come in! Come in! We're in the midst of rehearsals so you can see for yourself."

Kaze entered the building, curious to see what the peasant had gotten himself into. He found himself in a lobby constructed of rough boards. Goro led Kaze through the small lobby and into the rest of the building. It was a large room. The floor was crisscrossed with low railings, dividing it into sections. Each section had low-quality tatami mats on the floor. At the back of the room was a raised platform that was reminiscent of the platforms used for Noh performances, or by shrine maidens for dancing. Behind the platform was a large curtain with a crudely painted pine tree on it, forming a backdrop.

It was a theater.

Flickering torches illuminated the room, and on the platform a man and a woman were standing. They wore garish kimonos. Kaze was used to the stately refinement of Noh, where the actors were all men. They did wear sumptuous kimonos in Noh, but their faces were covered by masks that indicated what part they were playing. Kaze was surprised by the lack of masks on these players, and he was also surprised at the presence of a woman onstage.

In front of the stage, Hanzo was busy wrapping *omusubi,* rice balls covered with dried seaweed, in broad, green leaves to protect them. Evidently, Hanzo was in charge of selling snacks to the audience.

"The samurai!" Hanzo said. He dropped everything and rushed to Kaze, genuine pleasure showing on his broad peasant's face. He gave a deep bow, and Kaze returned the bow with a nod of his head.

"How did you get involved in this place?" Kaze asked Goro.

"After you gave us the money in Kamakura, we decided to come to Edo to have a good time. Hanzo and I argued about it, because he wanted to spend the money on a once-in-a-lifetime binge, and I wanted to start a business so we don't have to return to our little farm. We decided to compromise. We came to Edo and had a small binge. Before we could complete our binge, we met the former owner of this theater, who offered to sell us this. Hanzo and I argued some more, but we eventually bought it, thanks to the gold you gave us in Kamakura."

The part about Hanzo and Goro arguing was something Kaze could well believe. The two men argued like an old married couple. The two of them running a business was what Kaze found hard to believe.

"Have you ever run a theater before?"

"No, but the man who sold us the theater company said it's a gold mine!"

"And why did the mine owner want to give it up?"

Goro looked puzzled. He looked at Hanzo, who simply scratched his head. Kaze sighed. "Never mind. It doesn't matter."

"Well, I guess business has been a bit slow. The actors get part of the money the people pay, and they've been grumbling about it. I guess many women used to be in the show, but they're gone now. The only woman we have left is her," Goro pointed with his chin at the young girl on the stage. "She used to help the other women get dressed, but she says she's an actress."

Kaze shared some of the samurai view of morality. It was his heritage. But after years of wandering and countless contacts with peasants and other commoners, he understood that the earthy values of the heimin also had a place in society. Still, Kaze didn't quite approve of women onstage. He was sure that if this Kabuki got popular, the Tokugawa authorities would eventually ban women completely. As in Noh, the stage was the realm of men, even if they were playing the parts of women.

"In fact, that girl, Momoko, is helping us to build up business for the theater."

"How?"

"We're going to hand out leaflets to tell people about our big show. We had a woodblock cut with the information about our theater."

"What did it say?"

Goro looked sheepish. "I don't know. I can't read. I just had a woodblock man put down what he thought would get people to the show."

Kaze shook his head. Kaze wondered how many potential patrons couldn't read, either. Goro and Hanzo didn't seem prepared for any business venture.

The couple onstage seemed done with their rehearsals. The girl came off the stage and walked to Goro and Hanzo, apparently wanting to discuss something. In her tight kimono, she walked with the tiny, shuffling steps dictated by the wrapped cloth. Kaze judged her to be in her midteens. She used a wig and some makeup to look older, but her youthful features couldn't be masked. She was not pretty. She had a tiny pug nose, a mouth that was too wide, and a short neck; the exact opposite of classical beauty, which called for a straight nose, a small mouth, and a long, swanlike neck.

As she walked up to the three men, her gaze fixed on Kaze. Her steps slowed, and her eyes widened. She reached the men and stood before Kaze, mute, obviously taken with him. Kaze knew that some women found him attractive, but the girl's blatant fascination made him uncomfortable. He tried to ignore it.

"This is our friend," Hanzo said.

"I am Saburo," Kaze said. Goro and Hanzo looked surprised at the false name, but, for once, they kept their mouths shut.

"I am Momoko," the girl said. Momoko gave a deep bow. Kaze merely nodded in return, as was proper, considering the difference in their ages and social class.

"Excuse me. I didn't realize you had a guest," Momoko said. It was obvious she did realize it and had come forward only to get a better look.

Momoko thought he was thirty or so. He was obviously a samurai, probably a ronin, but he wore only a single sword. It was the long katana sword. He did not have a *wakizashi*, the samurai's "keeper of honor," the sword used for both close-in fighting and to commit seppuku, when necessary. His intense eyes were crowned by expressive eyebrows that made a definite V shape, and he had high cheekbones and a firm jaw. His skin was brown from an extended time outdoors. His expression was serious, but there was a small smile on his lips that made Momoko think he had a sense of humor.

Momoko was used to actors, who tended to be self-involved and vain. This samurai seemed to have no pretensions, and she could tell that her close scrutiny of him made him uncomfortable, not puffed up with the pride men sometimes had when they were attractive to women.

"I, ah, I'll come back later, when you're done with your discussion." She addressed this to Goro and Hanzo, but her eyes were fixed on Kaze. She turned and went back to the stage and the backstage area behind the curtain.

When she left, Kaze said, "Tell me, is there a back entrance to the theater?"

"No, Samurai-san." Goro looked surprised. "Why do you ask?"

"I am interested in the Little Flower Whorehouse, which is on the opposite side of this block."

"Are you, ah, a patron of that place, Samurai-san?" Goro was being discreet, at least for him.

"No," Kaze said. "But I am interested in seeing how its building is laid out."

Goro found the samurai's interest in the architecture of a whorehouse peculiar, but he had already found this particular samurai different from others of his ilk, and he didn't pry.

Have you found this Matsuyama Kaze yet?" Yoshida looked at his chief captain, Niiya, with a scowl.

"No, Lord, we have not. We are searching everywhere. If he is in Edo, we will find him."

"Do you understand how important it is that we find him?"

"Yes, Lord."

"It is a task that the Shogun himself has given me, Niiya. If I do it properly, other important tasks will follow. With Nakamura-san gone, there is no natural successor for the Shogun's favor. Others understand this, and many daimyo are now trying to bring themselves to Ieyasu-sama's attention. If I bring the Shogun the head of this Matsuyama Kaze, then my place in the new government will be assured. Do you understand what that means?"

"Yes, Yoshida-sama."

"Good. Have each district captain talk to every gambler, merchant, and entertainer. This Matsuyama Kaze is staying someplace in Edo, and someone must know about it. Do it quietly, however. This man will be hard to kill, and it will be easier if we can do it with surprise. Spread the gold around. Don't be stingy. Tell them that there is a thousand-*ryo* reward just for information about where he is. Tell them there's a ten-thousand-ryo reward if they bring us his head."

"Ten thousand ryo?" Niiya actually gasped.

"Yes. I have a golden opportunity to place myself in Ieyasu's favor, and I won't let mere money stand in the way of that opportunity. Someone will tell us where he is if the reward is big enough."

"Yes, Yoshida-sama!"

Okubo's hands trembled with excitement. He looked at the sword merchant. "If this is not genuine, it will go hard with you," he said.

The merchant masked his feelings and simply continued unwrapping the object. He unfolded the cloth and revealed the *daito*, the extra long sword, twice as long as a regular katana. It was normally used from horseback, but it could also be used on foot by a man who had trained with it. "I assure you, Okubo-sama, that it is a genuine Muramasa blade. Finding any sword made by

Muramasa is getting extremely difficult, and finding the long-bladed kind favored by you, great Lord, is almost impossible. As you know, the Tokugawas destroy Muramasa blades whenever they can. The blades made by Muramasa have a special enmity for the house of Tokugawa, even though Muramasa blades were made at least two hundred years ago. Ieyasu-sama's grandfather, Kiyoyasu, was killed by a Muramasa blade. Both Ieyasu-sama and his father were hurt by Muramasa blades. And when Ieyasu ordered his son Nobuyasu to commit suicide because he suspected his loyalty, a Muramasa blade was used to remove his head."

"I know of this history," Okubo said curtly. Now it was his turn to mask his feelings. It was precisely this enmity toward the Tokugawas, not the fine craftsmanship, that caused Okubo to covet a blade made by the master swordsmith Muramasa.

The man took a piece of tissue and used it to hold the sword's scabbard. Using another piece of tissue to hold the sword's hilt, he slowly removed the sword a small way from the scabbard and moved it about, letting the light play off the polished surface of the blade. There was a protocol for a formal sword viewing, and the man followed it exactly, removing the blade slightly more and once again showing its beauty. He never completely removed the blade from the scabbard, because it would be an impolite gesture to have a totally naked blade in the presence of a daimyo.

Okubo reached out and took the sword from the merchant. He touched the sword's hilt directly, not using the tissue. If he touched the actual blade, he would use a tissue, but for now he just wanted to get a feel for the blade and its weight.

"I can feel the power of this sword," Okubo said in wonder, more to himself than to the merchant. He drew the blade out from its scabbard. There was no convention of politeness that prohibited a daimyo from showing a naked blade before a merchant. Only when in the presence of another daimyo or the Shogun himself was a daimyo prohibited from drawing a sword.

"I, ah . . ." The merchant looked uncomfortable.

"What is it?"

"Well, Okubo-sama, you have already noted the unusual power found within Muramasa blades. They hunger for blood. But, great Lord, I would not feel comfortable unless I warned you that this power can have an effect on the owner of the blade, as well as the blade's victims. Muramasa blades have been known to drive their owners to rash action. They have been the ruin of more than one owner, and some swear they are unlucky. They have even been known to, ah, drive owners to madness."

Noting the look on Okubo's face, the merchant hastily added, "I have no fears selling this blade to a man of such exceptional strength and character as yourself, of course."

Okubo returned the sword to its scabbard. "My head of household will pay you," Okubo said.

"Thank you, Okubo-sama! Thank you." The merchant placed his hands on the tatami mat and bowed until his head touched the mat. Okubo waved the merchant away. When the man left the room, Okubo took the sword out of its scabbard and placed it before him. The polished blade gleamed with a cold malevolence. He stared at the long ribbon of steel. He could feel the hate and death radiating off the surface, filling the room with insanity. With such a blade, one could bring to closure a lifetime of enmity. One could aspire to any height, achieve any aim. One could even become Shogun.

Okubo shook his head, as if recovering from a dream. Perhaps he was already insane, he thought, daring to think thoughts that were forbidden and deadly.

Honda was also staring at something, but in this case he felt no power emanating from it. It was a simple, earthenware teacup filled with the frothy, bitter brew that resulted when tea was prepared in the formal way.

"Is something wrong, Honda-sama?"

Honda looked sharply at his companion, the man who had prepared the tea with nonchalant elegance. He was too sensitive to the moods of the people around him to make a man like Honda feel really safe in his presence.

"No, nothing," Honda said gruffly.

But, of course, there was something wrong. What he was engaged in went against his entire life. He was a rough warrior, and offering his life and services to the Tokugawas was the twin star that guided his actions. Now he was doing something that made him feel embarrassed and ashamed. Yet, with the changing order of Japan, he believed that he had to do this, and that he would have to change, too.

The Gods knew that Ieyasu-sama had changed. Honda was with Ieyasu almost from the beginning, when Ieyasu was a youth scratching to retain control of his own fief, buffeted by more powerful daimyo on all sides of him. Initially, Ieyasu had been cautious to a fault. They even invented a proverb about Ieyasu, "tapping on a stone bridge," to show his extreme caution in all things. He knew his limitations and refused to exceed them.

Then, as his fortunes changed, his attitude changed, also. Now it seemed like he accepted the awesome title of Shogun as something owed him for his years of struggle, scheming, and planning. But Honda knew the life of a man, any man, could be ended with a sword stroke, so all things of this earth were ephemeral. It didn't even take a sword stroke; Ieyasu had almost been assassinated by an unseen gunman sitting in a fire tower. True, there was no chivalry in such a killing, but Ieyasu would be just as dead if the bullet hit him, regardless of the conventions of bushido, just as Nakamura was dead. Honda snorted.

"Did you say something, Honda-sama?"

Honda looked up from his tea. He held the cup in two hands, one hand on the bottom, the other cupping the side, in the proper fashion. Despite his present circumstances, he wanted to show he was not a complete barbarian. "No," Honda said. He put his teacup down. "Come on," he said, "let's get on with it."

CHAPTER 9

Inky water that
mirrors only the surface.
What lies underneath?

Welcome, welcome!" The gap-toothed man at the door gave an oily bow, rubbing his hands together in anticipation as Kaze and the vegetable merchant entered. The merchant had insisted that he treat Kaze to a drink to thank him for his help with the gamblers, and Kaze had seen no graceful way to avoid his landlord's unwanted generosity.

The building looked like a large house, and there was no sign on the front. Like many buildings in Edo, it had a ramshackle, hastily built look to it. Much of the town was being reconstructed from whatever lumber and materials were available. The wood joinery, normally so meticulous and carefully fitted by Japanese carpenters as they put together a house like a giant puzzle, was sloppy and ill-fitted, because so much of the construction was done by inexperienced craftsmen. Only the rich, like the new daimyo flooding the city, could afford real craftsmen.

In the entry, Kaze took off his sandals and stepped up to the board floor. He was carrying his sword, having given up even the pretext of not being a ronin. After his encounter with the gamblers, it was obvious to the vegetable merchant and his household that he was not just a street entertainer.

"Just a drink tonight," the merchant said.

The man with the gap teeth, who wore a perpetual, if insincere, smile, led them into the depths of the building. Behind one of the ratty *shoji* screens that lined the hallway, Kaze heard the rattle of dice and a thump as the wooden dice cup was slammed to the mat in the room. A small shout escaped from a group of men as the cup was removed to reveal the results.

"Whose establishment is this?" Kaze asked.

The merchant gave a weak smile but didn't otherwise respond.

Oblivious to the merchant's discomfort, the gap-toothed man said, "This is Boss Akinari's place, Samurai-sama. Here you'll find the cheapest sakè and the fairest dice in all of Edo. Please enjoy yourself and come back. Your friend is a regular here. Most of our customers are regulars. That's because they know that Boss Akinari always runs a fair game."

Kaze looked at the merchant with one eyebrow raised. The merchant gave him a sick smile. The merchant had more than just a drink on his mind when he invited Kaze. Obviously, he was testing the waters to see if the arrangement he made with Boss Akinari's men was valid and to see if he was still welcome at the gambling house. He had brought Kaze along to provide some protection.

The man slid back a shoji screen. It looked no different from any of the others in the hallway, but in this room were a half-dozen men drinking instead of gambling. Kaze and the merchant found an unoccupied spot on the tatami mat and sat facing each other. They blocked out the others in the room, as Japanese are trained to do, creating their own private space in a crowded environment.

Kaze and the vegetable merchant ordered sakè, and the gap-toothed man scurried off. Soon he was back with an iron kettle filled with hot water. In the water were two porcelain flasks. He put the kettle down and handed the two men sakè cups; small porcelain saucers, decorated with a chrysanthemum, done in blue paint. The merchant filled Kaze's cup with sakè and, in the Japanese manner, Kaze returned the compliment and filled the merchant's cup.

As they were drinking, the shoji screen slid open and Nobu stuck his head in. The big wrestler looked around, apparently just checking things in the room. When he saw Kaze and the merchant, he seemed surprised. He dipped his head in a greeting, then gently closed the door.

In a few minutes, he returned. He walked up to Kaze, who looked at the large man with a quizzical look.

"Boss Akinari would like to talk to you," Nobu said.

"Me?" Kaze asked, puzzled.

"Yes. I told him about you, and he wants to have a drink with you."

Kaze shrugged and got up. The merchant also started to get to his feet, and Nobu put a hand on his shoulder and pushed him down. "No. Just the ronin," he said.

Kaze was led through the building to the back. The hall was just like the entrance, lined with nondescript shoji screens. Nobu slid a screen open.

Sitting alone in a dimly lit room was a large man in a blue kimono. He wasn't as big as Nobu, but his bull-like neck and massive arms proclaimed him a man not afraid to use physical force to implement his will. His head was shaved, in the manner of a priest, and he wore his kimono open, as you might on a hot summer's evening. Across his chest was a blue tattoo that outlined, in meticulous detail, the scales of a dragon. The tattoo showed clearly that this was no holy man. This type of tattoo was favored by palanquin porters and toughs, and the man sitting in the room didn't have the bowed legs of a porter.

The man looked Kaze over carefully. Boss Akinari was surprised that the ronin was just of average height. He expected a bigger man, considering how the ronin took care of three of his best men.

"Sit down. Have a drink," Boss Akinari said gruffly.

Kaze shrugged and sank to the mat.

As Boss Akinari handed Kaze a sakè cup and started to fill it from a flask, Nobu slid the shoji shut.

"I hear you gave my men a bad time," Akinari said, not bothering with the polite pattern of introduction.

Kaze took the cup and dipped his head in thanks. Then he took the bottle and poured Akinari's drink.

"It was more a lesson in manners," Kaze said.

Akinari gave a snort. Kaze couldn't tell if it was a laugh or comment. He sipped his sakè.

"That's good stuff," Akinari said, as Kaze took a drink. "Not the swill I serve to customers. After a few drinks, they can't tell the difference, anyway."

Kaze didn't respond. The sakè was better than what he was drinking with the vegetable merchant, but it was not top quality. Either Akinari didn't know the difference, or someone was cheating him on the sakè he was being sold. Maybe both.

"I wanted to talk to you to make sure my arrangement with the vegetable dealer will go smoothly," Akinari continued.

"Shouldn't you talk to the vegetable merchant about that?"

Another snort. Kaze still wasn't sure if it was a laugh or not.

"Nobu told me you're pretty strong. You're the guy who can disrupt things, not that mouse of a merchant."

"And what do you think I would disrupt?"

"Didn't the merchant tell you?"

"No. I just rent a room from him. I have no interest in his business."

Akinari hesitated, absorbing this information, then said, "To pay off his gambling debt to me, I've arranged for the merchant to haul things into the city for me, when he goes out to the country to buy vegetables."

"What kind of things?"

"Do you know what tobacco is?"

"That weed brought to Japan by the hairy barbarians, the Europeans? The one you smoke?"

"Yes. The foreigners introduced it to Japan a few years ago. Smoking it is quite good for the health. It's gotten popular with some people, but Ieyasu-sama hates it. He's banned it. Says he'll confiscate the home of anyone caught trading in it."

"And?"

"That makes it valuable! The people who like it can't seem to stop smoking it. I have a string of clients who will pay almost any price for it. Your vegetable merchant will make it easy for me to supply tobacco. He'll smuggle tobacco leaves into Edo under his *daikon, shiso* leaves, and other vegetables. I want to make sure you won't give us any trouble. Those tobacco smokers are real pigs about getting it, and I want a steady supply."

Kaze finished his drink. "The vegetable merchant is nothing to me. It will be inconvenient if his house is seized by the Tokugawa authorities for smuggling tobacco, but that's his concern, not mine." Kaze stood up. He again gave a small nod, not a formal bow, and said, "Thanks for the drink. I have to go now. I want to take a bath, and the public bathhouse in the neighborhood closes early."

Boss Akinari seemed surprised at Kaze's leaving. "Now, now," he said, "you're a good fellow. Why don't you take a bath here? We have our own bathhouse. I'll call a servant to lead you there."

Having your own bath was a luxury. Like most people in the lower classes, the vegetable merchant's house had a privy, but not a bath. Everyone in the household used a public bath, paying a few *sen* for its use.

Boss Akinari bellowed out for a servant, and the gap-toothed man opened the shoji and stuck his head in.

"Take this man to the bath," Akinari ordered.

Kaze thought, Why not? "Thank you," he told Akinari.

"No, it's nothing," Akinari said, waving his hand and giving the polite response for the first time in his conversation with Kaze. "I meant it when I said you were a good fellow," Akinari continued. "I can always use good men, especially if they're as strong as you. I have over a dozen men, but Nobu says you're something special. If you ever want a job with me, just say so. Say, what's your name?"

"Matsuyama Kaze."

Akinari's face remained impassive, but Kaze was puzzled because he thought he saw a flicker of recognition in the gambler's eyes. Still, the fellow was hard to read, and Kaze couldn't figure out what his reactions meant, so he didn't think too much of it. He followed the servant out of the room.

The surface of the water was a black mirror. The light from two paper lanterns reflected off the surface, hiding the depths in darkness. Wisps of steam emerged from the *ofuro* and rose into the air, disappearing into the dark light of the bathhouse. The ofuro was a large wooden enclosure, standing chest high, and filled with hot water.

Many bathhouses were open on one or more sides, especially if there was a view of a garden or some glimpse of nature. This bathhouse was an enclosed room, buried in the back of the gambling den. A sullen servant was sitting on a small stool. He looked up and gave a quick dip of his head as Kaze walked in with the gap-toothed man, who then left Kaze and returned to his post. The servant in the bathhouse didn't seem surprised that a stranger was walking in, and Kaze surmised that the gamblers often used the bath. Dedicated gamblers might gamble for days on end, so being able to soak in a hot refreshing bath would not be an unusual amenity.

With a minimal exchange of words, the servant helped Kaze strip off his clothes and sandals. The servant carefully folded Kaze's kimono and placed it on another stool, and invited Kaze to occupy the seat he had been perched on. Kaze sat as the servant carefully scrubbed him, using a rough cloth. Taking a wooden bucket with a handle attached to its side, the servant dipped into the ofuro to scoop out water to rinse Kaze off. As was the custom, Kaze would be clean when he entered the bathwater. There was no plumbing in the bath. The tub was filled by hand with buckets, and the water poured on Kaze was free to find its way between the slats of the floorboards and onto the earth beneath the building.

When he was thoroughly clean, Kaze stood and the servant placed the stool next to the ofuro, making it easier for Kaze to get in. The water was scalding, but Kaze eased himself into it with a welcome sigh. There was a bench seat in the tub, and Kaze sat on it, the steaming water coming up to his chin. The heat of the water flowed into his muscles, relaxing his joints.

"I'll be outside next to the firebox," the servant said. "If you need more heat, just pound on the wall and I'll put more wood on the fire." The ofuro's water was heated by a copper firebox that intruded into the side of the tub. The open side of the firebox was outside.

Kaze nodded his understanding and watched the servant leave. Then he immediately got out of the tub, took his sword, and placed it next to the tub. He held the scabbard and pushed on the tsuba, the sword guard, until he heard the click that indicated the sword was free of the friction point that held it into the scabbard. Some samurai took baths with wooden swords in their hands, so they would be instantly ready to fend off an attack. Kaze didn't do this, but he did want his sword, named "Fly Cutter" because of a trick that Kaze could do with it, close at all times. He got back into the tub.

Sitting in the water, Kaze closed his eyes. He was in that curious state where ignoring your surroundings makes you acutely aware of them. He let his mind drift, remembering his journey to the battlefield.

A year after Sekigahara, Kaze journeyed to the battlefield. He had never been there. Since he had no idea where the daughter of his Lord and Lady was taken, searching the central region of Honshu, the Kinki district, where Sekigahara was, was as good as searching any other part of Japan.

Although he was there to search for the girl, he also wanted to see the place where his Lord had died and where Japan had been transformed. What he found was a large, U-shaped valley, bordered by hills. The hills were covered with a wild profusion of unusually large wildflowers. They had intense colors, especially the red flowers, which were a deeper shade than any Kaze had seen before. A great number of foxes ducked in and out of the flowers, covering some hillsides so thickly that the foxes also looked like they were some kind of rust-colored flower.

In another place, Kaze might have found the scene charming, but he well understood what it meant at Sekigahara. The wildflowers were fertilized by the blood of thirty thousand men, draining their life into the earth. The year before, the foxes had feasted on the bodies of these men, growing fat for the winter so an unusually large number of them survived the snows and lived to breed.

All the abundant life around him came from death.

Sekigahara was astride the Nakasendo Road and only a short march from the Tokaido Road. Whoever controlled this area could control the movement between Kyoto, the ancient capital, and Ieyasu's domains around Edo.

The forces opposing the Tokugawas had covered the hills, and Ieyasu had marched his army into the middle of the valley. In addition, Ieyasu had decided not to await the arrival of his son, who had a third of the Tokugawa army. The son was diverted besieging a castle, and Ieyasu was furious at his tardiness. If Ieyasu won at Sekigahara, the stubborn castle captured by his son would have no meaning.

Normally, Ieyasu's battle plan would have been disastrous. His smaller army could be crushed on both flanks by the superior forces sitting on the hills on either side of him. But Ieyasu had bribed the commanders on the flanks to either stay neutral or to attack their supposed allies. Of all the forces loyal to Hideyoshi's heir that were bribed, the key was the men of Kobayakawa Hideaki, who sat on a hill and anchored the right flank of the army opposing Ieyasu. Kobayakawa was an adopted son of Hideyoshi, so his treachery was especially surprising and odious.

Survivors of the battle told Kaze that the night before, it had rained heavily, and during the early morning, the entire valley was covered with a dense fog. It was impossible to see either friend or foe. Kaze had been in several battles, and he could imagine what it must have been like.

Through the cold, damp fog, the thunder of the *taiko* war drums was heard. The deep sound of the drums, some as tall as a man, shook the earth if you stood next to them. Some of the drums had arrowheads inside them, to give them the mystic power to penetrate men's souls. The powerful drumming quickened the blood and put men into the mood to kill or be killed.

The battle was desperate, with both sides winning alternating advantage as the fighting surged back and forth. The opposing general, Ishida Mitsunari, was neither skilled nor a great leader, but he should have prevailed, based on sheer numbers and superior position. Instead, lord after lord refused his orders to attack Ieyasu's forces. At first, Kobayakawa simply refused to fight, too, but Ieyasu had a warning volley of musket fire sent his way, and Kobayakawa fell on the flank of his own army. By early afternoon, the hour of the Ram, the battle was lost.

And afterward?

Many committed suicide, because their cause was lost. Some fought to the last man. That's what Kaze's Lord did, along with his men. It is what Kaze would have done, had he been at Sekigahara. Others fled.

After Ieyasu won, it was time to count fallen comrades and view the severed heads of the enemy. At Sekigahara, Ieyasu viewed heads for hours, commenting on the various foes he had defeated. He knew most of them. Some were former allies, and others were longtime enemies.

Ishida ran from the battlefield, but after three days of starving and exposure in the area around Mount Ibuki, he was captured and handed over to Ieyasu. When he was given food and medicine, Ishida declared he would put Ieyasu to the trouble of killing him, instead of committing suicide. Ieyasu obliged.

While on his way to the execution grounds, Ishida was offered a persimmon, which he refused, he said, because it might upset his digestion. When someone expressed surprise at Ishida's concern for his digestion, considering the circumstances, Ishida said, "That shows how little you understand. You can't know how things will turn out, so while you are still breathing, you should take care of your body!" Ishida should have enjoyed the persimmon, Kaze thought, because his head was detached from his body just minutes later.

Kaze knew his Lord had died leading a suicide charge near the end of the battle. His Lord saw the traitors defecting to Ieyasu's side, and he knew the battle was lost. He took the samurai of Kaze's clan and plunged into the midst of the traitors, killing many of them before he was cut down himself. Kaze could imagine his Lord at Sekigahara, wearing his best suit of armor, the one with the blue silk cords, leading the doomed charge.

Sitting in the ofuro with his eyes closed, Kaze could picture that charge. He told himself that the drops running down his face were sweat, not tears. But they tasted like tears when they reached his lips.

Creak.

One of the floorboards outside the bathhouse made a sound. Kaze remained motionless. If it was someone coming to the bathhouse normally, then it would be easy to hear their steps as they approached. Instead, one or more people were trying to sneak up to the door.

The door was suddenly slid back, and a man charged into the bathhouse, his sword at the ready. Kaze instantly stood, reaching down and drawing his sword as he did so. All in one motion, he extracted his sword from its scabbard and swept it forward. The tip of the sword caught the man in the sternum and his own forward motion drove the blade in.

Surprised, the man crumpled at the edge of the tub, dying, as a second man entered the bathhouse. Kaze rolled out of the tub, landing on his feet with his back to the new assailant. As his feet hit the floor, he pivoted, with his sword cutting a flat arc that came around and caught the second attacker across the neck and shoulder. With a groan of pain, this man hit the floor, to join his companion.

Kaze stood, naked, and facing the door with his sword in the aimed-at-the-eye position. In the doorway, a third man stood, one foot on the threshold of the bathhouse, with the other still in the hall. He held his sword in one hand, his other hand on the edge of the door.

"Well?" Kaze said.

After a second's hesitation, the man slammed the door shut and started running down the hall for reinforcements.

Boss Akinari and a dozen of his men burst into the bathhouse a minute later. The two men on the floor were obviously dead, their dark blood covering the wet boards of the bathhouse.

"Where is he?" Akinari asked.

"He was here a minute ago," the third assassin said.

Akinari quickly looked at the room, his gaze alighting on the stool that had Kaze's kimono still folded on it, and the sandals next to them.

"He's run outside," Akinari said. "Fan out and find him!"

"But what does he look like?" one of his men asked.

"Look! His kimono is still here. He'll be naked and barefoot. How many naked men are you going to find on the street? Just find him and kill him! Scatter!"

Akinari and his men tumbled down the hallway, looking for a naked man trying to escape them.

In the silent bath, the echoes of their pounding feet dissipated and died. The glow of the paper lanterns cast deep shadows and made wavy orange streaks on the black surface of the water. Suddenly, from the middle of the ofuro, the surface of the water was disturbed. A head of black hair appeared, with the silver ribbon of a sword blade next to it. Kaze surfaced from the black water holding his katana.

He stood in the ofuro and listened, seeing if the hallway was clear.

Look at how he walks.
Is it the walk of a ghost?
Does the toe touch first?

Nobu entered his room. The shutters on the window were closed and the single candle he held hardly penetrated the gloomy darkness.

He sighed. He was tired. Like the rest of Boss Akinari's men, he had spent most of the night looking for the ronin. Unsuccessfully.

His futon was already spread on the floor. He lived in Boss Akinari's house, just like all the high-ranking members of the gang, and the servants would take out the bedding from a shelf every night and spread it on the floor of the plain room, ready for sleep.

Nobu was debating about going to get a bath before flopping down on the futon when a voice said, "Why did your Boss want to kill me?"

Nobu was a man not easily startled, but the voice coming from the dark corners of his own room made him jump. He held the candle up, so the light could penetrate the gloom. In the darkest corner, Nobu saw the dim outline of a man sitting. The figure moved his arm and into the yellow light of the candle the tip of an unsheathed sword appeared. The ronin!

"Why did your boss want to kill me?" Kaze repeated, letting his naked sword add urgency to the question.

"How did you get in here?" Nobu asked.

"I never left," Kaze replied.

"How did you know this was my room?"

Kaze pointed with his sword. "After the maids laid out the futons, it was easy to tell which one was yours. It's twice the size of a normal one."

"But—"

"I'm the one who stayed just so I could ask you a few questions," Kaze interrupted. "It is most impolite to ignore my questions as I answer yours. Now, why did Boss Akinari want me killed?"

"He wanted to collect the reward. He knows."

For a moment, Kaze thought that Akinari knew that he was a man wanted by the Tokugawas because of his ties to the Toyotomis. He decided to clarify this. "He knows what?"

"That you tried to assassinate the Shogun."

Now it was Kaze's turn to be surprised. He stayed silent, to see if silence would extract more information. It did.

Nobu licked his lips. Then he said, "I didn't want you to be killed, but the reward for your head is ten thousand ryo. No one could pass that up. There's a thousand ryo just for leading the authorities to you."

Even a thousand ryo was considerably larger than the reward for turning in a Toyotomi loyalist.

Kaze stayed silent for several more minutes, but Nobu didn't volunteer more. Finally, Kaze asked, "How does Boss Akinari know about this reward? I haven't seen notice boards posted around the city."

"The district captain told him. We give a payoff to him every month. Otherwise we couldn't operate a gambling den in this place. He said they don't want to post the reward on public notice boards yet, so you won't know and will be surprised."

Kaze was indeed surprised, but not because someone had suddenly tried to take his life. That had happened often enough. It was the thought that the Tokugawas had identified him as Ieyasu's would-be assassin that surprised him.

"Why do they think I'm the one who tried to kill the Shogun?"

"You were spotted near the place where the gunman hid."

The young captain who looked at Kaze so strangely when Kaze was doing his street act with the tops.

"Well, I didn't try to kill Ieyasu-sama," Kaze said conversationally. "If I had, he would be dead. But I suppose that doesn't matter if the authorities think I'm the one who tried to kill him. What a bother!"

Nobu looked like he was going to ask about what kind of bother it was, but Kaze stood up. He wasn't going to explain to the big wrestler about his quest to find the daughter of his Lord and Lady. Becoming the most hunted man in Edo would make it difficult to observe the Little Flower Whorehouse to see if the girl was still there, and to develop a plan to rescue her if she was. "What a bother!" he said again.

Kaze pointed to Nobu with his sword. "You're a good fellow, and I like you. I should kill you now, to keep you quiet. Instead, I'm going to walk out of here and I want you to treat our conversation as a dream. You must be tired, spending the night in the cold looking for me. I suggest you crawl onto the futon and go to bed. But whatever you do, please don't make me sorry I let you live. If you do, I promise I will do my best to come back and correct that mistake."

Then, without warning, Kaze took a cut at the candle. The sword moved with such speed that Nobu heard it more than saw it. A quick swish of air that seemed too gentle a sound to carry death with it. Nobu didn't see the sword hit the candle, but the light was snuffed out. Nobu could see the dying ember of the wick, fading to orange in the darkness. Incredibly, the ronin had cut off the burning wick of the candle, but left the rest intact.

Too stunned to move, Nobu strained to hear where the ronin was. He heard nothing, but suddenly, behind him, the door to his room opened. The dim light of the hall spilled into the darkened room. He turned to see who was entering the room and instead he saw the ronin leaving. Nobu's spine tingled at the thought of a man who could move so quickly and so silently. He watched the ronin's feet as he left the room. He wanted to make sure the ronin walked with his heel touching the ground before his toes. Ghosts walked with their toes touching first, and he wanted to assure himself that this ronin was a man, and not an *obake*.

After he was sure the ronin was gone, Nobu made his way to the bath. His body was covered with sticky, dried sweat. He tried to tell himself that the sweat had come from the search, but he knew he had not been sweaty when he walked into his room.

The bathhouse had been cleaned up. The bodies of the slain men were removed, and the walls and floor were still wet from countless buckets of water used to wash off the blood. Because of this extra effort, the attendant was not around. Nobu surmised that, like all of them, the attendant was tired after this extraordinary night. He stuck his hand into the ofuro and the water was hot enough, so he decided to take his bath without getting the attendant to help scrub his back and tend to the fire.

As Nobu started stripping down, he noticed that only one of the wooden stools was sitting on the bathhouse floor. There were usually two stools in the bathhouse, and Nobu was so large that he generally put the two of them side by side to sit on.

He looked around for the second stool, and found the pieces of it neatly stacked in a corner. Nobu was puzzled. In another corner of the bathhouse, he saw something curious. He went over and picked it up, holding it up to the lantern that illuminated the bathhouse so he could see it better. Someone had taken one of the legs from the broken stool and carved a Kannon, the Goddess of Mercy. Then the artist had placed the Kannon so it looked upon the place where the two men had died.

Nobu looked around and saw nothing else to explain the little statue. He looked back at the Kannon, seeing a face of infinite beauty and tranquility. Reverently, he placed the Kannon back in place.//

Kaze continued to move as silently as a shadow cast by a swinging lantern as he made his way back to the merchant's house. He had decided he would not spend the night, but there was something there he wanted; his sword-cleaning materials. It was common for a samurai to get his sword wet, in rain or when fording streams, but every samurai also took care of his sword, because the sword was an expression of his spirit and soul.

Kaze had just immersed his sword in water. Now he wanted to clean his sword and give it a light coating of oil, to protect it. "Fly Cutter" was precious to him. It was new, and he had never had a sword so lively and finely balanced. It was a natural extension of his arms, and was rapidly becoming part of his spiritual core.

Kaze approached the merchant's house and observed it for several minutes. All seemed normal, with light peeking out through tiny gaps in the shutters. Kaze crossed to the house and opened the door.

"Tadaima. I'm home," Kaze said.

The merchant's wife and the maid were sitting on the floor, whispering to each other across a low table. They looked up when Kaze entered, and gave an answering bow of their heads as Kaze dipped his head in greeting. He was puzzled that they were still up, but he didn't want to engage them in conversation.

Kaze made his way up the steep stairs, almost a ladder, to his room. Next to the folded futon sitting on a shelf was a bundle wrapped in a cloth. Kaze took the bundle and unwrapped it, taking out soft cloths and a small flask of oil. He carefully wiped down his blade, cleaning it. After he had cleaned it to his satisfaction, he took the flask of oil, poured some on a cloth, and coated the blade. He thought of disassembling the handle to clean the tang, but decided he didn't want to feel vulnerable while his sword was taken apart. He would do that when he had a safer place.

Just as he was sliding the blade back into its scabbard, he heard some footsteps on the stairs.

"*Sumimasen!* Excuse us! May we come up to see you?" It was the voice of the merchant's wife.

"*Dozo.* Please." Kaze was curious about what she wanted.

The wife and the maid came up the stairs, entering Kaze's small room and standing next to the stairwell, looking nervous. They were dressed in plain kimonos, but Kaze realized they were probably the finest kimonos they owned, because they were not patched. Clothes were expensive and were often given as a special present by a lord to a vassal. Most common people had their everyday kimonos patched in some way. Every other day he was in the house, Kaze had noticed the patches on the kimonos of the wife and servant, and he was curious about why they had apparently put on their best kimonos tonight.

"Well?" Kaze asked.

"My husband is still out . . ." The wife spoke haltingly, then stopped.

"Yes?" Kaze encouraged.

"And, ah, and . . ."

Kaze was puzzled. The two women looked at each other nervously, then back at Kaze. He smiled, to encourage the wife.

"And . . ." the wife began, before halting again.

"My mistress wants to say," the maid broke in, "that we are both grateful for what you did, saving us from the gamblers."

"Yes?"

"And, ah, and . . ."

Kaze was losing patience with the wife's halting explanation. He frowned. The maid saw this and once again broke in.

"Anyway, my mistress and I are so grateful that we want to show our gratitude by giving you a most exciting night."

"Exciting?" Kaze asked, puzzled.

By way of answer, the maid loosened her kimono sash and shrugged the garment off her shoulders. She was wearing the cloth wrap that served as a foundation garment and underwear beneath. She quickly undid the wrap and let that fall to the floor, too. She stood naked, giving Kaze a nervous smile.

Seeing her maid's actions, the merchant's wife did likewise, and in an instant, Kaze was confronted with two nervous and naked women. The wife had an arm across her breast and a hand across her loins, but the maid stood brazenly, looking at Kaze's reaction.

Kaze's reaction was surprise. Another surprise on a most surprising night. He was about to speak when he saw the eyes of the wife dart nervously toward the stairs. In an instant, he was on his feet, his sword drawn from its scabbard. He dashed to the stairwell and looked down it. Looking up at him in surprise was an armored samurai, creeping up the stairs, sword in hand, with at least a half-dozen men behind him.

Seeing Kaze, the samurai shouted and charged up the stairs. Kaze allowed him to get his head and shoulders past the top stair. The samurai took a cut at Kaze's legs with his drawn sword. Kaze dropped his sword blade to block the officer's blow; then he immediately twisted his blade to the side and thrust the point into one of the few places not protected by the armor, right under the samurai's chin.

The samurai grabbed at the blade as Kaze withdrew his sword, then immediately collapsed, knocking the two men behind him off the stairs and down on the remaining men on the ground floor.

The wife and maid shrank away from Kaze, snatching up their kimonos and huddling together in a corner of the room. They looked at Kaze with fear, uncertain about what revenge he might take. Instead, Kaze picked up his scabbard and ran to the shuttered window, opening it. Shoving his scabbard into his kimono sash, he started stepping out of the window and onto the tiled roof. Despite the sound of men running up the stairs, he paused before he completely exited the room, looking over his shoulder at the merchant's wife and the maid.

"It has already been an exciting night," he said. "You didn't have to add to it." Then, he added, "By the way, I would have turned you down."

There was a pale quarter-moon casting long gray shadows when Kaze went out on the roof. He looked down and was surprised to see hordes of soldiers rushing out of nearby houses and running to the vegetable merchant's house. Evidently the men on the stairs were just the vanguard of a larger party of troops sent to kill or capture him. Kaze surmised that Boss Akinari, unable to collect the ten-thousand-ryo reward, had settled for the thousand for turning him in.

It's not convenient to be the most wanted man in Edo, Kaze thought as he made his way up the roof and over the peak. He had seen red glows moving with several of the men and he knew that meant they had guns. He wanted to be on the opposite side of the roof from men with matchlock muskets.

Behind him, he could hear the men shouting and passing through the window onto the roof. The houses of Edo were jammed together, so often two, three, and even four houses had their roofs touching. The roofs were made of board and tile. Because of cost, board was the most popular, but there was talk of the Tokugawas requiring tile roofs, to cut down on fires. Many of the side streets and alleys were so narrow that Kaze thought he could easily jump them.

Kaze had left his sandals at the entry to the merchant's house, but he still had on his tabi socks and they were slippery on the sloping roof. He almost slid off the roof when he tried to stop and had to put one hand down to maintain his balance. As soon as he regained his equilibrium, he ripped one of the tabi off.

This delay allowed the first pursuer to catch him. Kaze caught the pursuer's blow on his blade, and his tabi-covered foot slipped, making it impossible for Kaze to immediately counterattack. Another man might have cursed this situation, but Kaze simply shifted his stance so his weight was primarily on his bare foot, which had much better purchase on the slippery slope.

His opponent was well trained and disciplined, the hallmark of a good swordsman. Kaze parried two of his cuts, but the other swordsman wasn't trying to press his advantage. Kaze realized that his opponent didn't have to. All he had to do was hold Kaze in place until his comrades arrived or a musketeer could get a shot from the ground. Despite his lack of a firm stance, Kaze went on the attack.

The other swordsman parried two of Kaze's cuts, but not the third. Kaze's sword caught him on the side of the neck, and the man fell to the roof, sliding to the edge, almost taking Kaze with him as he tumbled over.

Kaze still wanted to remove the other tabi sock, but he had no time. The next man out of the window was over the roof's peak and upon him. This man wasn't as disciplined or as good a swordsman as the first. Kaze dodged his cut and brought his own blade down across the man's forearm, slicing it in two. The man was holding his sword in two hands, and he looked down with surprise as suddenly he was holding it with one. He saw the severed arm hit the roof and a look of befuddlement passed across his face, the shock, pain, and reality of the situation not yet registering.

Not waiting to see the man's reaction, Kaze immediately ripped off the other tabi and started running across the roof. The merchant's house was so close to his neighbor's that Kaze was able to easily step from one roof to the other without breaking stride. Behind him, he could hear shouts and running feet.

At the end of this roof, Kaze had to make a short leap to cover the distance across a side street. As he did so, he heard the crack of a musket firing. Kaze didn't feel the ball whistle past, but he knew the shot was aimed at him. On the next roof, he changed direction, jumping to a roof behind the house he was running on. He looked over his shoulder and saw at least three samurai in pursuit. He knew that was just the vanguard and that there would be others.

He ran up the slope of the new roof and over the peak. He cut to the left and started running again. Behind him he heard one of his pursuers crest the roof and start after him. With sandals on, however, his pursuer didn't make the change in direction in time, and he skidded off the roof, falling down to the street below with a yell. Probably not high enough to kill a man, Kaze thought, but the fall certainly resulted in broken bones.

Kaze ran across three more roofs. Though he could keep ahead of the men pursuing him across the rooftops, he couldn't run faster on the uneven and steep roofs of Edo than the men pursuing him on the ground. As he changed directions, the men on the ground fanned out, searching for him. Sometimes his pursuers on the rooftops shouted directions to the men on the ground, and sometimes the men on the ground directed the pursuers on the roof. Occasionally, a musketeer on the ground fired a shot at him, but none of the shots came close, and they may have been fired more as a signal to the other men of Kaze's location than as an attempt to hit him.

As Kaze ran, he tried to anticipate an end game, and none of the possibilities looked good. With the number of men pursuing him, he couldn't fight them. Even if he killed several of them, there were more to replace them. He could open one of the occasional attic windows, like the one in his room, but then he was likely to be trapped between the pursuers on the roof and the pursuers on the ground: not a pleasant alternative. Lacking a better plan, he continued to cross the rooftops, leaping the gaps between roofs, pulling ahead of the pursuers behind him, but not outdistancing the ones on the ground.

He came to the end of a string of three roofs and recognized where he was. Ahead of him, across the gap of a major street, were warehouses lined up along one of the many canals that cut through Edo. Kaze stood and looked at the gap ahead of him. The distance was long, and he was winded. He put his sword in its scabbard, looked over his shoulder at the men chasing him, and risked running backward, so he would have a running start at the leap. He stopped, and just as the first of his pursuers had almost caught him, he started running forward again, this time at full speed, toward the wide chasm between the roof he was on and a roof on the other side of the wide street.

He reached the end of the roof and launched himself into space, flinging himself into the nighttime void, stretching forward to bridge the gap between the two roofs. He flew through the air, sustained only by his determination to elude his pursuers. He landed on the edge of the other roof hard, the impact knocking the wind out of him as he skidded across the tiles.

Behind him, he heard one of his pursuers yell, "I'll get him!

Make sure the men on the ground surround the warehouses."

Kaze looked over his shoulder and saw one of the pursuers running toward the gap. The man launched himself into space as Kaze had done, intending to clear the street and reach the safety of the warehouse roof. But Kaze was barefoot and wearing a kimono. This man had sandals on, and he had the extra weight of a helmet and armored jacket. He fell short of the roof, one hand barely reaching the roof's edge and grabbing desperately at a tile. The tile was yanked out of its mud base and the man, still clutching the tile, fell to the ground with a thud. Out of instinct, Kaze peeked over the edge of the warehouse and looked down at the body crumpled on the street below. It lay very still.

The pursuers on the ground reached the scene and two of them, in the red glow of the fuses on the matchlock muskets, stopped and took aim. Kaze withdrew his head from the roof's edge as the muskets fired. This time the shots were close enough for Kaze to hear the lead balls whizzing by.

Still gasping for air, Kaze crossed the roof to get near the canal side. He reached there, looked down, and realized that there was a street even wider than the one he had jumped between the warehouse and the dark waters of the canal. With the wind knocked out of him, Kaze couldn't make another long jump at that moment, and he lay back on the roof, staying out of sight and trying to regain his breath.

Below, he heard the noise of men as they surrounded the warehouse. In a few seconds, he heard the clatter of a horse arriving on the scene. Obviously, the officer in charge.

"Where is he?"

"He's up there on the roof, sir!"

"Are you sure?"

"Yes, we have men on the roof on the opposite side so he can't go back, and all four sides of the warehouse are surrounded."

"Can we get men on that roof?"

"Apparently not, sir. Kojima tried jumping it from the other side and fell. He's hurt pretty bad—"

"Yakamashii! Shut up! I don't want a health report when all you men couldn't trap one lone ronin. Just get a party of men into that warehouse and see if there's any way to the roof. Bust the door down if you have to. You and you! Go to the nearest fire station and get their ladders. Bring them here and we'll send men up to the roof from two different sides. And you! Get me my gun. I'll guard the canal side of the building. Go around the entire building and make sure the other musketeers are spread out and ready, in case he shows himself. Is that clear?"

Several voices shouted, "Hai! Yes!" Then Kaze heard the sound of running feet.

Kaze was impressed. Whoever was in charge of the operation was a good officer. In a few minutes, the officer's efficient planning would soon flush him out from the warehouse roof, one way or another. Kaze decided he would be flushed out in the best way possible for him, and not in the ways the officer had planned.

With the musketeers set and ready, there was a good chance he would be hit when he tried to jump to the canal. He shrugged one arm out of his kimono sleeve and crawled to the edge of the roof. He took the scabbard out of his sash and stuck the tip into the loose sleeve. He started lifting the sleeve slowly. In the dark of the night, the black mass of the sleeve would look like someone peering over the edge of the roof. Kaze had barely gotten the sleeve raised when there was the crack of a gun. He was surprised to feel the tug on his scabbard as the cloth of his sleeve was shoved back. At the report of the first gun, two other muskets at other sides of the building were fired, out of sheer nervousness and tension, because it was impossible for the musketeers to see anything.

Kaze now had a few seconds before the muskets could be reloaded. He jumped to his feet and took a quick look down. A man in an officer's helmet was furiously reloading his musket. Holding his sword in one hand and the scabbard in the other, he summoned all his strength, took two quick steps, and jumped into space.

The officer was sure he hit the figure on the roof, so he was surprised when his quarry jumped up before the echoes of the musket died down. He was even more surprised as the man jumped off the roof. Sword and scabbard in each hand, with one sleeve of his kimono flapping behind him, the man looked like a *tengu,* a quarrelsome creature that was half man and half bird, and able to fly.

While reloading his musket, he followed the arc of the man's jump as he sailed over his head toward the canal. The man made it to the canal water with no distance to spare, entering the black water with a tremendous splash that threw water high past the edge of the canal. The water caught the pale moonlight, transmuting it from black to silver as it sparkled in the air.

The officer finished loading his gun and ran to the edge of the canal. He couldn't see the man, but he fired into the center of the splash, hoping to hit him. In seconds, other musketeers had run up to the canal's edge, and a ragged volley of shots pierced the blackness.

Some of the men ran down the canal to a bridge, crossed over, and lined the opposite bank. All the men were observing the dark water, waiting to see a head pop up. The officer reloaded his musket and waited along with the rest, hopeful to get another shot at the ronin. Even against the darkness of the water, he was confident he would hit the man's head as soon as it broke the surface.

But it didn't break the surface.

After many long minutes, the officer wondered if his shots or one of the other shots had killed the man after he entered the water. He ordered torches brought, and he told his men to secure boats and long poles, so they could probe the murky waters of the canal to see if they could find the ronin's body.

CHAPTER 11

A piece of bamboo,
small finger holes, a soft breath,
and divine music.

This is a disaster," Hanzo said.

"Well, it was your idea to take the money the ronin gave us and get a business," Goro said accusingly.

"*Baka!* Fool! It was your desire to spend the money on a spree. Now we have a business!" Hanzo replied.

"A failing business! Why didn't you check this? How can you buy a business without knowing about it? No wonder the former owner sold it to us! He saw a fool coming."

"You agreed to it, too. That makes you just as big a fool!"

"So you admit that you're a fool!"

"I admit nothing. It's just that—"

The knocking at the door of the theater sounded like blows on a taiko drum, reverberating in the empty theater and causing the two peasants' eyes to grow round with surprise.

"Who's that?" Goro asked in a whisper.

"I don't know. Go see."

"I don't want to see. Why don't you see?"

"Why should I see? Why don't you—"

The knocks were repeated, even more insistently.

The two men looked at each other.

"Why don't we both see?" Hanzo suggested.

Goro nodded and followed his partner to the theater door. Goro removed the stick that acted as a lock and slid the door open a few inches. He gasped and jumped away from the opening.

"What is it?" Hanzo asked.

Pointing a shaking finger, Goro said, "Look!"

Tentatively, Hanzo peeked through the open slit of the door. There, in the pale light that spilled out through the slit, Hanzo saw an apparition. It was in the shape of a man, with its kimono dripping wet and hanging loosely on its body. A sword was stuck in its sash, and its face was obscured by wet hair. Two eyes glowed out, watching Hanzo like a hawk watches a mouse.

"What's the matter?" the apparition said.

Hanzo started, but then recognized the voice. "It's the samurai, Matsuyama-san!" he exclaimed. Goro put his head next to his partner's, confirming the identification despite the figure's appearance.

"You look like a ghost!" Hanzo answered.

The figure smiled.

"Don't smile!" Hanzo said hastily. "It looks even worse when you smile."

"Well, then, open the door and let me in, or I will be a ghost. If the authorities don't see me, then the cold will kill me."

Hanzo slid the door open and allowed Kaze into the theater. Then he slid the door shut and locked it.

"What happened?" Goro asked the samurai.

"I went for a moonlight swim," Kaze said. He had swum underwater to the darkness under the bridge. That allowed him to surface and take a breath. "I did most of my swimming underwater tonight." Seeing Goro's puzzled face, Kaze added, "I had to stay underwater or I'd have been killed."

"Killed! By who?"

"By you, if you don't allow me to get out of these wet clothes."

Kaze was amused. Behind the curtain that hung across the theater's stage was another world. In a corner, bamboo baskets held wigs and small props. In the center of the backstage area, tatami mats were laid, with small chests that held makeup of various sorts. Along the walls were bamboo poles hung with costumes of all varieties. Kaze had selected a samurai's costume, but much gaudier than any he would have actually worn.

Hanzo took a small kettle from a firebox and poured Kaze a cup of tea.

Kaze took the cracked cup gratefully, sipping at the bitter liquid with relish. "*Oishii!* Good!" he said.

"So why did you have to go swimming, Samurai-san?" Goro said.

"If I tell you, it may be dangerous," Kaze replied.

"The first time we met you, you said it might be dangerous. Didn't we do good with that danger?"

"You did very good."

"So tell us."

Kaze considered for a moment. He didn't know if he could trust these two, but he needed a base of operations in Edo. He decided that he should tell the two men about the reward, not as a test, but because undoubtedly notice boards would spring up all over the city by morning. Now there was no advantage in keeping the reward a secret. "If I tell you, I must also ask you to resist the temptation of a thousand ryo."

"A thousand!" Goro spluttered.

"Now, now, let's not get excited about money we don't have," Hanzo said to his partner. "This samurai was kind to us and treated us with honesty and respect. No other samurai has done that for us. I think we should help him."

"Yes, but a thousand ryo . . ." Goro muttered.

Scratching his chin, Kaze said, "Actually, I think if you can kill me, you can earn ten thousand ryo."

"Ten thousand ryo!" Now it was Hanzo's turn to splutter.

"This man is a devil," Goro said to Hanzo. "For ten thousand ryo a man would kill his own beloved *obaasan*! If a man would kill his own grandmother, how can he expect us not to do something with him?"

Kaze smiled. "You might find me a little harder to kill than your beloved grandmother," he suggested.

"Now calm down," Hanzo said. "The samurai is obviously teasing us. No one could offer ten thousand ryo as a reward. That's impossible!"

"But with our business failing, even a few ryo would help."

"Is your theater in trouble?" Kaze asked.

Goro put his hands to his head. Hanzo looked at Kaze and said, "We were cheated when we bought this theater. We were told it was a big moneymaker, and it was, but only because the Kabuki allowed women to do lascivious dances onstage. The Tokugawas recently banned that, so now we have to depend on actors to bring in the crowds." He sighed. "Now the actors do plays that are like Noh dramas, but they're not really trained in Noh, and the audience doesn't seem too interested in it anyway. I was told the audience was mostly men, but without the women dancing, we seem to get only a few family groups. We don't know what to do. We thought we'd just buy the theater and collect the money, but now we'll lose everything."

Kaze shook his head.

Hanzo sighed. "Well, we can settle this in the morning. Don't worry, Goro and I won't do anything to turn you in. We have a room at a boardinghouse near here. We'd invite you there, but it's a small room and—"

"Don't worry," Kaze said. "I'll be quite comfortable here. We'll talk in the morning again."

"All right," Hanzo said. "Come on, Goro, let's let the samurai sleep, and we need rest ourselves. We have to figure out what we're going to do to save this failing theater, and with it our money."

Hanzo and Goro left, leaving Kaze alone in the dark theater with a single lantern to pierce the murky gloom. Kaze found a robe in one of the costume baskets, and he used it to cover himself as he stretched out on the floor. He blew out the candle and lay in the dark, thinking about his next moves and what he would have to do.

As long as the Tokugawas thought he was the assassin, he would never be able to rescue the girl. If he stood on the street observing the Little Flower brothel, eventually someone would become suspicious and report him to the authorities. He didn't have money or proper clothes, so he couldn't walk into the brothel, pretending to be a customer, to look for the daughter of his Lady. In its way, the Little Flower Whorehouse was as tough a fortress to crack as mighty Osaka Castle itself.

As Kaze lay in the darkness, he became aware of a tiny patch of starlight high on the wall. It came from a vent on the back wall of the theater that allowed smoke from lanterns and hibachis to escape. A bamboo lattice covered the vent, keeping out birds and bats, but between the bars, Kaze's sharp eyes were able to make out individual stars in the sky. Without a pattern to guide him, Kaze wasn't sure what stars he was looking at, but it comforted him to know that, through those tiny holes in the bamboo lattice, the stars that had accompanied him on all his journeys were once more looking down at him.

From the lattice grill, Kaze also heard the faint, plaintive sounds

of a bamboo flute, the shakuhachi. The high-pitched, breathy
notes of the flute floated above the crude roofs of Edo and wove
themselves through the starlight. Kaze didn't know the tune being
played, but he did know it was a song of loss and sadness. He
closed his eyes and allowed himself the luxury of dropping his
guard for just one moment, immersing his being in the slow
rhythm of the music.

Kaze thought of the story in *Uji shui monogatari*, which told of
Fujiwara Yasumasa, who was walking across a desolate marsh one
moonlit night. To while away the time, he started playing his flute.
Unknown to him, a dangerous bandit was hiding in the under-
brush, waiting to kill and rob him. Through the mastery of his
flute playing, Yasumasa mesmerized and overwhelmed the robber,
charming him into submission as he fell under the flute's spell.

Kaze snapped himself to attention. He did so not because he
had heard a sound but because he realized he was in a state of
reverie where he would miss a small sound, if there was one to
hear. Not hearing such a sound could cost him his life. He was
not afraid to die, but he wanted his death to have meaning, and
being killed because you dropped your guard while listening to
flute music was not a meaningful death. Kaze drew his sword
closer to him and thought of the death of Takeda Shingen.

While besieging Noda Castle, owned by Ieyasu's clan, Shingen
heard that a flute player played each night from the castle walls.
While he played, both sides stopped fighting and listened to the
plaintive melodies. Shingen decided to hear this music and had a
place set up for him near the castle walls, behind a reed screen. A
musketeer saw the preparations and made preparations of his
own.

The musketeer set up his gun so he could shoot at the reed
enclosure, even in the dark of night. He waited until the flute
player was in the midst of his concert and fired one bullet into

the enclosure. By luck, he struck Shingen himself, although at the time the musketeer didn't know it. Mortally wounded, the wily Shingen gave orders to keep news of his death hidden for three years.

Now Kaze was accused of trying to kill Ieyasu in a similar manner, with a musket. Kaze was almost insulted that they thought he used a musket. Any peasant could be trained to point a musket in the direction of the enemy and fire.

The muskets were the "gift" of the hairy barbarians from Europe, and Kaze wished they were banned from warfare in Japan. A peasant armed with a musket could kill a superbly trained samurai, turning the value of years of samurai training and swordwork upside down. Kaze's own training had been intense, especially during the formative years when he studied under the Sensei, his teacher.

Almost all Japanese art was taught by a master to a pupil, from painting to dancing to fencing. Over and over again, Kaze was drilled in the physical actions that somehow turned into mental and spiritual lessons. Over and over again.

The pattern of attack and defense was repeated endlessly. The purpose was to teach Kaze proper *kata*, or form, and Kaze's Sensei seemed to have an inexhaustible fund of patience as he persistently practiced the same moves. First Kaze attacked the Sensei using the same precise sequence of moves; then Kaze was in turn attacked by the Sensei, repeating the exact moves Kaze made. As Kaze increased his mastery of the sequence of attack and defense, the Sensei drastically increased the speed, dancing their repetitive ballet at ever higher levels.

Once, when he was ten, Kaze was frustrated by the endless practice, and he dared to swing his sword with anger. Another would not have detected the emotions behind Kaze's sword cuts, but the Sensei immediately stopped the practice. He glared at Kaze and said, "Baka! Fool!"

The Sensei never swore, but he made the word "fool" sound as scornful and withering as any torrent from a drunken samurai. Kaze's face burned red, and he hung his head in shame. It was the Japanese way for the novice to learn from the master, but it was also the Japanese way for the novice to accept the pace of teaching set by the master, and never show frustration.

"I'll teach you the most important thing you can learn in a fight," the Sensei said. "Until you defeat yourself, you cannot defeat others. If you fight from anger, frustration, or pride, you cannot win. You must fight from nothingness, letting the sword seek its own path. If you let your emotions rule you in a fight, even if you overcome your enemy, you have not won. Can you understand that?"

"I think so, Sensei."

"As you get older, you'll have more cause for rage. It's a sad part of life that the passage of time is the accumulation of pain. When that happens, you'll not only understand this lesson better, you'll have more need of it."

Kaze had taken that lesson to heart, and had never again vented his emotions through his sword.

This particular practice was an especially long and tedious one. Finally, convinced that Kaze had learned as much as he was going to that day, the Sensei stopped. Gratefully, Kaze sat on a log at the edge of the meadow they were practicing in and he reached for a jug of water. "*Mizu*, Sensei?" Kaze asked.

The old man, who seemed hardly winded, gave a negative nod of his head. Kaze uncorked the jug and poured the water down his throat. The water was cold and sweet, as refreshing as water taken directly from a mountain stream. The Sensei was six times older than Kaze, but Kaze had stopped being embarrassed that

KILL THE SHOGUN   113

the old man seemed to have resources of stamina that far exceeded his own. The wellspring of the Sensei's strength was his spirit, not his body, and Kaze knew he had a considerable amount of growth before his spirit could even approach his teacher's.

"Can you tell me something, Sensei?" Kaze asked after he had caught his breath.

The Sensei nodded his head slightly. Kaze knew this was his signal to continue.

"I practice each pattern until I learn it precisely. If I meet some-one in a duel who recognizes what pattern I'm using, won't it give them an advantage to know my next move?"

"Yes."

After a silence, Kaze dared ask for more elucidation. "Then why do I practice the patterns so precisely?"

"So you can learn to be creative in your fencing."

Kaze pondered that, and at the risk of being called stupid by the Sensei, he asked, "But won't the precise repetition of patterns kill any creativity I have?"

"Then whatever creativity is inside you deserves to die. You practice patterns to learn technique. That technique is necessary to allow the freedom to create. You cannot project power without a sound base, and you cannot show creativity without a mastery of basic technique. When you have mastered that technique, you can transcend it and combine the basic moves of sword fighting into marvelous new combinations. But first you have to be so grounded in basic technique that you no longer have to think of it. That is what makes a master fencer."

"When do you think I'll master technique?"

"Never."

Kaze sighed. Dealing with the Sensei was sometimes like talking to a Zen priest. Seeing the frustrated look on the boy's face, the Sensei said, "Why do you think I say that?"

Kaze thought for several minutes, then finally said, "Because you are constantly practicing, despite your years with the sword. When you spar with me, you are not only teaching me, you are also reviewing all the basic subtleties of the patterns. You are correcting me, and at the same time reminding yourself. You always say that no man can achieve perfection, he can only strive for it. If that's true, then the striving must continue forever, because our goal is to achieve perfection of mind, spirit, body, and sword."

"Good."

The flute music stopped. Kaze looked up at the lattice opening, hoping that the music would start again, despite its melancholy theme. But silence filled the night air, and Kaze eventually realized that the music for the night was finished. He sighed and drew the robe closer around his shoulders. Just before drifting off, he wondered if the choice of a musket as the assassination weapon had any significance. Unlike Shingen, Ieyasu had been lucky, and the bullet had missed him and hit Nakamura. Kaze wondered if the conditions of the assassination had promoted that luck.

CHAPTER 12

*Gray hair does not mean
wisdom. Sometimes it doesn't
even mean great age.*

Yoshida had very little faith in luck, although he had to admit that the ronin he sought must have the devil's own luck. He turned to Niiya and frowned.

"You had almost a hundred men," Yoshida said. It was a statement, not a question.

"Yes, Lord."

"And this one ronin was still able to elude you?"

"I don't know, Lord. I have had men dredging the canal with poles since he disappeared, but that canal is subject to tidal surges, and it may be possible that his body was washed quite some distance from where it landed."

"It's also possible that the body pulled itself out of the water and walked to a warm bed."

"I'm sure I hit him with a musket shot," Niiya said emphatically. "I was waiting for him to poke his head out over the edge of the roof. The light was poor and his head only poked up less than the span of a hand, but I'm sure I hit him. I don't miss what I aim at."

"You hit him, but he still had the energy to leap over a wide street and into the canal?"

"I don't miss what I aim at." Niiya's words were spoken slowly and his eyes were locked on Yoshida's. Yoshida decided he had pushed too hard.

"I'm sure you did. No one knows the accuracy of your marksmanship better than I." He turned back to the map of Edo. It was late at night, almost morning. The map was illuminated by the soft light of a paper lantern. Like most Japanese maps, it was a perspective view of the city, with individual buildings shown. The scale was approximate, with artistic considerations ruling cartographic ones. Edo was growing so fast that any map drawn was obsolete before the brush left the paper. Like forest mushrooms, hovels and shacks sprang up on open soil in the space of a morning. Lords and officials confiscated entire sections of the city, forcing all who lived there to move. Yoshida had heard a story of one particularly unlucky fellow who had been forced to move five times in the last year. He had an uncanny knack for placing his house on land that would soon be given to a daimyo or temple.

Except for the anchors of the rivers and Edo Castle, the entire city was in constant flux. The Tokugawas had even leveled Kanda Hill to fill up some of the swamps that made Edo such an unhealthy city before the Tokugawas took over the area a dozen years before.

"We have men searching all up and down the canal," Niiya said, tracing the path of the water channel on the map with a calloused finger. "If his body is in the water, we'll find it. Here, where the canal joins the river, we've put up a net so the body can't wash out to sea."

"And if you don't find the body in the water?"

"Then we will put up notice boards all over the city telling of the reward."

Yoshida thought for a moment and said, "Put up the notice

boards at first light. If we find the body, no harm will be done, but we should try our best to get another hint of where he's hiding. There's no value in keeping our search secret anymore."

"What name should we use on the boards?"

"He is using the name Matsuyama Kaze, so use that. Also list his former name. His former name was stricken off the list of official names after Sekigahara, so it has no meaning, but perhaps someone would know him under his former name."

Niiya bowed. "All right, my Lord."

"I think we should also try to search any quarter where this Matsuyama Kaze might be spotted."

"To do that, we will need the help of additional men."

Yoshida frowned but said, "All right. I'll ask Lord Honda, Lord Okubo, and Lord Toyama for help. That should give us plenty of men to search any section of the city."

Niiya nodded his agreement. "I'll go and have the notice boards prepared," he said.

When Niiya left, Yoshida turned back to the map of Edo. Since he was a small boy, Yoshida had loved the planning of campaigns. He would lead groups of other boys in mock skirmishes, sallying forth on a stick horse with a toy sword. In winter, he would supervise the building of elaborate snow forts, and then lead the defense or attack on the fortress. Even in the quiet moments of the evening, Yoshida loved playing *shogi*, Japanese chess, or *go*, a strategy game played with black and white stones.

Of course, as the son of a daimyo, Yoshida was expected to be the leader of his contemporaries, but he discovered very early that he relished this role. Other sons of highborn nobles took leadership positions, but even as a boy, Yoshida felt they did this because of who they were born to, not who they were.

Like all Japanese, Yoshida set great store on the value of lineage and birth. Yet recent history had shown that birth did not guarantee power and ability. Oda Nobunaga was the man to start the unification of Japan after hundreds of years of clan warfare. He was the daimyo of a minor, albeit strategically placed, domain in central Japan. His was not considered one of the great families.

Nobunaga's successor was Hideyoshi. Hideyoshi was a peasant who raised himself to become the ruler of the land by virtue of his original mind and extraordinary abilities. People who could not accept that a peasant could become ruler now said Hideyoshi was the illegitimate son of a court noble, but Yoshida doubted this. Hideyoshi honored his mother, in true filial fashion, and his mother was a simple peasant woman. The idea that this common peasant could be the concubine of a court noble was ludicrous.

Then there was Tokugawa Ieyasu, the Shogun. Until recently, the Tokugawas had been considered a good, but not great, family. It was a family much like Yoshida's own. Now Ieyasu claimed he was a descendant of the Minamotos, which allowed him to obtain the hereditary title of Shogun, a title Hideyoshi couldn't claim because of his common birth. Ieyasu had richly rewarded the priest who "discovered" this family connection to the Minamotos. Yoshida was sure that if the opportunity ever presented itself, he could find a priest who would discover a link between the Yoshidas and the Minamotos, too.

So although Yoshida still thought birth was important, he realized that ability was more important in this modern age. That's why he was so anxious to show his abilities to Ieyasu during this assassination crisis.

He had planned the ambush at the vegetable seller's house with Niiya as soon as the gambler Akinari came with the information about where Matsuyama was staying. He had not been able to stay for Matsuyama's return, but he knew of Niiya's intelligence and skill, and had absolutely no doubts about his loyalty.

But despite Niiya's having almost a hundred men waiting for the ronin, the man had managed to elude his carefully set ambush. No, Yoshida corrected himself, perhaps Niiya was right, and the ronin had been wounded, and it was only a matter of dredging his body out of the canal. Luck had been with him thus far, with Ieyasu-sama giving him the opportunity to lead the search for the ronin, so perhaps luck would be with him now, and the ronin was dead.

But, just in case he wasn't dead, Yoshida returned to his map of Edo to see what would be the best way to search the city.

Toyama was also up early in the morning, but he was not busy doing anything, save for worrying. He was lying on his futon, looking at the dark creases in the ceiling boards, all outlined by the light of the lantern in his room. He had dismissed his favorite concubine earlier in the evening, not able to muster up the energy for lust. He had tried to look over dispatches and letters from his home domain, but even this activity required too much thought and concentration.

Toyama was a maelstrom of emotions, all involving Tokugawa Ieyasu. He had contempt for Ieyasu, because Toyama's family was much better than the Tokugawas, yet he now found himself a vassal of the new ruler of Japan. In fact, Ieyasu's family had been known as Matsudaira until Ieyasu had received permission to change it, so, although the Tokugawa name was an ancient one, it was one that actually belonged to the powerful parvenu for only three decades.

Toyama also had fear of Ieyasu, because the new ruler had shown a willingness to demote daimyo who displeased him to a lesser fief, or to even invite them to commit seppuku and enter the void. He hated Ieyasu because of the power that the new Shogun wielded, yet he wanted Ieyasu to like him, so his current fief and lifestyle would at least remain untouched.

"Damn that Ieyasu! Why did he have to survive that assassination attempt?"

As soon as the words passed his lips, he was sorry he said them. *Kabe ni mimi ari, shoji ni me ari,* Toyama's mother would say. Walls have ears, shoji have eyes. It was treason to even think such a thing. To say it out loud, especially in a place far from your home castle, was an invitation to join the great beyond. Most of the servants were hired in Edo, so there was no guarantee that there wasn't a Tokugawa spy among them. In fact, knowing the suspicious Ieyasu, it was almost certain that there was at least one spy among them. Toyama cursed, but this time silently.

It was frustrating that he couldn't think of an idea that would help cement his position with the Tokugawas. He knew he was on shaky ground with them because he only reluctantly supported them, and only after it was clear Sekigahara was a resounding Tokugawa victory. Then he had an idea. Ieyasu had said it himself. Toyama smiled and was at last able to close his eyes and sleep. His last thought before drifting off was that he couldn't wait until he had an opportunity to reveal his idea. //

The next morning, Kaze woke early and took off the costume he slept in. He put his own kimono on, but as he did so he looked at its sleeve. As he thought, there was a hole from a musket ball in it. He felt lucky his scabbard wasn't hit by this shot. Kaze placed his little finger through the hole and wriggled it around. He put on the kimono and laughed.

Kaze had never been backstage at a theater before, so, out of curiosity, he looked through the various baskets and costumes around him. What he found made him think.

The street was bustling with people, and business was brisk. The rice cake seller had his stand set up at a strategic location, and he was enjoying the fruits of the notoriety. His stand consisted of a waist-high wooden tower. At the top of the tower was a copper box where he burned charcoal, and in the sides of the tower were handles for carrying it around, as well as drawers for merchandise. Painted on the sides of the tower were kanji and pictures of what he was selling, so both the literate and illiterate could understand.

A man hobbled up to the stand. The stand operator looked at him. He had muscular arms and shoulders, but the flowing beard and hair that stuck out from the straw hat he was wearing were white, and he hobbled along with the help of a stick.

"So many people here, *neh*?"

The voice wasn't exactly old, but it wasn't young, either. The stand operator decided to err on the side of politeness to an elder and responded, "It's been this way for several days, *ojiisan*."

"Is that yagura over there the fire watchtower where the assassin who tried to kill Ieyasu-sama hid?"

"Yes, grandfather, and that castle wall over there is where Ieyasu-sama and the other great lords were standing when the shot was fired. That spot at the bottom of the dry moat is the very place where Lord Nakamura ended up after falling off the wall. That's why all these people are here. They're curious to see the exact location of such an infamous deed."

"As am I, as am I," said the old man. He looked at the yagura, a small watch-box placed on top of a construct of poles, and looked over to the wall of the unfinished castle. "That's quite a shot," he said. "No wonder the assassin missed Ieyasu-sama and killed Nakamura-sama."

The vendor scratched his head. "I wouldn't know about that," he said. "I never fought in any battles. Is that a long shot for a musket?"

"Yes. In fact, a regular musket probably wouldn't carry that far. I would think it would require a gun by Inatomi Gaiki to carry a musket ball that far, with any hope of accuracy."

"Inatomi?"

The old man cackled again. "*Gomen nasai.* Excuse me. Just shop talk from an old soldier. Inatomi is the best matchlock musket maker in all of Japan. Only he could make a gun that could shoot that far."

"I was here on the day of the assassination attempt," the vendor said.

"So was I," replied the old man, "but I left before the shot was fired."

"Well, you missed the excitement then. People were running around everywhere, soldiers everywhere, it was nothing but confusion. When they found the dead watchman in the yagura, they brought the body down and just laid him out on the street. It was awful. His throat was cut and his head was flopping back when they brought him down the yagura ladder." The vendor shuddered.

"No one heard the watchman cry out when the assassin went into the yagura?"

The vendor frowned. "No, I didn't hear anyone say they heard the watchman."

"So the watchman didn't cry out when an armed stranger entered the yagura?"

"No, I guess he didn't. That's strange."

"And no one noticed a man carrying a musket after the assassination attempt?"

The vendor scratched his head. "No, I didn't hear of that, either. That's also strange, isn't it? You'd think someone would notice a man carrying a musket."

"Yes, you would."

"Well, it doesn't matter. They know who the assassin is, anyway, and there's a huge reward for his head."

"How do you know that?"

The vendor pointed. "See that big crowd over there? They're reading the notice board that was put up, telling of the assassin and the reward."

The old man looked in the direction the vendor pointed, and said, "Thank you. I think I'll go over there and see for myself."

"Say, what about some nice hot rice cakes before you go?"

"Gomen nasai. I'm afraid my teeth aren't good enough to eat them." He cackled.

"They look plenty good enough to me," the vendor said rudely as the old man walked away.

The old man walked to the back of the crowd. Someone in the front was reading the notice board out loud for his illiterate brethren.

". . . the aforementioned assassin is to be turned into the authorities immediately. Anyone found protecting this man will receive death, as will five of his neighbors. If you tell the authorities of where he is, so he may be captured, you will receive a thousand-ryo reward." A gasp came from the crowd at the mention of the sum. "If you bring the authorities his head, you will receive a ten-thousand-ryo reward." The reader had to stop, because instead of just gasping, the crowd went into a frenzied buzz of conversation that drowned out the reader's voice.

Kaze, who was wearing a disguise he put together at the theater, patiently worked his way closer to the notice board. The clothes, white beard, hat, and hair allowed him to pass as an old man if he was not too closely scrutinized. He took the chance of having someone in the crowd inspect him at close quarters so he could read the notice board for himself.

His eyes swept across the *hiragana* letters on the board. Hiragana was used instead of kanji for notice boards. With hiragana, the words were written phonetically, and it was possible to sound out a word, even if you weren't familiar with it. Although an expert could discern the various strokes that made up a particular kanji character, it was easier to read with hiragana.

They had both his former name and Matsuyama Kaze on the board, and they had a description of him. Fortunately, there were thousands of samurai who could fit the description given. Kaze had not been certain about Nobu's assertion that there was a ten-thousand-ryo price on his head, but there was the reward amount clearly written on the board, with Lord Yoshida's name authorizing it. No wonder Boss Akinari had tried to kill him. Kaze wondered how firm Goro and Hanzo's resolve to shelter him would remain, once they had both the reward and penalties listed on the board read to them.

Kaze turned and started walking out of the area, remembering to hobble and lean heavily on his stick.

CHAPTER 13

The master is death.
It conquers the finest hands
and the keenest mind.

Inatomi."

"What about Inatomi?" Ieyasu asked, fixing his eyes on Toyama.

Toyama was so anxious to parade his idea before Ieyasu, he had blurted it out at the first opportunity. Yoshida, Okubo, and Honda, who were also at the conference, looked at him peculiarly, because such an outburst was both unseemly for a samurai and a sign of lack of control.

Toyama licked his lips, then he cleared his throat. "You said yourself, Ieyasu-sama, that the distance for the assassination attempt was extremely long for a musket ball to carry, and that only a gun by Inatomi Gaiki could be used. Inatomi's guns are rare and expensive, and he probably hasn't made too many of them. This Matsuyama Kaze is a ronin, and could never afford a gun by Inatomi. He may be the assassin, but there may also be others in the plot. Inatomi lives nearby in Ueno. I think we should go to him and ask him who has bought his guns. It may not give us the exact plotters, but it will give us a list that we can examine. By concentrating on Matsuyama Kaze, we may be allowing equally guilty parties to escape."

"Ridiculous!" Honda exploded. Toyama actually flinched. "Knowing who has an Inatomi gun tells us nothing. I have one of his guns myself, and so does Ieyasu-sama."

"No," Ieyasu said quietly. "It's actually a good idea. Our efforts to find this Matsuyama have so far failed." Yoshida blushed. "It might be good to try another approach. Sometimes you're too direct, Honda. It you've assaulted the front of the castle a dozen times with no success, walking through the back door is the best thing you can do."

"It's just a total waste of time," Honda objected. "I'm still against it."

Ieyasu ignored his blustery general. "Yoshida-san."

"Yes, Ieyasu-sama!"

"Take a squad of men to the gun maker's house. Toyama-san is right. I do think only a gun made by Inatomi could have been used in the assassination attempt. Get me a list of who Inatomi-sensei has sold his guns to. He takes such care with the manufacture of his weapons, I don't imagine he's made that many of them. If nothing else, the list will give us a basis for identifying lords who may be in conspiracy with this Matsuyama Kaze."

"I'll be happy to send my men," Okubo offered.

"No, I want Yoshida-san to do this," Ieyasu replied.

"Immediately, Ieyasu-sama!" Yoshida got to his feet and strode out of the room.

Honda glared at the retreating daimyo, while Toyama basked in the thought that his idea had been a good one.

Two hours later, Kaze trudged up a hill in Ueno, still disguised as an old man. After seeing the assassination site, he also had come to the conclusion that only a gun by Inatomi Gaiki could have been used, and he wanted to talk to Inatomi. He stopped for a moment, leaning on his walking stick and getting his bearings.

He walked over to a roadside shop and asked directions to Inatomi-sensei's house. Kaze used the title sensei, which meant teacher, to indicate that he knew that Inatomi was also a master.

Getting directions, he made his way down the road to the house of the well-to-do craftsman. He stopped at the door and entered. The house would be a sales outlet as well as a residence, so he had no compunction about entering. The entryway was a dirt square, surrounded by the house floor, which was a raised wooden platform. Here visitors were expected to stop, remove their sandals, and get properly greeted by servants or a member of the craftsman's family.

He called out, "Sumimasen! Excuse me!"

Silence met his greeting. This was unusual. A craftsman's house was always occupied, because it was also a place of business.

"Sumimasen!" Kaze shouted, thinking that perhaps he wasn't heard the first time. Again, no response.

Kaze sat on the raised floor and removed his sandals. In the air he smelled smoke. It wasn't the pleasant smell of a charcoal fire, but something more acrid and pungent. He decided to investigate. Fire was the great fear of all Japanese households. With paper and wood houses, this fear was not idle. Every Japanese city had periodic and disastrous fires, and in the pantheon of crimes, arson was considered the most heinous, next to treason.

As Kaze walked through the house, there was an unnatural silence to it. The house was a large one, one that would house a master, several apprentices, and a support staff of servants. In such a house there would always be a natural buzz of activity as people went about the business of daily life. This house was lifeless, and Kaze wondered where its inhabitants were, and why they had abandoned the house during the middle of the day, leaving a fire burning.

He walked from the entry into a sitting room, where Master Inatomi probably greeted important guests and conducted business. It was a spacious, twelve-mat room with a beautiful wooden rack along one wall. On the rack was a matchlock musket, made by Inatomi-sensei.

Kaze's weapon was the sword, and he was an expert at judging a blade with a single glance. He was not as familiar with muskets, but even his relatively inexperienced eye could see that this weapon was also a work of art. The barrel was a sleek tube, with decorative engraving on its side. The matchlock mechanism was as finely made as a delicate porcelain sakè flask. A curved piece of steel held a rope fuse, which was lighted when the gun was to be fired. When the trigger was pulled, the lighted match was pushed into a hole and ignited the gunpowder in the barrel. The short wooden stock was beautifully grained and shaped, and polished to a high gloss. The weapon was an expert amalgam of deadly function and aesthetic craftsmanship.

Past the sitting room, Kaze entered a hallway. It went the length of the house to the back. It was there he found the first body.

It was a woman in her late thirties. She appeared to be a maid, dressed in a common gray kimono. She was lying on her face, one hand twisted behind her back, reaching for the terrible cut that stretched from her neck to her waist. Someone had cut her down as she ran. Kaze checked briefly to make sure she was dead, then continued walking down the hallway.

In a room that was an office, he found the source of the smoke. The room had sliding screens along two walls. These were shoved back, revealing shelves. If the room was used as a bedroom, the futons, pillows, and other sleeping gear would be kept on the shelves, ready to be brought out each night at bedtime. In this room, the shelves were used to store various papers, either folded or rolled into scrolls. Most of the papers were knocked off the shelves and spread on the floor. Kaze glanced at them, using his walking stick to move them slightly so he could get a better look at them. They seemed to be a mixture of personal correspondence, business records, and diagrams of matchlock gun designs. In the center of the room was a copper box, filled with sand and used to burn charcoal in the winter. The smoke came from this box.

Kaze walked over and looked at the ashes left smoldering in the box. The fragile paper embers were still red. The flames from the paper burnt in the box had only recently died. Kaze surmised they were business records, perhaps listing who owned the guns made by Inatomi Gaiki. Obviously, someone else had realized that the choice of weapon would form a link that might lead to the assassins, and they had taken steps to break that chain.

He found another dead woman in the kitchen, but didn't find the real carnage until he walked out of the back door of the house.

At the back of the house was a garden in the Chinese style. The carefully shaped azalea bushes were woven between serpentine paths of clean, white gravel. The yard was encircled by a high, bamboo fence. Against one wall of the fence were large rocks, chosen and artfully placed to give the illusion of a distant mountain range. It was a fine garden, perfectly in keeping with the artistic sensibilities Kaze saw in the craftsmanship of the musket.

The white gravel paths were stained red by the blood of bodies spread around the yard. Most of the bodies were on the main path, which led to a workshop at the back of the garden. The bodies of another woman and three men were sprawled across the path, each twisted in the pain of their death agony. Kaze paused to put on a pair of the wooden geta that were by the back door. These were raised wooden slippers, left conveniently for the use of people leaving the house, where they were in their tabi socks, and going out to the garden and workshop.

Kaze stopped for a moment to examine the cuts on the bodies. He could tell from the slashes that they were made by several men, not a single swordsman. He saw cuts made by at least three different styles of swordsmanship. The men were good swordsmen but not experts. Against unarmed women, servants, and apprentices, it didn't require much skill.

Kaze walked sadly to the workshop knowing what he would find.

The workshop had a large forge, filled with glowing charcoal, much like the forges used by swordsmiths. In the workshop were a variety of files and jigs that would not be used by swordsmiths; the particular tools of the gunsmith. Kaze glanced up at the corner of the workshop and saw a shrine to the God of the Forge. Then he looked down.

There were two other young men in the workshop, and a gray-haired older man: Inatomi and two apprentices. The face of Inatomi looked surprised, even in death. The slashing cut that half severed his neck must have come suddenly, perhaps from someone he knew. It was probably the signal to start the slaughter of the rest by samurai who stood outside the workshop, guarding the other members of the household in the garden. Two women had apparently managed to flee, one making it to the kitchen before she was cut down and the other almost making it outside the house before she was killed in the hall.

Nine people killed so a tenuous link to the attempted assassination of Ieyasu could be broken. Nine people, including a master who could craft beautiful objects like the musket that Kaze saw in the front room of the house. Life was fleeting. Kaze knew that. And all was an illusion. Kaze knew and believed that, too. But it seemed a colossal waste to snuff out the talent represented by Inatomi and his household.

If you were a dancer, a musician, or an actor, your skills died with you. Even if people talked about your skills after your death, this talk would be a mere shadow of the actual act. Even swordsmen fell into this category, Kaze reflected. Once you ceased to exist, your art ceased with you. If you were a poet, painter, or artisan like Inatomi, some of your creations would exist after your death, but the real art was in the steady hands, the intelligence, the sense of balance and proportion, and the skill to create new poems, pictures, and beautiful objects. This creative ability died with the artist, and even if the work of the artist lived on, this work was now circumscribed by a finite body of work. Nothing new would ever be created by this particular artist, to surprise, delight, and enlighten new audiences.

Kaze sighed. He decided to do something out of respect for the skill of Inatomi-sensei that he usually only did to propitiate the souls of people he had slain. He looked about the workshop and found a piece of fine chestnut wood. Perhaps Inatomi-sensei was going to use it for a musket stock. On a workbench, Kaze found a knife and, amid the carnage and bodies around him, he sat in the doorway of the workshop and started to carve the wood.

Yoshida rode up to Inatomi's house, leading ten mounted samurai. As he reached the front of the house, one of the samurai leapt off his horse and rushed forward to hold the reins of Yoshida's stallion.

"Captain!" Yoshida said.

A samurai rode forward. "Yes, Yoshida-sama?"

"Go in and tell Inatomi-sensei that I have arrived. Tell him it is on business from the Shogun himself!"

"Yes, my Lord!" The captain rushed into the house, but returned a few minutes later, puzzled.

"There doesn't seem to be anyone in the house, my Lord."

"Ridiculous! Even if Inatomi-sensei is out, his servants or apprentices will be here."

"I called several times, but no one came to the door to greet me."

"Did you look in the house?"

"No, Yoshida-sama, I thought—"

"Idiot! We're here on the Shogun's business! Take some men and search the house. Find out why there's no one to greet us."

Chagrined, the captain motioned to three samurai to dismount and follow him. They entered the house, pausing to remove their sandals at the doorway out of habit and respect. In moments they found the dead maid.

All the samurai took out their swords. "Follow me," the captain ordered. They quietly made their way through the house, pausing at the office and the kitchen with the second body, and into the back garden. The captain sucked in his breath at the sight of so many bodies in the garden. In the doorway of the workshop at the end of the garden, a flash of movement caught his eye. He signaled his men to follow him, and they didn't bother to stop to put on the geta. They made their way across the garden, their feet, clad in only tabi socks, muffling their footsteps. They carefully approached the workshop door.

As they reached the doorway, the captain was able to see more bodies in the workshop. He also saw a living person doing something peculiar.

There was what seemed to be an old man placing a wooden statue on a workbench. The figure wore an old but respectable kimono and a farmer's woven straw hat. Wisps of gray hair peeked out from the edge of the hat and partially obscured the face of the figure, but the man's muscular arms didn't look like the wasted limbs of an ojiisan. The captain looked at the statue and was surprised to see it was a Kannon, a statue of the Goddess of Mercy, carved from chestnut wood. The serene face of the Goddess looked out at the carnage in the workshop and garden, providing some grace to the souls of the slaughtered.

"*Oi!* You!" the captain said. "Stay where you are. I want to talk to you about what happened here."

Without showing the slightest surprise at the captain's shout, the old man smoothly placed the Kannon on the shelf and reached forward for a shovel that was sitting next to the forge. He scooped out a shovelful of the forge's contents and tossed it out the door of the workshop.

Puzzled by this action, the captain told the samurai with him, "Get him."

With their swords naked, the three samurai rushed forward, only to start hopping about as they approached the workshop door. The red-hot coals from the forge burnt through their tabi-clad feet.

In the seconds this bought him, the old man picked up a walking stick and charged out of the shop. His wooden geta shielded his feet from the hot coals.

Still recoiling from the burning coals, the lead samurai took an off-balanced, one-handed cut at the old man. The old man used his stick to knock the sword blade out of the way; then he rapped the wrist of the samurai with a sharp cut, as neatly executed as any fencing teacher using a wooden *bokken* practice sword. The captain heard a crack as the stick hit the samurai's wrist, and the samurai, his wrist broken, yelped and dropped his sword.

"That's not an old man," the captain barked. "Kill him!"

The man reached down to pick up the dropped sword, and a second samurai took a vicious cut at his arm. The man smoothly changed the movement of his arm, causing the blade to miss by the smallest of measures. Then he picked up the sword and brought it up in time to parry a blow by the third samurai. His agility and balance, perched on the wooden geta, was amazing.

Instead of sparring with the two samurai, the man charged the captain. In one hand he had the sword, in the other the walking stick. The captain took an overhead, two-handed cut at the man.

The man met the blow with the sword, bending slightly to absorb the shock with his upraised arm. Before the captain could disengage his sword, the walking stick came round and struck the captain in the side of the head. The captain collapsed, knocked senseless, as the man bolted into the house.

CHAPTER 14

The wind in my face.
The horse in fluid motion.
Freedom on four hooves.

Yoshida was still in front of the gunsmith's house, waiting impatiently for the captain to report back. He was about to send other samurai into the house to see what the situation was, when a man burst out of the front door of the house, brandishing a sword in one hand and a stick in the other. He had the hair of an old man, but the quickness and agility of a man in his prime.

Yoshida opened his mouth to shout an order to the remaining samurai, but before sound could escape his lips, the man took a cut at the reins of his horse. The sword cleanly cut the reins, which were still being held by the samurai on the ground. This samurai, in shock, looked stupidly at the limp cords hanging from his hand.

The man immediately hit Yoshida's horse on the rump with the stick. Frightened, the horse bolted, carrying Yoshida off down the road at a full gallop. In ancient days, samurai were trained to ride horses without holding the reins, so they could shoot a bow and arrow at a full gallop. With the emphasis on the sword and the musket, the art of mounted archery had been diminished for all samurai, and Yoshida could only grab at his horse's mane in an effort to bring the animal under control.

Yoshida's samurai were frozen for an instant, uncertain if they should ride down the attacker or chase after their Lord. This instant was all Kaze needed. He sprang to the saddle of one of the unoccupied horses, just as two samurai burst from the house, adding to the confusion. Pulling on the reins to wheel the animal about, Kaze set off down the road in the opposite direction from Yoshida's fleeing mount.

Three samurai decided to pursue Kaze, and the rest set off to catch Yoshida and bring his runaway horse under control.

As Kaze thundered down the road, he looked over his shoulder and saw his three pursuers. The fastest was approaching him rapidly, mounted on a better horse.

Kaze was riding toward Edo. With the expansion of Edo, the village of Ueno was eventually becoming a satellite of the capital, and the road between the two was fairly populated. As the horsemen rode down the road, peasants, servants, and merchants scattered like leaves before an approaching whirlwind. Kaze knew that when he reached Edo, the crowded streets would end the pursuit, and the samurai chasing him could count on help from the many officers patrolling the streets of the city. From that, Kaze also knew he would have to settle things quickly.

As the lead samurai caught him, Kaze slowed slightly to bring the samurai next to him. Kaze didn't want the samurai behind him, where he could slash at the horse's hindquarters to cripple Kaze's mount. The samurai drew his sword and took a cut at Kaze's head. Kaze ducked and threw the walking stick at the samurai with all the force he could muster. The samurai ducked, but not quickly enough. The stick caught the samurai across the forehead. He wobbled in the saddle for several strides of the horse, then neatly slid out of the saddle, falling to the dirt road in a sprawl.

Kaze quickly shifted his sword to his other hand, just in time to parry a cut by the second samurai, who had just caught him.

Kaze blocked a second cut, then shifted his weight so he could lean out to one side of the horse, closer to the samurai. Kaze quickly brought his sword upward, striking the samurai in the side. The samurai looked uncomprehendingly down at his flank, just starting to spurt blood. As the pain struck him, a cry burst from his lips and his horse immediately started to slow down, no longer spurred on by kicks in the side from its rider.

Kaze spun in his saddle and looked at the third samurai. Using the first finger on his sword hand, he crooked it and motioned to the samurai to come forward for his turn. The samurai looked at Kaze's urging, then glanced over his shoulder at his two companions, one a receding dot sprawled on his back in the road and the other a man clutching at his side, trying to staunch the flow of blood. His eyes wide with fear, the samurai looked back at Kaze and shook his head, declining Kaze's invitation to come forward and fight. Instead, he simply started slowing his horse, allowing Kaze to outdistance him as he fell farther and farther behind.

Outrageous!" Yoshida was in a rage, all semblance of control gone. "A master craftsman and his entire household slaughtered! Four samurai confront one unarmed man in the garden, and the man disarms one of them and gets away. The man attacks me, cutting the reins of my horse as easily as he could have cut me, and no one stops him. He steals one of our horses, and three samurai can't catch him. Fools! What kind of samurai are you? I should have the lot of you slit your bellies, and kill your families, too, just so your stupidity won't be perpetuated in our clan!"

The entire party of samurai he took to Inatomi's house were lying before him, literally prostrate on their bellies to show their remorse. Three had bandages on their feet to cover the burns, and one of these had his wrist bound tight in a splint. The captain had his head bandaged, with fresh blood still soaking through.

Another samurai, one of the riders, had made an involuntary groan as he prostrated himself, his back twisted by his fall from his horse. The only man missing from the party was the one who'd had his side slashed. The doctors said he was too ill to move, although they did say he would live. It was amazing how much carnage one man could inflict on a party of trained warriors.

"I will commit seppuku to atone for the failure on myself and my men," the captain said.

Yoshida snorted. "You truly are an idiot," he said with contempt. "You men know what this devil looks like. If you kill yourselves, then we're left with no men in our clan who know this old man."

"Yoshida-sama," the captain said, "I don't think this was an old man. I think it was a much younger man dressed in the clothes of an ojiisan. Somehow he had white hair, but I'm positive it was not a man whose age matched his hair."

Surprised, Yoshida said, "It was a younger man?"

"Yes, Yoshida-sama."

Yoshida rubbed his chin. This was an interesting piece of news. "Do you think it could be this Matsuyama Kaze in a disguise?" he asked.

"I don't know, Yoshida-sama, but he fought like the demon this Matsuyama Kaze is supposed to be."

Yoshida didn't know what this Kaze looked like. Ieyasu-sama, Okubo, several of Okubo's officers, and a few others knew Kaze's face because they had seen him at Hideyoshi's sword tournament, but Yoshida had not thought to take someone with him who knew the man he was hunting when he went to Inatomi's house. Yoshida looked at Niiya, who was also in the room, and said, "What do you think of this development, Niiya?"

Niiya shook his head, surprised. "It's amazing. Still, if the man at Inatomi's was Matsuyama Kaze, it makes for an interesting twist."

"Yes, it does," Yoshida agreed. Then, looking at his cowering samurai, Yoshida said, "As for you, get out of my sight. Don't slit your belly in the mistaken belief it will reduce my anger. I need men who know the face of this devil; otherwise I will have to depend on someone like Okubo-san to identify this man when we finally take his head. After all the embarrassment this man has caused us, I want to be able to settle this affair myself, without help from others. I want to present Ieyasu-sama with this man's head, and I want to make sure I give him the right one. Now get out!"

The samurai pulled themselves into a kneeling position and scooted out of the room backward, bowing the entire time to show their contrition.

Niiya walked over to the opening the samurai exited from and slid close the screens for privacy. He approached Yoshida, and Yoshida said, "Ieyasu-sama will be interested to know that it might have been Matsuyama who slaughtered Inatomi and his household. Okubo-san mentioned that the ronin had done something similar in Kamakura."

Niiya nodded his head, and said, "We have another interesting bit of news."

"What is that?"

"The other night, when Matsuyama escaped us by jumping into the canal, a man going to his privy in the middle of the night caught a glimpse of a strange figure. It was a man, soaking wet. The man only got a brief glimpse, but it could be this Matsuyama."

"You never found the body in the canal?"

Niiya's face burned red. "No, Yoshida-sama. I was sure I hit him. I never miss what I aim at, but I guess it was not a serious hit."

Yoshida said nothing about Niiya's assertions about his marksmanship. He had seen enough evidence to know Niiya was not just boasting idly. Instead, he asked, "Where was this man?"

"In Ningyo-cho."

That afternoon it started to rain. Kaze had abandoned the horse at the edge of Edo. It would either find its own way back to its stable or a patrol would find it. Now he stood on the street, watching the Little Flower Whorehouse carefully. He was still in the disguise of an old man, in a rain-soaked and threadbare kimono. Rain dripped down the sloping sides of his peasant's hat, forming a watery curtain that hid his face. He had wanted to find another disguise, but he felt none of the other costumes in the theater would pass muster on the street. They were suitable for a stage performance in the flickering glow of paper lanterns, but they didn't look realistic in the daylight.

The Little Flower was tough to solve. It had only one door, and there seemed to be a servant guarding that door constantly. Kaze would get a glimpse of someone just in the doorway, occasionally letting vendors in who delivered food, sakè, and other supplies. Kaze could, of course, force his way into the house, using his sword, but that wouldn't tell him if the girl was there, or where she might be located in the house.

There seemed to be no outside windows, although Kaze was sure that the house would have screens that opened into inner courtyards for ventilation and light. By getting on the roof, Kaze could enter the courtyards, but he would again have the problem of knowing if the girl was there and where she was kept.

It was a difficult problem, and one Kaze decided he would have to think about some more. He shuffled off down the street, returning to the Kabuki theater. As he walked away, another figure watched him intently. Kaze was very good about knowing his environment, sensing when he was being watched and when enemies were near. But the watcher was also good. Extremely good.

His entire life was devoted to both keeping out of the eye of those who might hunt him, and keeping track of those he would hunt. His natural excitement at having spotted Kaze was tempered by his knowledge of how truly dangerous this man was. //

When they received the commission, the men assigned to the task studied a drawing to identify Kaze. It wasn't a portrait in the conventional sense, but a sketch of Kaze's face drawn to highlight points of identification. Did his earlobes join the head, or did they hang free? What was the exact shape of his jaw? What was the curve of his eyebrows? With a few strokes of the brush, a ninja who had seen Kaze at Hideyoshi's sword tournament was able to create an identification drawing. The Koga clan, like all ninja clans, tried to remember the faces of the men of exceptional fighting ability, as well as the faces of the great daimyo. The former were likely to be with the latter, and a ninja had to identify both.

In addition to eyes, the ears of the ninja extended everywhere, especially in a busy city like Edo. The man already knew of the dripping wet man spotted in Ningyo-cho. He also knew of Yoshida's encounter with an old man of exceptional fighting qualities at Inatomi-sensei's house. He surmised that the two might be the same: a young man disguised as an old.

Therefore, he was already looking for an old man when he passed the ojiisan standing in the rain. There was much one could do with clothes, posture, and gray hair to give the appearance of an old man, but no one could disguise their hands. Another, not trained to the state of alertness of the ninja, might have missed the fact that the old man's hands were much too young for the wet gray hair peeking out from the straw peasant's hat. Even fewer would notice that the hands had the calluses of a swordsman. Yet a glance at the old man's hands as the ninja passed him told him that the muscular ojiisan standing in the rain was not what he appeared to be.

Showing extreme caution, the ninja followed Kaze down the wet street.

The actor in us.
We play parts throughout the day,
sometimes on purpose.

Hanzo rushed into the theater. He made his way past the half-empty floor and up to the stage, going behind the curtain. "All of Ningyo-cho is blocked off!" he exclaimed to Goro and Kaze. "Soldiers are going from building to building, searching them!"

"What are they looking for?" Goro asked.

"Obviously, me," Kaze said.

The two peasants looked at the ronin with wide eyes. "If you were going to collect on that reward, now is the time to run to the soldiers and tell them I'm here," Kaze continued. "If you help conceal me, you will become conspirators with me, and will be putting yourself in as much danger as I'm in."

The two peasants looked at each other. Peasants were supposed to be masters of guile, and Kaze knew from contact with them that most peasants could be secretive and ruthless. These two seemed incapable of guile, however, and Kaze could see a whole range of emotions stream across their faces: surprise, fear, greed, uncertainty, and, finally, resolve.

"You are the only samurai who has ever treated us like men," Hanzo said. "All others of your class have treated us as creatures lower than the beasts in the fields." Looking at his partner, Hanzo said, "What do you say, Goro? Let's help Kaze-san."

"Hai! I agree!"

Hanzo looked around. "Maybe we can cover you with some of those costumes and baskets," he said. "We can do it in a private corner when the actors are busy putting on their costumes."

Kaze shook his head. "No. Under a pile of baskets or costumes is the first place they'll look." He glanced over at the low chests of makeup used the by actors. "I have a better idea."

The squad of soldiers marched down the street, two or three of them breaking ranks to check each shop and house. Darkness had fallen, and the street was illuminated by the warm glow of torches and lanterns. The soft yellow light clashed with the hard reflections thrown off by spear blades, armor plate, and drawn swords. The curious gathered on the street to gape at the unusual sight. Curious or not, each person, whether on the street or in a building, was looked at by the soldiers. If a man of the right age and build was discovered, he was led to a nearby group with one of the soldiers who had seen Kaze at Inatomi's house.

A runner approached the leader of a squad marching down the street toward Goro and Hanzo's theater. "Anything to report, sir?" the runner asked.

The captain shook his head and winced. It was the officer whom Kaze had hit with the stick, and his *atama,* his head, still hurt. "No. Tell Yoshida-sama we haven't found anyone suspicious yet, except the usual collection of whores and gamblers." The runner scurried off to report as the squad approached the theater.

"Ka-bu-ki," the captain read off the cloth banner over the door. "What's that?"

"This is where the loose women were dancing, sir. Remember? We closed them down two weeks ago. They've reopened with new owners. I looked at them, and they seem to be doing some kind of plays, but none of the women are dancing lewdly."

"Women onstage!" The captain shook his head, uncertain of what was becoming of the world, then regretted it. He held his head steady for a few seconds, until the dizziness and pain subsided. "I'll take a squad in here myself. I know what the dog looks like, and it will be easy for me to identify him if he's hiding here."

The captain entered with a half-dozen spearmen. In the lobby, he met a nervous peasant who apparently was the manager or owner of the theater.

"Your name?" the captain demanded.

"I am called Hanzo, Captain-sama." Hanzo bobbed up and down so low his head almost hit the ground. As a peasant, Hanzo didn't have a last name. Only samurai and nobles were afforded the privilege of a last name. Watching the constant bowing of the peasant made the captain's head hurt more. He aimed a well-placed kick at the peasant, hitting his leg and causing the fool to land with a yelp on the floor. Not bothering to see the result of his kick, the captain led his men into the theater.

The theater was sparsely populated. The floor was covered with a grid of low wooden walls, no higher than a man's calf, forming box seats. Only a few of the boxes had people in them, sitting on tatami mats. Although the theater was nearly empty, the patrons who were there seemed fascinated by the action on the stage. Most of the boxes had food of some sort, either bought at the theater or carried in by the audience, but not a bite was taken, because all eyes were on the stage.

There a man and woman were center stage, with a shamisen player and *tsuzumi* drum player to the side of the stage, providing a musical counterpoint to dialogue being declaimed by the two actors.

The woman was dressed in a gaudy red-and-yellow kimono, and her face was covered in white makeup, with high, arched eyebrows painted on her forehead and painted red lips; redder than the brightest red *tsubaki*, camellia. She was kneeling on the stage. Even with the makeup, the captain could see this was no beauty, and he surmised that the women who were dancing lewdly at the theater had moved on to other, and more direct, occupations. Still, even though she wasn't a beauty, there was something in the way she held her body and tilted her head that gave the captain the impression that she was strangely attractive. The pose of her body made the captain understand that she was playing a well-born young maiden.

The ability to communicate age and station in life with a few subtle gestures was extraordinary, but it was the other man onstage, dressed as a monk, who riveted the audience, and for good reason. The man wore a wig with black hair wildly flying up, and his face was painted pure white, like the maiden's. On this white face was painted a bold pattern of black lines, intended to show the deep wrinkles of an old man. It was a surprising and flamboyant makeup, unlike anything the captain had seen before.

The monk shuffled across the stage, looking up to the sky and sniffing the air.

"Lo, these many years I have stayed in the mountains," the monk declaimed. "I was brought to the mountains by my revered Sensei when I was but a child. He taught me the holy sutras and the ways of the ascetic. I have never known the company of others, save for the few men who have visited me on this mountain. I have lived a holy life, pure and chaste, and far from the temptations of the flesh, and I know little of the ways of men. It has been a lonely life, and one without company, save for a few wandering monks and an occasional woodcutter."

The soldiers stepped over the low walls that made up the box seats in front of the stage. Surprised patrons looked up as the soldiers methodically went from enclosure to enclosure, looking each patron in the face to make sure none matched the description of Kaze. The performance didn't stop, and if the actors and musicians were surprised to see the soldiers in the audience, they didn't show it.

The monk crossed the stage and stumbled across the kneeling woman. Reacting in surprise, the monk looked at the audience and said, "But wait, what kind of man is this? His face is fairer than any other I have seen. His hair is long and thick and silky and it smells of flowers. His kimono is colorful but oddly shaped and soft. He is unlike any other man I have seen in my lonely mountain retreat. Who are you, stranger?"

The maiden made no reply and modestly hid her face. A few members of the audience snickered, and even the captain smiled.

"Now this is a strange fellow!" the monk continued. "I wonder why he is so oddly shaped and lumpy. Could he be concealing something under his robes? I must investigate!"

The audience started giggling as the monk walked up to the maiden and stood behind her. She maintained her silence, demurely looking at the ground.

"Can you tell me why you are here, stranger? Are you fleeing someone, or perhaps you are lost?" the monk asked. The girl remained silent.

"Well, then perhaps you will not object if I search you, to see what you are carrying under those robes. Those objects may give me an idea of who you are and why you have disturbed the solitude of my mountain."

The monk bent and placed a hand on the maiden's neck. He

looked up at the audience. "This is interesting. The stranger has skin as smooth and fragrant as the petals of the *botan*. It is not rough and coarse as my own skin or the skin of other men."

He dipped his hand into the maiden's kimono, cupping a breast. "Unusual! This man has a large lump growing on his chest!" He shifted his hand as the audience broke into laughter. "There are two lumps on this strange man's chest! Whatever could they be?"

After fondling the maiden for a moment, the monk said, "More and more puzzling! There are tiny nubs on the tips of these mounds of flesh, hard as pebbles and curiously pleasing to rub!" Even the soldiers searching the audience kept glancing up at the stage, laughing along with the crowd.

"Ah, by the Gods, I must investigate this situation further!" The monk dropped to one knee so he could insert his hand deeper into the maiden's kimono.

"Yes, this man has a flat stomach with no further lumps, but it is soft as a downy futon and not hard as my own is. Now to investigate further!" The monk pushed his hand even deeper into the kimono of the woman and assumed a look of total shock and befuddlement, the outrageous makeup on his face amplifying his amazed expression. The audience was near tears from laughter.

"Oh terrible fate! Oh calamity! This man must have been the victim of a dreadful accident! Deep in his groin I feel the proper hair of a man, but the poor fellow is missing his *chinchin*!" At the use of childhood slang, the audience burst into a new wave of laughter. The soldiers had stopped even making a show of questioning the audience, and were standing around, looking at the stage and laughing.

The monk stayed frozen, a look of complete befuddlement on his face. After the laughter died down, the maiden finally broke her silence.

"Ah, gentle hermit, I can see you are not familiar with the ways of the world! I am an *onna*, a woman, and what you are feeling is my *bobo*." The country vulgarity set the audience to howling again.

When the laughter subsided, the monk stood and said, "This is a most wondrous thing, this woman! But why would the Gods make woman so different from man?"

The maiden turned her head to look at the monk. From her kneeling position, when she turned she was staring pointedly at the monk's crotch, her nose just inches away. She waited for the audience's laughter to build at her close inspection. Finally, when the laughter subsided, she cleared her throat and said, "I may be missing a chinchin, but I see your *futomara* is large enough for both of us." At the use of a colloquialism for a large penis, the wave of laughter from the audience, which had subsided temporarily, suddenly reached a new crescendo. When the audience had quieted enough for her to be heard, the maiden said, "With such a futomara, the jade gates of the bobo may provide one with a new and pleasurable way to find enlightenment. It can be a new way to heaven."

"Can that be true? Can finding enlightenment be as simple as the difference between man and woman? How can that be done?"

"Show me to your hermit's hut and I will demonstrate the process," the maiden said. "I have been fleeing from an unhappy love affair, but I see now that the Gods have guided me to this remote spot so I can do charity work! It will be a blessing to enlighten this innocent monk in the ways of men and women."

The monk helped the maiden up. Taking his hand, the maiden led the befuddled monk off, stopping to give the audience a sly and knowing look before continuing offstage. The laughing audience gave the performers a hearty round of applause.

Despite his headache, the captain was laughing as hard as the rest of the audience. Pulling himself together, he gruffly shouted to his men, "Come on! We don't have time for this foolishness!" He turned and stomped out of the theater. Reluctantly, the men followed.

CHAPTER 16

Five silent shadows
cross the flat gray, nighttime street.
Death blends with blackness.

Momoko looked at Kaze with bright eyes.

Kaze was removing the outlandish makeup he had put on to disguise his face. He had decided that the best place to hide was in plain sight, and the best way to do that was to call attention to himself in a way that actually hid his identity. Like many warriors, Kaze had been trained in the classical Noh drama, often taking part in Noh performances. It was the mark of a civilized man. Before he became Shogun, Ieyasu had often danced Noh, even taking roles where his paunch had been put to good use for comic effect, inviting the assembled audience to laugh at him. Of course, this buffoonery had another purpose. By acting the clown on the Noh platform, Ieyasu had put more than one potential enemy at ease, diffusing suspicion and causing foes to underestimate the shrewd man scampering and clowning on the stage.

He had done this for the Hojos, the clan that Ieyasu and Hideyoshi eventually deposed from Edo and the rich Kanto plain, and he had also done this for Hideyoshi, whose house he eventually defeated. When Ieyasu acted the clown, it sometimes preceded serious business.

Kaze had acted a scene from the Noh play *Dojoji*, although the risqué actions and words had been added extemporaneously. Momoko had picked up on Kaze's intent immediately, playing the scene to great effect. She had been surprised that the ronin had wanted to act in the Kabuki, and even more surprised at his talent for it. She did not know Kaze's desire to act in Kabuki was motivated by the need to elude the searchers, and that his comic flare came from the same core of icy intelligence he had when he was under pressure.

As Kaze finished removing his makeup, he looked over at Momoko, who had been looking at him the entire time. "Well?" he said.

Momoko still had her white makeup on. It emphasized her pug nose and plain face, but Kaze thought her lack of physical beauty was reduced by the force of her sparkling personality. Momoko meant peach and, filled with happiness tonight, she certainly was as sweet and luscious as her namesake.

"Saburo, this is the best night of my life," she said.

Kaze raised an eyebrow, a bit nonplussed by her declaration, especially since she used the false name he had given her. Seeing his surprise, Momoko explained.

"I've always wanted to be someone special; that's why I wanted to try this Kabuki," she said. "I know I'm not a beauty, and I don't have any special skills with musical instruments or the brush. My poetry is embarrassingly bad." She looked down. With her white makeup on, Kaze couldn't tell for sure, but he thought she might even be blushing. "Even my cooking and my, ah, my other, ah, womanly skills, aren't very good. I've never even really had a boyfriend. But tonight I did feel special. It was glorious. When I heard those people laughing so loud at you, I decided to see if I could make them laugh, too. And I can! Each of those laughs was like a shower of sakè. It made me drunk with happiness. It was all because of you." She bowed a deep, formal bow. "Thank you!"

Kaze was about to say it was nothing, in true Japanese fashion, but he realized that if he said that, it might diminish the importance of the moment for Momoko. So, instead of saying anything, he simply returned the bow, just as deep, and just as formally.

The ninja was surprised. He thought the search of Ningyo-cho by Yoshida's men would end the possibility of completing his contract that night. Not that he thought Yoshida's men would catch the target, of course. He knew Yoshida's men and he had a good idea of the capabilities of the target, and he was confident that in any game of cat and mouse, it was the target who would be the *neko* and Yoshida's men who would be playing the part of the *nezumi*. It did not surprise him when his spies reported that Yoshida's search of Ningyo-cho had been a failure.

Now that Yoshida's men had gone, the target, this Matsuyama Kaze, had left the theater and was walking about the streets of Ningyo-cho. What surprised the ninja was that Matsuyama was being followed by a young woman. She left the theater moments after Matsuyama and was making a clandestine effort to track him. The ninja signaled to his partner, who was hiding down the street, to gather the rest. The partner, like all of them, was dressed in the black pants, shirt, and hood that allowed him to blend into the night. Then the ninja started following the target and the girl.

As he followed, he decided that this unusual development could be an advantage. The girl trailing the target would act as an effective shield. The ninja was confident of his ability to follow someone unnoticed, but when there were five of them, it would be impossible for that many men, even ninja, to follow a man of Matsuyama's capabilities without drawing attention to themselves. With the woman between them, he was sure Matsuyama's attention would be drawn to her clumsy attempts to stay hidden, and he would not notice the gathering of death forming behind him.

Matsuyama seemed to be wandering the streets, seeing if the woman would get tired of following him. A hand was placed on his arm, and the ninja knew his four companions had arrived. He placed his fingers into the palm of one of them, and used his fingers in a silent code, instructing his companion to take two others and get ahead of Matsuyama, so they could trap him in a side street. With a scratch and tap of his finger in the palm of the other, he also instructed him to make the call of the *tsugumi*, the thrush, as a signal they were ready.

The other ninja touched two of his companions on the arm, and the three of them ran off down a side street to circle around and get ahead of the target.

He and the other ninja continued following a short distance more, when the target stopped and looked pointedly behind him. Perhaps he was tired of being followed and decided to confront the girl. Regardless, the ninja froze and blended into a shadow, just in case the target realized there were others on his trail. The ninja's companion, who was relatively young and unseasoned, continued moving forward, much to the ninja's annoyance. His young companion was too distant to touch, and he didn't dare make a sound, so all he could do was watch his young charge continue to creep forward.

Suddenly, there was the call of the thrush from ahead. Instantly, the target drew his sword and stood sideways in the street, so he could see both before and behind him, his weapon at the ready. The ninja cursed at the bad position he found himself in, with his companion too far ahead, but at the same time he had to admire the alertness of the target, sensing that the bird's call in the midst of a city like Edo might be the harbinger of something dangerous.

All semblance of stealth abandoned, the ninja and his companion drew the short, Chinese-style swords they had strapped to their backs, and started running toward the target. As he reached the woman, she half turned in surprise at the sound of running feet, and the young companion, who was several paces ahead of the ninja, struck her at the base of her neck with his open hand, Okinawan style. The woman immediately collapsed to the street.

The ninja was about to yell to his companion to slow down, because he wanted the men in front and behind the target to arrive at exactly the same time, but he saw it was too late to curb the impetuousness of youth. He would arrive a split second before the others.

The target used this timing error to his advantage.

He parried the young ninja's blow with his sword. Then, instead of going on the offensive with the young ninja, he pivoted around and caught the lead ninja on the other side of him. This man thought he would have an easy kill while the target was engaged with the young one, but instead he was caught by surprise by the pivoting movement and the target's sword slashed across his midriff.

The target didn't stop his pivoting movement with the success of his attack, however. He spun completely around in time to have his blade parry a second cut from the young one.

Again, instead of going on the attack, he turned his attention to the other side of him and swung his blade at the other attackers, catching a ninja jumping over the body of his slain companion. Not waiting to see the success of his attack as the mortally wounded ninja fell to the ground, he turned his attention back to the young one in time to parry a third blow.

"Get back!" the ninja ordered. The young one obeyed orders and the remaining ninja on the other side did, too.

The ninja took out his knife. Ninja were known to be experts in all types of throwing weapons, and the ninja expected a fighter as good as this samurai to react. The samurai did react, but in an unexpected fashion.

Normally a samurai fought facing an enemy with both hands on his sword. At the sight of the knife, this samurai simply turned his body to the side, holding his sword in only one hand and presenting the smallest target possible. The ninja smiled. He was an expert and could hit something as small as a plum with a thrown knife. Simply turning to present a smaller target was not a good defense. It was the first mistake this target made in the fight.

With a quick motion, the ninja brought the knife back and threw it. The samurai stepped back quickly as the knife was thrown, and although it cut the kimono of the samurai, it did not strike home.

Surprised, the ninja realized that the samurai's movement was not a mistake, but a brilliant defense. The human body was only as wide as a hand span. An expert knife thrower will aim for the center of the target, so one only has to move a small distance to have the knife miss a vital spot.

"Give me your knife!" the ninja called to his young companion. The other ninja tossed over his knife.

The ninja now had to guess which direction the samurai would move, forward or backward. If he guessed wrong, the knife would miss completely. If he guessed right, the samurai would be wounded or dead. The samurai stepped back the last time, so the ninja guessed he would step back again, because that might be the direction he found most comfortable for moving quickly. The ninja brought back the knife and threw it.

The knife grazed the back of the samurai's kimono, but didn't strike flesh. The samurai had not moved. The ninja realized that the samurai perceived that he would understand why his first throw had missed, and that he would compensate with his second. With the thrower expecting a moving target, the samurai had simply stood firm and let the throw's compensation cause it to miss him.

It was as if the samurai could read his mind, anticipating his moves. For the first time in his life, the ninja became fearful of another man's fighting ability.

Suppressing his emerging doubts, the ninja shouted, "At my signal!" The others knew what he meant, but so, apparently, did the samurai. He stepped back slightly, still standing sideways in the street, so his back was protected by the wall of the building behind him. This meant that the three of them would be approaching him from the front, instead of from both sides.

The ninja hesitated, to assess this new development, but before the ninja could shout his signal to attack, the samurai abandoned the defensive posture he had just adopted and moved to the offense. He stepped forward quickly to the younger one, using the young one's body to block the ninja from taking a cut. The younger one took another slice at the samurai. The samurai blocked it, but this time he followed through, and after the parry he twisted his blade to one side and slashed the younger one across the neck.

Without wasting a moment, the samurai turned and blocked a blow from the ninja behind him. The samurai took a cut at the ninja, then a second and third. The third found its mark, and the man fell to the ground, mortally wounded.

As if he were moving to the choreographed sweeps of a dance, the samurai spun around and parried the last ninja's cut, which an instant before had been aimed at the back of the samurai.

The ninja stood on guard, watching the samurai, waiting for an opportunity. The samurai did the same, his sword at the aimed-at-the-knee position, as if he was inviting an attack from the remaining ninja.

Suddenly, from behind him, the ninja heard a female voice calling, "Saburo!" The target's name was Matsuyama Kaze, and the ninja was momentarily confused by the strange name being shouted by the woman, who had obviously recovered from the blow given her. He risked a quick turn of his head to see if this Saburo was coming up behind him. Convinced his back was clear, he turned to the samurai just as the samurai's sword cut into his flesh. The ninja staggered backward, then fell to his knees as he felt his strength draining from the cut across his side and stomach. Even in his dying state, the ninja couldn't help but admire his target, who had shown no hesitation between thought and action, between opportunity and conclusion. "Superb!" the ninja managed to gasp before dying.

CHAPTER 17

*Infatuated
sighs and sad puppydog eyes.
Young love. A bother!*

Saburo!" Momoko came running down the dark street, her feet making the characteristic shuffle sound of someone running in a kimono. She stepped around the bodies that littered the ground and threw her arms around Kaze's neck.

Surprised, Kaze took one hand off his sword hilt and patted her on the back. "Don't worry, Momoko. The ninja are all dead now. They can't hurt you."

Momoko pulled back. "I'm not worrying about them hurting me," she said indignantly. "I knew you'd kill them! I'm just worried that you're hurt."

Kaze smiled. "You have a lot of faith in me. There were five of them."

"They hit me and knocked me down, so I didn't know how many of them there were, but when I regained my senses I could see you had already defeated all but one of them. You were fantastic!"

Kaze smiled. "Youthful enthusiasm."

"I'm not that young," Momoko said. Then, taking advantage of the fact that her arms were around Kaze's neck, she kissed him fiercely. It was a clumsy, sloppy kiss, but what Momoko lacked in technique, she made up for with vigor.

Kaze put a hand on her chest and gently pushed her away. "Five men just died," he said. "It's frightening how youth can ignore death to indulge lust."

Momoko drew herself up, as dignified as any court lady. "I kissed you because I was happy that you survived," she said. "It wasn't lust."

"Whatever it was, let's leave this place before a patrol comes by and discovers us. It would be inconvenient to have to explain five dead bodies."

Momoko nodded and started rushing off.

"Slow down," Kaze said. "If we run, we'll attract attention from anyone who sees us. If we stroll, no one will take notice."

Momoko slowed down and dutifully started following Kaze a pace behind, just like a wife. Her face was flushed with excitement from the night's events, but just as if she were onstage, she played the role of the Edokko housewife perfectly.

"Why were you following me?" Kaze asked when they had left the street with the dead ninja.

"I just didn't want the night to end. It was so wonderful for me. When you took off your makeup and abruptly left, I decided to see where you were going. I was curious."

"About what?"

There was a moment's hesitation. "I was curious to see, ah, if you were visiting a woman, or maybe even—"

"Even?"

"Well, maybe you were visiting a boy. A lot of samurai like that. I wanted to know if that was the case with you."

Kaze shook his head. "The young people these days are incredible. Haven't you been told that a maiden of your age should have some modesty?"

"I'm not a child," Momoko said.

"Then you should feign modesty. You're not a strumpet."

"Remember, until a few weeks ago, the Kabuki dancers at the theater were females doing the most lascivious dances. After the performance, they would entertain patrons, sometimes right backstage. I was always backstage helping them dress or picking up costumes after the performance. I'm not experienced, but I've seen plenty."

"Maybe too much," Kaze said.

Kaze had left the theater to look for a convenient way to get on the roof of the Little Flower, to see if he could look down into any inner courtyards and get an appreciation for the layout of the building. Within moments of leaving the theater, he knew he was being followed, and seconds after that he knew the follower was Momoko. Although she had a gift from the Gods when she was onstage, this gift did not extend to an ability to mimic clandestine operations. Initially, Kaze thought a little wandering would discourage the girl, but she was persistent, and Kaze decided a confrontation and lecture were in order.

Instead of being the teacher in this situation, however, Kaze learned a lesson. Skilled ninja can hide anywhere, even behind a mere slip of a woman. Kaze was so focused on Momoko that he didn't even realize so many men were surrounding him until he heard the tsugumi call. Kaze was not a city dweller, but he understood that this call was unusual in a city like Edo, especially at that time of night.

He and Momoko walked back to the Kabuki theater. Momoko's imitation of a wife on the journey somehow irritated Kaze. When they got to the theater, Momoko proceeded to stir up the charcoal fire in an earthenware container, which served as the only source of heat for warmth and cooking. She poured water, which was obtained from a communal well in the neighborhood, into a teapot, and commenced to heat it. Kaze shook his head. It was as if it were a totally normal part of Momoko's daily routine to witness a battle between one man and five ninja, and now it was time to sit back, relax, do some domestic chores, and have some soothing tea.

As Momoko busied herself with chores, Kaze rummaged through the theater props until he found a suitable piece of wood. It was a branch that must have been used as decoration. No matter. Taking out his katana, he cut the branch to the proper size. He sheathed the katana and took out his *ko-gatana,* the small knife he kept in a holder that was built into his sword's scabbard. He sat by the fire and started to carve.

Momoko was curious, but she kept quiet and let Kaze work. Under Kaze's practiced hand, the wood took shape rapidly, a figure emerging from the grain in quick order. When he was done, he put the statue of the Kannon on the floor before him.

"Would you like some *ocha,* tea?" Momoko asked timidly. She had remained silent, allowing Kaze to work the entire time.

Kaze nodded, and Momoko handed him a chipped cup of the bitter green brew. Kaze sipped at the scalding liquid and sighed.

"Can I see it?" Momoko asked, pointing to the statue.

Kaze handed it to her. She examined it closely, as if the planes and curves of the wood would reveal something about the soul of its maker.

"It's a beautiful Kannon," she said.

Kaze gave a brief nod to acknowledge the compliment.

"Is this modeled after someone you know?"

Again, Kaze nodded.

"Your, ah, your wife?"

Kaze shook his head no.

Momoko looked at the statue again. "She is extremely beautiful."

"Yes, she was."

"Oh, has she grown old now?"

"She will never grow old."

"How is that possible?"

"She's dead."

"Oh. I'm sorry. Was she as gentle and serene as you've made her in the statue?"

"Yes. She had a remarkable quality for making you feel happy and calm. Most women make men happy by getting them excited, but she had a loving grace about her that washed over all in her presence."

"Were you in love with her?"

Kaze sighed. "I couldn't be in love with her. She was the wife of my Lord."

"But Saburo . . ."

"Momoko, I'm not Saburo. My name now is Matsuyama Kaze. I was once a samurai in the service of my Lord, and now I am a ronin, a wave man, a wandering samurai."

"Matsuyama Kaze . . ." Comprehension washed across Momoko's face. "Are you the man who tried to assassinate the Shogun?" she blurted out.

"No."

She looked a little relieved.

"I am, however, the man the authorities want for trying to assassinate the Shogun."

"But—"

"The authorities think I tried to kill Ieyasu, and ended up killing Lord Nakamura in the assassination attempt. I actually didn't do either."

"But if they're looking for you, why are you still in Edo? Saburo, ah, Kaze, you must leave here for somewhere safe!"

"Where in the entire realm is it safe for a man suspected of trying to kill the Shogun? More important, I have business in Edo."

"No business is worth your life!"

"To me it is."

"Please leave Edo right away! I'll, ah, I'll go with you. Just to keep you company. The authorities won't suspect a man and, ah, his young wife."

Kaze smiled. He was going to remark on the transparency of youth, but Momoko's drawn face, so filled with fear of the authorities for Kaze's sake, plus her boldness in declaring, albeit indirectly, her love for him, made him soften his statement.

"It would probably be good for me to leave Edo for a short while, but not for the reasons you want. This city is interesting, but I can't think here. I want to go to a place where a bird's song doesn't mean an attack, a place where I can breathe clean air and find trees that are free to all, instead of locked up behind the walls of a great lord's Edo villa. I have to consider what to do next, and I can't do it in this city."

"I'll go with you."

"No, you'll stay here. I'll be back shortly, because I have to finish my business here in Edo. It's a sacred pledge, and I must complete it. But before I can do that, I must think, and that requires me to be alone for a while. Besides, Goro and Hanzo need you. They're hopeless businessmen, and this theater will fail if they try to run it by themselves. They have good hearts, but weak minds. You have a good heart and a good mind, and you love this Kabuki. You'll help mold and invent it, and I'm sure you'll be a great success. It is your karma to be here, not wandering the roads with me."

"But—"

Kaze was already on his feet.

Momoko grabbed the statue of the Kannon. "At least let me keep this, as a remembrance of you."

Kaze reached down and gently took it from her hands. "No. This has a purpose. On my way out of town, I'll stop at the place where the ninjas died and place it where she can look over the site, and soothe the troubled souls of the men I killed."

At the tears forming in Momoko's eyes, Kaze snapped, "Don't cry. It's pathetic, and I hate pathetic people!"

Momoko wiped her eyes with the sleeve of her kimono, and actually managed a smile, although it was a forced, stage smile.

"I'll be back in a few days." Kaze stuck his sword in his sash. Then he said, "I'll carve you something else someday. Something more suitable for a woman of your remarkable talents." Momoko's false smile metamorphosed into a genuine one.

"Good," Kaze said. He took the carved statue of the Goddess of Mercy and left.

Look within yourself.
Block out all thoughts and worry.
Hear your beating heart.

Toyama was in a rage. He had spent the morning in his villa's study, writing instructions to his retainers in his home fief and notes to relatives. None of the correspondence discussed his growing anxiety over his position with Ieyasu or his desire to distinguish himself when others, like Yoshida, Honda, and Okubo, seemed to be getting ahead in the new order that was coming from Ieyasu's Shogunate.

Toyama was also anxious to hear from the ninja he had hired to kill Matsuyama Kaze. As soon as he heard Kaze was dead, Toyama intended to tell Ieyasu, disclosing his role in hiring the ninja. Yet despite days of waiting, he had heard nothing.

The only comfort Toyama had was that Yoshida, with all the power of the Shogunate's troops behind him, was doing no better. Toyama delighted that Yoshida's search of Ningyo-cho had disclosed nothing, despite the effort he put into closing off that quarter of the city and sending troops to examine every house, business, and alleyway.

Buoyed by that thought, Toyama had decided to treat himself to a walk in the garden before he finished his correspondence. It was a fine day. Toyama was told that Edo was hot and humid in the summer, and dreary in the winter, but today, one of the last days of fall, the weather was glorious. Above, the clouds looked like white swirls on deep blue silk, and in the luxury of his garden, he was insulated from the bustle of the city.

Toyama returned to his study refreshed. On the low desk he was using to write, he found a letter. Toyama was puzzled. When he left, he was sure that the desk had been clear, save for a few sheets of fine paper, an ink stone, a stick of ink, and some fox hair brushes.

Toyama called out, and one of the guards in the hallway slid open the door.

"Yes, Lord!"

"Did one of the servants just deliver a letter?"

"No, Lord. No one has come down the hallway."

Toyama waved a hand to dismiss the guard. He knelt on the low cushion placed before the writing desk and picked up the letter. It was not placed in an outer wrapping, like some formal correspondence might be. Instead, the letter was folded tightly until it formed a flat strip, and then the strip was folded over into a decorative knot. "Lord Toyama" was written on one of the paper ends coming from the knot. His name was written in proper kanji, using a very thin brush and a fine hand. Toyama undid the loose knot, then unfolded the paper. Inside was a note in the squiggly lines of hiragana, written with the same brush and fine hand.

To Lord Toyama—
   Five have died, but the target still lives. The contract has been completed, but was not successful.

The note was unsigned, but Toyama knew who it was from. The ninja! He let out a shout of frustration and anger that caused the guard to slide the door open again.

"Lord, is there something wrong?"

"No! Close the door, you fool!" The guard hastily did as he was ordered.

Those peasant murderers would not be allowed to get away with this, Toyama fumed. He looked at the words "The contract has been completed" and "not successful" and threw the letter down. Toyama would go to Ieyasu. He would explain what happened, and how much money he had paid these ninja. Then he would enlist Ieyasu's support for a campaign to exterminate these assassins and spies. Why, it wouldn't surprise him if the attempted assassination of Ieyasu had really been a ninja plot. It was just like them to strike from hiding, when the victim would least expect it. He would show them that they couldn't trifle with a Toyama! With Ieyasu's help, he would hunt them down, every one of them, and rip the guts from their women and children before he crucified the men. He would be merciless! No amount of begging or pleading would deter him from exacting a terrible vengeance on the ninja, wiping them from . . .

Toyama's eyes fixed on the letter, lying crumpled in a corner where he had thrown it. A terrible thought entered his head. "Guard!" he bellowed.

The door slid open instantly. The guard, his eyes wide with fear over his Lord's inexplicable actions, said, "Yes, Lord!"

"Are you sure no one was in my study?"

"Yes, my Lord. There are two of us. We would certainly know if someone had entered your room."

A chill seized Toyama's spine, and he actually felt the flesh on his arms rising to chicken skin. "All right," he said breathlessly. When the guard continued to look at him, seeing if he was possessed, he simply waved him away.

Toyama was possessed. Possessed with fear. A ninja had managed to penetrate his villa, delivering a letter to Toyama's study unseen and unheard, in the few minutes available when Toyama left his study to walk in his garden. Toyama had heard many legends of ninja magic. Even without magic, he also knew the ninja were incredibly tenacious.

He remembered the rumor of how Uesugi had died. A ninja dug a tunnel under Uesugi's garden, directly under the privy next to Uesugi's manor. The tunnel exited right under the hole in the wooden floor of the privy, intersecting the deep shaft dug to hold human waste. The ninja crawled down the tunnel and waited, in the stinking darkness, for days, until Lord Uesugi finally used that privy to relieve himself. Then the ninja had thrust a sword up Uesugi's backside, impaling him and causing him an agonizing death.

At first, the servants thought Lord Uesugi had had some kind of terrible seizure, until they saw the blood gushing from his bottom. Afterward, Uesugi's guards discovered the tunnel and were able to piece together how their Lord was killed. The official story was that Uesugi had died of a sudden fit while going to the bathroom, but six guards committed seppuku in apology for the successful assassination. Toyama thought this was a waste, because who but a ninja would conceive of such a terrible way to kill a man? How would you defend a lord from such a thing?

If Toyama declared a vendetta against the ninja, they would undoubtedly reciprocate. He would forever be fearful about using a privy. But even such a bizarre precaution couldn't save him from the ninja's revenge. He looked at the crumpled-up letter and realized that it had been delivered in a specific manner to serve as a warning.

Toyama slid over and picked up the letter with a trembling hand. He opened it and stared at the phrase, "Five have died." What manner of demon was this Matsuyama, that he could kill five of the ninja devils?

•   •   •

The demon Matsuyama was sitting in a pine tree, looking at a flower. He had walked the entire night and most of the morning. Edo was large and growing larger by the day, but it wasn't so large that one couldn't escape the city and its satellite villages on foot. One direction being as good as another, Kaze had started walking toward Fuji-san, that snowcapped slope of perfection seen in the distance from Edo.

Passing farms and villages in the still, early morning hours, he came to rolling hills, thick with woods. This was what he was seeking.

Kaze could taste the scent of the trees on his tongue. If they were pines or cryptomerias, it was a heady taste of pitch and tar. Kaze's favorite was the cherry, which created a faint perfume that entered his nostrils and dispersed its sweetness to his very finger-tips.

Following a boyhood habit, he picked a wildflower, then scaled one of the trees that had a sturdy branch growing parallel to the ground, and sat on the branch in the lotus position, his sword across his lap. He looked down at the flower, focusing on it. It was an old trick.

By focusing on a specific object like the flower, one could block out the clutter that filled the mind. Then, when one stopped think-ing about the specific, one was not consciously thinking at all. This state of non-mindedness led to revelation and understanding. Paradoxically, non-mindedness opened up the consciousness to new thoughts, approaches, and insight, drawing from the entire universe of enlightenment, instead of the narrow circle of self that usually confined thoughts.

When he had satisfied himself with his inspection of the flower, really not knowing if it took a minute or an hour, he dropped the flower from his perch in the tree and watched it tumble to the ground. It turned madly, responding to the vagaries of the gentle wind that stirred the air. How like our lives, Kaze thought, so at the mercy of circumstances, illness, war, and the actions of others. With his head down and his soul in a state of repose, he stared at the ground, not really focusing. He did *kanki-issoku,* quietly exhaling completely through his mouth, using his stomach, then inhaling through his nose. He meditated, opening his mind to solutions to the problems facing him, depending on the deeper resources of his spirit instead of the finite abilities of his mind.

When Kaze stopped meditating, it was night. He was surprised to find himself surrounded by darkness, with the hard points of stars splashed across the sky. If someone had approached him in his meditative state, he would have been instantly alert. But to the natural cycle of day into night, he remained oblivious.

Kaze dropped out of the tree, landing on his feet as lightly as a cat. His muscles were sore from inactivity, but by maintaining a proper *zazen* posture, even while perched on a branch, he was not as stiff as he would otherwise be.

He found himself a grassy spot under the tree and wrapped his kimono a bit tighter. Hugging his sword in his arms, he lay down to sleep, happy at being outdoors once again, far away from the city.

He was surprised at the conclusions he had come to about the attempted assassination of Ieyasu. He was also surprised at his plan for rescuing the Lady's daughter from the Little Flower Whorehouse. Before drifting to sleep, he marveled at what thoughts came to you when you simply put yourself into a state to receive them.

What was on top is
now crawling on the bottom.
Reversal is life.

Is gambling a profitable business?"

Nobu gave a start at the voice in his room, but this time he knew exactly where to look. Just as before, the ronin was sitting in the darkest corner of the room, looking relaxed and at home. This time, his sword was still in its scabbard, sitting next to him on the mat.

"How did you get in here?" Nobu said.

Kaze pointed to the window, frowning at a question he thought should be obvious.

Nobu moved the lantern he was carrying between them, so he could see the ronin better, and sat his bulky body down on the oversized futon he used.

"Why do you want to know how much money is in gambling?"

"Because," Kaze said, "for the first time in my life, I have a use for money."

"Gambling is usually the best business," Nobu said. "Better than flesh and even better than stealing. With flesh, a man can become sated and will eventually leave the whorehouse. The fever for gambling can't be quenched. It's better than stealing because you eventually end up with all of a fool's possessions. When you rob his house, you can only carry off some of his things. Besides, they crucify you for stealing, but only beat you up for gambling. If you cross the proper palms with payoffs, you can even avoid the beatings."

"So this business makes a lot of money?"

"Not as much as it should."

"Why?"

"Because Boss Akinari is greedy. As greedy as the fools who lose everything gambling here. If someone wins too much, Boss Akinari arranges for him to disappear. Word gets around about that kind of thing, you know, and it really hurts business. Most of the big gamblers have stopped coming here, and they've gone to other gambling houses. That's why the Boss is getting involved with things like tobacco. There's no need to get involved with that evil weed. The Boss claims it has many health benefits, but, like their religion, I think it's just another bad thing those smelly Europeans have introduced to Japan. If Boss Akinari would just show some patience, everyone's luck turns eventually, and the big winner this month will be begging for a loan next month. That's what makes gambling such a good business to be in. We don't have to branch out into tobacco."

"Why don't you point that out to him?"

Nobu hesitated. There was something about this ronin that he liked, however, so he decided to be frank with him. "If anyone in the gang looks like they're getting too independent, Boss Akinari makes them disappear, too."

"It sounds like Akinari is not a very good boss."

Nobu shrugged.

"Perhaps Boss Nobu would do a better job for this gang."

Nobu started, then saw the ronin was serious. "You're a devil, Matsuyama-san," Nobu said. "It's not healthy for someone to start thinking like that. Besides, it would be disloyal for an underling to think about deposing his boss."

"Nobunaga got rid of Imagawa, and Ieyasu, who was an Imagawa vassal, joined him, to their mutual benefit. Akechi, a vassal of Nobunaga's, assassinated him. Hideyoshi said he was avenging Nobunaga's death, but he eventually displaced Nobunaga's sons as ruler of both their clan and Japan. Ieyasu was Hideyoshi's chief daimyo, but he deposed Hideyoshi's son and now rules as Shogun. A vassal replacing his boss is a common enough thing nowadays."

"And what about you? Were you loyal to your lord?"

"Well, yes," Kaze admitted. "But I'm a bit old-fashioned. That's just me. It doesn't mean you have to be."

"You are a devil!"

"Perhaps, but perhaps also a sensible devil, Boss Nobu."

"Boss Nobu," the big man said, muttering the words to himself, savoring their novelty.

The door to Nobu's room slid open. The big man looked startled, and Kaze looked at the door with interest, to see what was developing. It was a woman, one of the servants of the household. She held a tray with a teapot and two steaming cups of tea.

"I saw you had guests, Nobu-san, so I thought you might like some ocha," the woman said.

"How did you—" Nobu started.

Before he could finish his question, the woman shouted, "Now!" She threw the tea tray at Kaze.

Kaze diverted his face to avoid the scalding tea, but he didn't jerk himself out of the path of the tea, as another man might. Instead, he reached out to grab his sword. The tea splashed against his arm, sending a shock of pain as the liquid burned his skin.

As part of the plan, the woman threw herself down on Kaze's scabbard as soon as she had thrown the tray. She trapped Kaze's arm and weapon under her body.

Before Kaze could push her away, the room was filled with men, smothering the ronin with a tsunami of flesh.

Boss Akinari sat on a raised dais, like a noble. He had a *yojimbo*, a bodyguard, standing next to him with a sword for protection. Akinari also had a sword stuck in his sash, and sitting before him on the dais was Kaze's sword, "Fly Cutter."

Kaze's arms were being held by two burly men. The only other person in the room was Nobu. Kaze's arm hurt from the hot tea, but otherwise he only had a few bumps and bruises.

"I had Nobu's room watched, on the chance that you would return to talk to him. I'm very pleased you did," Akinari said. "Your head will mean a great deal of money to me. But before I turn you over to Yoshida-sama for the reward, I think it's fair to settle some scores. You killed two of my men the first time I tried to take your head."

"I'm sorry I killed your men, but it would have been inconvenient to lose my head," Kaze said.

Akinari frowned. "I'll teach you to be disrespectful to me. Nobu, hit him."

Nobu looked at Akinari and shrugged. He turned to Kaze and drew back his huge fist, hitting the ronin in the stomach. It was like being hit with one of the battering rams used to burst castle gates. Kaze gave an "Oooff" and fought to get his breath back.

"As I said, you killed my men. Then you embarrassed me by fooling me into thinking you had escaped, when you actually wanted to stick around and talk to Nobu."

Kaze looked at Nobu, and whispered, "He doesn't trust you. That's why he had your room watched. You said Akinari made men disappear. You're next." His whisper was even lower than normal; the effects of Nobu's blow to his stomach.

"What's he saying?" Akinari asked, unable to make out Kaze's whisper.

"Just some nonsense, Boss," Nobu said.

Akinari snorted. "Then you embarrassed me with Lord Yoshida, escaping from the vegetable merchant's house. That cost me a thousand ryo. Still, your head will bring me ten thousand, so maybe it has all worked out for the best."

"You'll never see a penny of that," Kaze whispered to Nobu.

"What is he saying?" Akinari asked petulantly.

"It's just more nonsense," Nobu responded.

Akinari looked at the men holding Kaze. "What is it he's saying?" he asked.

"He's saying you don't trust Nobu, Boss," one of the men said.

Akinari remained silent for a moment, then said, "Nobu, it's suspicious this man wanted to talk to you twice. Now you can prove your loyalty by doing the job of beating him up before we take his head. Hit him again."

Nobu nodded, then struck another blow, this time to Kaze's side. Kaze almost expected to hear the crack of a rib, but instead he just felt pain from the hammering.

"Look at him," Kaze gasped. "He doesn't trust you. Soon you'll be as dead as me."

"Why are you just hitting his body?" Akinari asked Nobu. "Why not his face?"

"I want Yoshida-sama to be able to recognize him when you take his head in for the reward. Blows to the body can be just as punishing as blows to the face."

"Nonsense. Smash his face up. And be quick about it!"

"It's a test." Kaze smiled through the pain at Nobu. "He wants to make sure we're not friends."

"I'll show him we're not!" Nobu said. He brought his fist back, and took careful aim at Kaze's face.

"Boss Nobu," Kaze said.

Nobu hesitated a moment, then he brought his fist forward with all his strength. The fist flew past Kaze's face and caught one of the two men holding Kaze squarely in the cheek. This time, Kaze did hear the crack of bone. The surprised thug crumpled to the floor instantly.

With a grace that seemed impossible for a man of his size, Nobu dove toward Boss Akinari. Akinari and his bodyguard started drawing their blades, but Nobu was not trying to reach the gambling chief. Instead, he snatched Kaze's sword from the floor, turned on his side, and threw the sword and scabbard back to the ronin.

Kaze caught the sword with the hand recently freed by Nobu knocking out the man holding it. Without taking the sword from its scabbard, Kaze brought the scabbard down across the head of the man still holding him. As he felt the man's grip loosen, Kaze yanked his other arm free and grabbed the scabbard.

He drew his sword, and got the blade extended in the aimed-at-the-foot position, just in time to block a cut at Nobu, still lying on the floor, made by Akinari. Akinari's blade was close to Nobu's face when Kaze's blade intercepted it. The eyes of the big man grew wide as the two pieces of steel met just a finger's width from his skin. The clang of steel filled the small room, and Nobu took advantage of the small reprieve to roll away from Akinari and the yojimbo.

The yojimbo stepped past Akinari and attacked Kaze with an overhead cut. With his sword so low to the ground after protecting Nobu, Kaze couldn't parry the blow, so he took a lesson from Nobu and dove to the ground, rolling to one side as the cut flashed past him. As he rolled, Kaze reached out with one arm and slashed the yojimbo across the chest and belly.

The yojimbo let out a cry of pain and staggered backward, eventually falling to the floor. Kaze quickly finished his roll just as Akinari rushed at him. Kaze was in a crouching position and put his sword up to stop Akinari's blow. Akinari brought his sword back for a second blow as Kaze forced his way to his feet. Then, making a classic diagonal cut across Akinari's neck and shoulder, Kaze killed the gambler.

Breathing hard, Kaze glanced over at Nobu, who was shakily getting to his feet. Then he looked around and said, "Quite a mess." He looked at Akinari and told Nobu, "You'll need a coffin." Glancing at the yojimbo, who was clutching at his wound and turning white with shock, "Maybe two." Kaze walked over to the yojimbo to see if he should deliver another blow to put him out of his pain. The yojimbo stopped breathing, taking the decision out of Kaze's hands. Kaze saw the other two were still unconscious.

"I think we're all better off with Akinari in the void. He'll be reincarnated, but with the life he led, it's probable he'll come back as a particularly annoying mosquito. I'm sorry about the yojimbo, though," Kaze remarked. "He was just doing his job. I wish he had done it less well, so I didn't have to kill him."

"I said you're a devil, and it's true! Boss Akinari suspected me because of your habit of sneaking into my room to talk to me. Now he's dead."

"Better him than you," Kaze pointed out. "Boss Nobu," he added.

Nobu scratched his head. Then he smiled. "I suppose you're right. You're still a devil, but this might work out to everyone's advantage. Except, of course, for Akinari and the yojimbo."

"What about the rest of Akinari's men?"

"They're my men now. Those two are still out, and the yojimbo is dead. No one knows what happened here except the two of us. I can say I slipped and hit the wrong guy, and then you managed to get free and kill Akinari and his yojimbo. No one will challenge me if I take over and blame all this on you. If that one"—Nobu

pointed with his chin at the man Kaze had knocked unconscious—"dares to mention that I'm the one who threw you the
sword, then he'll be sorry. As far as the gang is concerned, you're
the one who did it all."

"Happy to be of service, Boss Nobu."

"Now I can be of service to you. You said you needed money."

"Yes, and some help with other things."

"There would be plenty of money if I could deliver your head
to Lord Yoshida." Nobu grinned, to show he was making a joke.

Kaze also smiled. "As I told the late Boss Akinari, it would be
inconvenient for me to lose my head now. If I get some money
and help from you, I am close to fulfilling a quest, and also dis-
covering who actually tried to kill Ieyasu."

Nobu sat on the dais recently occupied by Akinari. Ignoring
the unconscious men and dead bodies in the room, he said, "Tell
me more."

Crush a young flower.
Does it give you such pleasure?
A perverted act.

Irasshai!" The servant greeted the man at the door to the Little
Flower Whorehouse with an enthusiastic shout. He also gave the
man a close examination, because he was a stranger.

He was dressed in good but not sumptuous clothes, in the style
of a merchant. He looked to be in his early thirties, with muscular
shoulders and arms. He was not carrying a sword, so he was a
commoner. Outside, the ink of night had painted the street. Some
establishments had brightly lit lanterns hanging in front of them
to advertise that they were open and to guide patrons to their
door. At the Little Flower, however, only the light that discreetly
spilled out from the door marked the entrance.

"How can I help you, sir?"

"I understand that you cater to, ah, special tastes at this establishment. Fresh taste. Young taste."

"Well, yes sir, we do. However, you must understand that such
entertainment is very expensive. I am sure the esteemed gentleman
is very prosperous, but since you have not honored us with your
presence before, I want to advise you that an evening's entertainment might be very dear."

The merchant reached into a sleeve and brought out a pouch. He poured out some of the contents into his palm, and the servant's eyes lit up at the sight of gold. "Welcome, welcome, sir!" The servant slid open an inner door. A guard at the door immediately looked up, ready for trouble. The servant gave him a sign that all was well and asked him to fetch the owner of the brothel because an important—that is, rich—guest had arrived.

Within minutes a woman in a fancy black-and-yellow kimono arrived, with two young serving girls trailing her. "I am Jitotenno," she announced, sitting on the tatami mat. She bowed until her head touched the ground. Her posture was humble, but Kaze suspected the woman was not. Her name, which had been taken when she entered the Floating World of prostitution and entertainment where few people used their own names, was the name of an empress who had ruled Japan a thousand years before.

The serving girls helped remove the man's sandals, which looked new, and replace his tabi socks, which also looked new, after washing his feet. While they did this, the brothel owner cooed over the new customer, making small talk and flattering him.

Kaze was the customer. After getting money from Nobu, he had gone from the gambling house back to the theater Nobu offered to put him up at the gambling house, but Kaze decided it wasn't wise to dangle too much temptation in front of Nobu, and simply said he would make his own sleeping arrangements. Kaze didn't want his head removed by Boss Nobu, and he was careful he wasn't followed to the theater.

At the theater, he had a tearful reunion with Momoko. At least it was tearful on her part. He was surprised that both Goro and Hanzo seemed happy to see him again. Kaze looked over the costumes at the theater but didn't see anything he thought was suitable for the part he was going to play, so he gave Momoko money to buy an appropriate merchant's outfit.

The Little Flower Whorehouse was a fortress, so the best way in was through the front door. To do that, Kaze knew he needed money. With money, all barriers would fall, and he could get them to usher him into the building and show him its inhabitants.

"It is most fortunate the gentleman arrived now," Jitotenno said. "We are about to have a viewing."

"Viewing?"

"It is an opportunity for our esteemed guests to see the children, and to select the dear one they would like to be with. As you can guess, our clients demand freshness and newness from our children. Since we run only the finest establishment, I have many agents looking for orphans and other children that we can introduce to our clients. We always have new children for our guests."

Kaze's heart sank, not only at the thought of a steady parade of new flesh coming through the Little Flower, but also at the thought that the child he was seeking might have already been sent away.

He was led to a veranda facing an inner courtyard, open to the sky. As Kaze had suspected, this was how the Little Flower provided light and air to the building. Three other men were already sitting on the veranda, comfortably ensconced on *zabuton* pillows, drinking sakè served to them by a young girl. The courtyard was lit by several torches and, although it was mostly white sand, it was tastefully landscaped with rocks and a few evergreen plants.

Kaze was seated comfortably and given a saucer of sakè. He gave a polite bow to the other three. They bowed back but didn't say anything. Apparently the Little Flower was not a place where adults engaged in much conversation. When Kaze was settled, the showing began.

Jitotenno walked to the left side of the courtyard and slid back a shoji screen, revealing two musicians. One man proceeded to hit a *shime daiko* drum, and the other man held a staff festooned with bells, shaking it in rhythm to the drumming.

Jitotenno continued walking around the veranda. At the far wall she slid back another screen. A half-dozen children spilled out of the room behind the screen and into the courtyard. There were three girls and three boys, and Kaze judged their ages to be between seven and nine. Two of the boys engaged in a mock sword fight with light bamboo poles, and the third started fussing with a kite he carried, although it was obvious he wasn't going to fly it in the confined courtyard. Two of the girls knelt in the sand and started playing cat's cradle with a piece of string, and the third started bouncing a shuttlecock on a decorative *oibane* paddle.

Normally, a group of children playing would bring joy to Kaze's heart, tinged with sadness over the loss of his own children in the war that made Ieyasu Shogun. In this case, there was only sadness. The play of the children had no spontaneity or laughter. It was a carefully rehearsed sham to display human flesh.

Kaze closely examined the faces of the girls. It had been years since he had seen the child, but none of these girls looked even remotely like Kaze's former Lord and Lady. Kaze's heart, which was already low at the sight of these children, sank even lower when he saw that none of the girls was the child he was looking for. For the first time in almost three years of searching, Kaze was discouraged.

Kaze looked at the faces of his three fellow customers, and he had to fight to keep a look of revulsion off his own face. The others were watching the children intently, two watching the girls and one watching the boys. On their faces were expressions of pure lust, the kind of lust a drunken teenage boy might have when he went to a brothel to lose his virginity. To see this expression on the faces of grown men when they were looking at children disgusted Kaze.

To Kaze, once a child was past infancy, it was a small person. The child was expected to work and learn and contribute to the household, especially if it was a farm household, as most were.

Even though a child was a small person, there were many things that a child could not do until they had gained the experience of years. A girl might be married at fourteen, but at the age of the children in the courtyard, they were supposed to be years away from the mysteries of sex. To see how grown men could view such unformed beings as sexual partners was beyond Kaze's understanding.

Jitotenno, who had moved to the right side of the courtyard, raised her hand, and the musicians stopped playing. The children immediately dropped their toys and sat on the sand, in a clearly rehearsed move.

"Now, esteemed guests, I would like to present to you the most delicate flower of the Little Flower. She is our most favorite entertainer, and has been for years, Little Chrysanthemum, Kikuchan!" She dramatically slid open a screen and a frail girl stepped out of the room and onto the veranda. She was dressed in the finest silk kimono, a deep red with a pattern of yellow and white chrysanthemums on it. A matching obi was tied, and her hair was dressed as if she were going to a shrine on New Year's Day.

Kaze's breath caught in his throat. Her face was a younger image of the Lady's. The same smooth cheeks, the same small mouth, the same delicate eyebrows that perfectly accented the eyes. Those eyes, however, were not the Lady's eyes. The Lady's eyes were always lively and full of joy. This child's eyes, her daughter's eyes, were dull and lifeless. Her look was distant and withdrawn, as if by crawling into some secret place inside her, the child could also withdraw from the life she was leading. It was a younger version of the face Kaze carved on the Kannons he used to ease the dead, but without the peaceful grace and tranquility.

Kaze had found the child.

He wished he had brought his sword with him—although he knew that he would have had to surrender his sword at the door of the brothel—just so it would be nearby in case he decided to abandon his plan and cut his way out. Kaze knew that there were probably several thugs someplace in the house, but he didn't care. No one would stop him from saving this child, now that he knew she was here.

Kiku-chan took a shakuhachi, a bamboo flute, from her obi sash and brought it to her lips. She started to play. It was a slow, plaintive melody that carried across the courtyard with surprising power. The music filled the space and spilled out of the top of the courtyard and into the open sky. Once again, Kaze's breath caught.

It was the same melody Kaze had faintly heard that night in the theater. Slow, haunting, ineffably sad. Through that music, floating across the roofs until it barely reached the theater on the other side of the block, Kaze had made contact with the daughter of the Lady and had not even realized it. Tears formed in his eyes.

Kiku-chan continued her playing for several minutes; then she put her flute back into her obi sash, gave a deep bow to the men on the veranda, and went back into her room. Jitotenno slid the screen back into place.

That was the signal for the other children to leave the courtyard and line up on the opposite veranda, where they could easily be selected by the guests. Kaze glanced over and saw that, despite the smiles plastered on their faces, the eyes of the children were apprehensive and even fearful.

Jitotenno walked over to the four men and bowed deeply. "I hope you have seen someone who will make your stay in our house a little more pleasant," she said.

"I'll take the flute player," one man said immediately.

Jitotenno bowed again. "Kiku-chan, because of her great beauty and refinement, costs four times the amount of the other girls available."

"I'll still take her," the man said.

"I'll double it," Kaze spoke up.

Jitotenno's eyes widened slightly; then she looked at the first man.

"If you give me credit, I will pay a bit more," he said.

Kaze took out his money pouch and jingled it. He would normally never do something as crude as this, but he felt in this company the gesture was suitable.

At the promise of so much cash, Jitotenno said to the first pedophile, "I will let you stay with one of the other girls at a discount, and the next time you visit us, I will make sure you spend the night with Kiku-chan. I hope that is satisfactory. After all, Kiku-chan is not a virgin, despite her virginal appearance, so you will not lose any advantage by letting this gentleman spend tonight with her. In fact, you will have your pleasure with both Kiku-chan and another of these adorable children, and at a substantial savings. I hope this will be acceptable?"

The man, not liking the arrangement but seeing the logic of it, grunted his assent to the offer.

"Good. Let me take this esteemed gentleman to Kiku-chan, and then I will return to see what girl or boy you other gentlemen have chosen to take your pleasure with."

Kaze stood, and Jitotenno led him around the courtyard to Kiku-chan's door. She slid open the door. In the room, lit by two paper lanterns, a futon was already spread on the tatami mats and a small hibachi with a pot of water and several flasks of sakè stood next to it. Kiku-chan sat on the futon, her hands in her lap, looking very small and vulnerable. She looked up at the opening of the door, her face registering resignation that she had a "guest" for the night, and not really caring who the guest was.

"For your safety, esteemed gentleman, we have guards who will watch the door all night." This was a warning, so that Kaze wouldn't try to sneak out without paying when he was done. "You can do whatever you like with the child tonight. Please excuse me for saying this, but if you cripple or kill the child, you will have to pay us for either the loss of her services or blood money. Otherwise, please enjoy her." She ushered Kaze into the room and slid the door closed behind him.

Kiku-chan watched him closely. She had gone beyond the point of being wary with the guests, and was simply trying to see how rough he might be with her.

Kaze sat down on the tatami, a distance far enough away that he thought she might feel safe.

"Do you want some sakè?" she said.

"No."

She sat silently, waiting for what would occur next.

"Do you remember me, Kiku-chan?"

"Have I entertained you before?"

"No. From before you were Kiku-chan." Kaze spoke her real name. "From the time you were a child with your mother."

She looked surprised at Kaze's statement, but said, "I am Kiku-chan. That girl you named is dead. Her mother is dead. All her clan is dead. She has no one. Kiku-chan is at least alive, even though she has no one, too."

"That's not true, Kiku-chan. You have me. I was sent by your mother to find you."

"My mother is dead!"

"Yes, I know that. I was with her when she died. Before she died, she told me to find you and rescue you."

Now the child looked wary. She had been told so many lies in recent years that she knew not to believe this one.

"Yes. It's true. I will get you out of here."

"How?"

"I can't tell you that. But it will be soon. Trust me."

Kiku-chan's face clearly showed she didn't trust anyone.

"Why don't you try to sleep?" Kaze suggested. "Perhaps something will happen tomorrow."

With a knowing look, the little girl stood up and started removing her fancy kimono. "Keep your inner kimono on," Kaze said. Kiku-chan looked puzzled, but did as she was ordered. When she was done removing the elaborate obi, the fancy kimono, and the decorative pins from her hair, Kaze said, "Now sleep. Don't worry. No one is going to touch or harm you tonight."

Like an automaton, the young girl got under the futon cover, with her head on the small wooden pillow-block that was placed next to a full-sized, adult pillow block. Kaze could see a tension in her neck and shoulders, and from her breathing he could tell she was not really asleep. He wondered if she expected him to fondle and molest her in her sleep, and also wondered what manner of man would do such a thing. Eventually, as Kaze stood vigil watching her, Kiku-chan's breathing became more regular, and the child finally fell into slumber.

Once, during the night, the child woke with a cry, her arms flailing, as if she were trying to beat someone back. Kaze, who had not slept, decided it would be best for him to stay where he was and not to try to touch or comfort her. She sat up and looked around, and upon seeing Kaze, fear briefly flashed across her face, until she remembered who he was. Then she regained her icy composure. Without a word, she lay down and closed her eyes again.

In the morning, the child awoke and sat up, looking at Kaze again with those wide, distrustful eyes. In his years of wandering, Kaze had concentrated his thoughts on his search for the child. He had not given consideration to what would happen when he found her. Partly this was because he was not sure he would find her. He could easily imagine wandering the length and breadth of Japan without finding her, until he became too enfeebled by age or he was killed. Partly it was because it was simply not in his nature to worry about endless possibilities that might not come to pass. He did think about future strategy, but in the context of a warrior planning a campaign, not as a man enumerating the possibilities of the future. Now that he had found the child, Kaze realized that the unfolding possibilities of the future could become a reality, and he would have to cope with the novel burden of protecting and healing a damaged child.

The sound of footsteps came from the veranda, and Kaze moved to the futon and messed up his side, so it would look like he slept there. There was a discreet call from the door, "*Sumimasen! Ohayo gozaimasu!* Good morning! Can we enter?"

"Come," Kaze said.

Jitotenno and a maid were at the door. The maid was holding a tray with a hearty breakfast on it; miso soup, rice, and a small grilled fish.

"I hope you had a marvelous night," Jitotenno said.

"It was very satisfactory," Kaze replied.

"Excellent," Jitotenno said. "The maid will serve you breakfast. I will take Kiku-chan now, then return when your breakfast is over."

Kaze looked at the Lady's daughter, loath to let her disappear from his sight now that he had finally found her. Jitotenno interpreted this look as one a lover might give to a paramour, and took Kiku-chan by the hand and led her out of the room. Kaze sat down and ate the breakfast, thoughtfully considering what would happen next.

After he was done, Jitotenno returned to the room and announced, "Now, if the esteemed guest would like to settle the bill . . ."

"Of course," Kaze said, handing Jitotenno a cloth pouch of coins.

Jitotenno took the money with a bow and left the room. Kaze did not get up to go. In minutes, Jitotenno returned to the room, a dark cloud across her painted face.

"There must be some mistake," she said. "Most of the coins in this pouch are copper. There are only three gold coins. You said you would pay double for Kiku-chan's services, and the money in this pouch doesn't even cover her regular fee."

"I'm very sorry," Kaze said. "That is all the money I have."

"Come in here," Jitotenno said. Two thugs entered the room. They were muscular and evil looking.

"Beat this dog," Jitotenno said sharply. "And when you're done beating him, throw him out into the street. If he ever returns here, kill him."

She left as the two thugs commenced to kick and hit Kaze. Kaze protected his face, but made no effort to defend himself. The thugs were strong but not very skilled, and Kaze knew he would come out of this with no more than bad bruises, so he simply sat on the mat and endured a beating he knew he could stop, even without his sword.

When the thugs finally tired of punching and kicking him, they yanked Kaze to his feet and dragged him from the room to the front of the house. They continued dragging him right out into the street, administering another round of kicks and punches while shopkeepers and people walking on the street stopped to watch the show. When they were done, the thugs looked at the gathered crowd and announced, "This man didn't have enough to pay his bill!" They walked back into the Little Flower, one thug pausing to pick up Kaze's sandals and throw them out the door. They hit Kaze as he picked himself off the dusty street.

Kaze put on his sandals and a large crowd milled about, waiting to see if there was going to be more entertainment. When he was ready to go, Kaze stood and said in a loud voice, "Despite this rude parting, I thank Jitotenno for her hospitality! It was useful to a man in my circumstances, even if she threw me out when my money ran dry!"

Then he pushed his way through the crowd and started walking away. Near the edge of the crowd, he stopped to adjust his sandals. As he did so, he spoke to the large man standing in the doorway of a shop. It was Nobu.

"The child is there. Her name is Kiku-chan."

Then Kaze continued walking, trying to work out the soreness he felt from the beating.

I should be put in charge!" Honda was never one to mince words. Ieyasu, Okubo, Toyama, Honda, and Yoshida were in council again, to hear a progress report on the search for the man who had tried to assassinate Ieyasu.

"Yoshida-san has tried to find one man for days, with no success. He even searched the entire Ningyo-cho district, using hundreds of men, with no success. That very next morning, five ninja were found dead in Ningyo-cho, proving the assassin must have a large gang there, but Yoshida-san couldn't discover them. No one man could kill five ninja. It's time to let someone else try. As long as that man is free, Ieyasu is in danger. Yoshida-san tried. He failed. Now let me do it, Ieyasu-sama."

Before Ieyasu could make a decision, Niiya appeared in the doorway of the room, bowing on one knee, in proper military fashion. Ieyasu looked surprised.

"This man is Niiya," Yoshida said. "He is my chief captain. What is it, Niiya?"

"I beg forgiveness for interrupting such an important conference," Niiya said, "but I have a report that I know you will want to hear immediately. The ronin, Matsuyama Kaze, has been spotted. We know where he's been hiding!"

"Where?" Yoshida asked, excited.

"In Ningyo-cho, as you suspected, Yoshida-sama," Niiya said. Yoshida gave Honda a look of triumph.

"The dog was in hiding in a whorehouse that specializes in providing children."

"A pervert as well as an assassin," Honda grumped.

"Evidently he ran out of money, so they threw him out this morning," Niiya continued. "We have already closed down the whorehouse and arrested everyone in it."

"Good, good! Ieyasu-sama, please excuse me. I would like to go see abut this development, and personally supervise as we question the inhabitants of the whorehouse."

Ieyasu waved his hand, dismissing Yoshida. He and Niiya left the room. As they walked down the halls of the Shogun's villa, Niiya said, "I'm sorry for interrupting you, Yoshida-sama."

"It couldn't be better timed. Honda was about to take over the investigation. After all our careful planning, it would be a shame if that old dog snatched the victory from us at the last moment. Okubo is remaining strangely silent on this, especially since he has a personal grudge against this Matsuyama, and Toyama is a fool. Only Honda is a threat to make me look bad in this, especially since we're so close to capturing this Matsuyama. When did he leave the whorehouse?"

"This morning. The fools in the whorehouse made a spectacle of throwing him out. Countless people saw it, and all confirm that the man matched the description of Matsuyama."

"How did you find out about it?"

"One of our informers told me. A gambler. He used to work for the gambler that told us that Matsuyama was staying at that vegetable merchant's house. His boss had an accident, so he's taken over the gang. He wants to get back into good standing so we'll leave his gambling house alone."

"What do the people at the whorehouse say?"

"They claim that Matsuyama was only a guest for one night, and that he didn't pay his bill, which is why they beat him up and threw him out."

"Do you believe them?"

"No. Matsuyama has been hiding for days. He needs a place to hide in the city, and that whorehouse would be perfect."

"Have you started torturing them yet, to see if they change their story?"

"No, Yoshida-sama. I thought I'd wait for you."

"Good. I'll make those dogs tell me the truth, or kill them in the process. I must find that Matsuyama, or Honda will end up as the most important daimyo in Ieyasu's new government!"

I thought I'd save you a walk."

Nobu started, then spun around to see a komuso walking just behind him, the basketlike headgear just inches from his face. The komuso lifted the basket to reveal his face. It was Kaze.

"You! You're always sneaking around to surprise me. Why do you do that?" Nobu demanded.

Kaze grinned. "Gomen nasai. I'm sorry. I was born in the year of the Monkey, and liking mischief is a fault of mine. I even enjoy sitting in trees. I can't help it. I also enjoy seeing you jump. It's amazing to see a man as big as you who is also light on his feet." He dropped the basket back into place to mask his face.

Kaze looked at the small figure walking next to Nobu. She had on a bright blue kimono, although her hair was a bit disheveled, because no one had prepared it that morning.

"Hello, Kiku-chan. I said I would get you out of that place."

Kiku-chan viewed the strange figure with suspicious eyes and gave no greeting.

"I thought we were going to meet at the temple?" Nobu said.

"Yes. As I said, I thought I'd save you some walking." By meeting Nobu unexpectedly on the route to the temple, Kaze also thought it would make it harder for Nobu to spring an ambush, just in case the lure of the reward on his head was too great.

"As you can see, here she is."

"Good. Did you have any trouble?"

"No. Yoshida's men were so happy to get the report that you were at the Little Flower that they would have given me all the children, if I had asked. They were happy to hand Kiku-chan over to me. Now they probably think that I'm a pervert," Nobu sniffed.

"And the other children?"

"They've been given to monasteries and nunneries to raise. They'll be safe enough there."

"And the rest?"

"Well, they let the servants go, but Jitotenno and her thugs are going to have a hard time of it. They'll be lucky if they escape with their lives."

Kaze nodded his satisfaction. Everything had worked out exactly as he had planned, including the rescue of all the children from the whorehouse. "Then I suppose this ends our business, Boss Nobu."

Nobu scratched his head with a large hand. "I suppose so. You're a devil and a troublemaker, but somehow I think I'll miss you. If you manage to survive and ever get back to Edo, come say hello. We'll drink together."

"I'll do that. Now that I've got Kiku-chan, I intend to take steps to see I'm not as hunted as I am now. I don't mind it, but it will make it hard for me to find a suitable home for Kiku-chan if every Tokugawa samurai thinks my head is worth ten thousand ryo."

"What do you intend to do?"

"You know that information you got for me?"

"The question I asked the guard captain?"

"Yes."

"How will that help you? I just thought you were curious."

"I am curious, but that's not the reason I wanted to know."

"You can't mean that he's involved in the attempt to assassinate Ieyasu-sama!"

"No, he wasn't involved in an attempt to kill the Shogun."

"But—"

Kaze took Kiku-chan's hand and started walking down the street, leaving a puzzled Nobu looking after him. Nobu shouted, "You are a devil! Now I'll be puzzling about what you meant all day!"

Kaze looked over his shoulder, lifted the komuso headgear, and gave the big man a grin.

As they walked together, Kaze, who was used to years of walking roads alone, made no attempt to make conversation with the child. Kiku-chan wore the tall, black lacquered geta that were favored by courtesans and prostitutes, so she almost came up to Kaze's shoulder. She watched the ronin warily as they made their way through the crooked streets of Edo, which were not laid out on a grid, Chinese style, like Kyoto. The twisting streets were designed to confuse invaders, making assaults on Edo Castle, found in the heart of the city, difficult.

Even though the streets were confusing, Kiku-chan slowly understood where the strange man was taking her. Suddenly, Kiku-chan slipped out of the stiltlike geta and started running. Without a second's hesitation, Kaze pursued her, shouting, "Kiku-chan! What's the matter? Come back!"

The young girl didn't heed the words of the man. Instead, she used her small body to slip past people on the street, weaving between pedestrians as she gradually pulled farther and farther away. Kiku-chan had learned that the words of men were not to be trusted. Even when they spoke honeyed phrases, they eventually ended up hurting you and using you for their pleasure.

She risked a quick glance over her shoulder, but the man was nowhere to be seen. She didn't slacken her pace until she had run past several streets. Then she stopped and looked behind her, searching the crowded streets of Edo to see if the man was approaching.

"Why did you run?"

Kiku-chan spun around and saw the man with the basket mask was right behind her. The big man had called him a devil. Maybe he was. She started to run again, but his hand quickly reached out and held her arm. It was a gentle grip, but one that would not be broken, no matter how much Kiku-chan twisted or struggled.

"Why did you run?" he asked again.

"You're taking me back there!" she spit out.

Kaze looked at her kindly, although he realized she couldn't see his expression with the komuso headgear on. It was impossible to imagine what kind of life she had led for the last few years. She had been the pampered plaything of sick men, given fine clothes and then abused. It was good she still had the spirit to run away. It showed she had not been completely broken.

"We are going to Ningyo-cho, but not to the Little Flower. We're going to a place near it, where you can be safe. I have other business to take care of in Edo, but I can't do it until I know you will be properly cared for, if I'm not in a position to help you. You know, a few nights ago I was in the place I'm taking you to, and I could hear your flute. It was so full of sadness that I think I understand some of what you're feeling. I know it will be hard for you to trust me, but remember, I was sent by your mother. Even though she is in the next life, your mother still loves you, and she wants me to protect you. She would not send you someone you couldn't trust."

Tears filled the child's eyes. Kaze picked her up and started carrying her in his arms. In a confused blubber, Kiku-chan said, "I left my geta back there."

"I know. We'll buy you proper sandals, and clothes that aren't as fancy, but suitable for a girl of your age. Those geta were the shoes of a prostitute. You are no longer a prostitute. It's proper for us to leave those shoes behind. You are no longer part of the Little Flower. You are Kiku-chan, the daughter of my Lady, and you're safe now."

CHAPTER 21

Hate is a killer.
It kills others and our souls.
Yet, it's so human!

Is this your daughter?" Momoko was fussing over Kiku-chan,
but clearly curious about the relationship between the girl and
Kaze.

"She is my responsibility," Kaze said. "For a while, I would like
her to be your responsibility."

"Me?"

"Yes. Goro and Hanzo have good hearts, and they'll help. I
have to do something, and I want to make sure Kiku-chan will be
taken care of if I don't succeed. You are the person I can trust
with that responsibility, especially if I don't come back."

"What are you talking about? Are you going to do something
dangerous?"

Kaze smiled. "It can't be more dangerous than five ninja trying
to kill me, yet here I stand, still alive."

"It is dangerous."

"Life is dangerous. If I don't do this, then it will continue to
be more dangerous than it needs to be." Kaze took the remaining
gold he had received from Nobu out of his sleeve, gold he had

withheld from Jitotenno to provoke an incident that would get attention. He handed the coins to Momoko.

"Here," he said, "take this money and do two things. First, get Kiku-chan some different clothes: clothes suitable for a child of her age, so she doesn't look like she's going to a bawdy house. Next, rent me a horse."

"A horse?"

"Yes. Make sure I can get it at any hour of the day or night, and make sure it's at a stable on the west side of Edo Castle."

Momoko looked at the gold coins. "This is more than it will take to do that. What do you want me to do with the rest?"

Kaze looked at her strangely, and Momoko realized that a samurai rarely concerned himself with money. He let his wife do that. By giving her his money, Kaze was extending a kind of intimacy to her. She blushed.

"Keep the money," he said patiently. "If I don't come back, you will need the money for Kiku-chan. If I do come back, you can use the money to help the theater and Goro and Hanzo. Just don't tell them you have it, and don't tell them who gave it to you. The last time I gave them money, they were banging their heads on the ground with bows of gratitude. It was disgusting. I don't want to see that again."

"But Goro and Hanzo won't need the money. The theater is doing better, thanks to you."

"Oh?"

"Yes. The actors are using the wild makeup, like you did, and the people love it. We can't show passion on the stage, but we can talk about it, and women seem to like that even better than showing it. I've also had the idea that we should include sword fights in our plays, after seeing you with the ninja. I'm sure that will be popular, too! Here. Take the money back. You'll need it."

Kaze frowned. Momoko knew she was spoiling the moment,

and she cursed her inability to really understand how the samurai mind worked. Talking to a samurai like Matsuyama-san about money was very bad manners, especially after he had entrusted you with handling his money for him.

"Sumimasen. I'm sorry," she said, with a deep bow. "I'll get the clothes and arrange for the horse."

Kaze sat in the valley where two roofs came together, hidden from the ground but still able to watch the temple. He had been watching for a day and a night and a second day, only leaving briefly to answer calls of nature or to take a drink from the communal well, late at night when he wouldn't be seen. He had a small store of toasted rice cakes he brought with him, the kind of rations he might have on a hard military campaign.

As in a military campaign, Kaze didn't consider waiting as wasted time. Every warrior knew how to act, but the good ones also knew how to wait. Timing in a campaign, battle, or fight was crucial. Action and waiting were a natural balance, like breathing in and breathing out. Kaze knew his waiting and watching was just the prelude to action. Of course, Kaze also knew that his waiting might be in vain. Thus it was with battle plans, where sometimes waiting came to nothing because an expected situation didn't develop.

During the first day, he saw the man he was waiting for. He was staying in the temple because of Edo's housing shortage. Kaze was able to identify him by the crest on his helmet, which Nobu had described to him. He seemed to be going about his normal duties, so Kaze had no interest in him then.

In the depth of the second night, in the early morning, at the hour of the Tiger, Kaze did have an interest in the man. His waiting paid off. He saw the man leaving the temple with two companions. They were on horseback, and what interested Kaze was that he carried a musket and he was not wearing his insignia. He and his companions were dressed as charcoal burners.

They must be going into the woods, Kaze thought, where their costumes would allow them to blend in. On the day of the attempted assassination, Kaze was sure he had worn his uniform. With so many soldiers rushing about after the shot was fired, another soldier was almost invisible in the crowd, even one carrying a musket. That's also why the yagura watchman didn't cry out when an armed man entered his watch platform. It would not be unusual for a uniformed officer to want to get a good observation perch. It's also why no one noticed him leaving the scene of the assassination attempt.

Kaze watched what direction they took leaving Edo, and quickly got off the roof and rushed to the stable where his horse was waiting.

Following people undetected on horseback was harder than following them on foot, especially since Kaze didn't want them to get too far ahead of him. But the darkness helped as they crossed the farms and villages that surrounded Edo, and by the time the dawn arrived, they were off the roads and into the woods to the northwest of Edo, where the trees could screen Kaze.

The trio proceeded into the forest, to a point where the thick groves of trees were broken up by meadows. Then they stopped, with two of them moving forward on foot while the third held the horses.

Kaze tied his own horse and circled around the man holding the horses. Moving with the silence of an experienced hunter, he crept up to the two men, who seemed to be sitting behind a large rock, waiting. Kaze sat and waited, too.

• • •

This is my favorite time, Honda." Ieyasu was anxious to get to the hunt. Behind him, several horses with packs that supported perches for birds trailed, led by the bird's trainers. They were followed by a half-dozen mounted bodyguards.

The hawking party broke out of the forest and into a meadow. It was one of Ieyasu's favorite hawking sites, and he ordered the birds forward, so he could decide which one he wanted to fly first.

Ieyasu looked up at the blue sky. "It's a perfect day for the birds," he remarked.

"It won't be a perfect day for the prey," Honda grumped. "Today they'll die."

"To live is to die," Ieyasu said, quoting a proverb. "Besides, when you have to die, it's probably best to die on a day such as this one. When it is my time to go to the void, I wish it would be on a day just like today."

Kaze watched one of the men pop his head up over the top of the rock, and then say something to the one with the musket. The man with the gun took out his flint and steel, and set the cord on his musket burning. He was getting ready to shoot. Kaze looked in the meadow in front of the rock and saw a party out hawk hunting. He realized the two men on horseback were Ieyasu and Honda.

The man with the musket stood and started taking aim. He was using the most modern gun and technology available. Kaze chose a more ancient weapon. More ancient even than his sword. He picked up a fist-sized rock and threw it with all his strength.

The rock hit Niiya in the side of the head just as he pressed the trigger of his musket. The burning cord hit the touch hole, and the musket fired with a loud crack that shattered the silence of the meadow. Niiya collapsed, his musket ball flying harmlessly into the air.

Niiya's companion drew his sword and turned to face Kaze, just as the ronin ran from his hiding place to the rock. The man was a good swordsman but not an excellent one, and the duel was over in an instant, the man falling dead to the ground from a cut across his neck and shoulders as Kaze rushed past him.

Kaze wanted Niiya alive, and he knelt down next to the prone man, loosening the man's jacket sash and using it to tie up Niiya's hands. Across the meadow, Kaze could see Honda and Ieyasu's bodyguards springing into action, riding at full tilt toward the sound of the shot and the rock. Honda joined them, the old warrior acting instinctively to defend his Lord. It was over a hundred paces to the rock, so Kaze was able to quickly tie Niiya's hands as the samurai charged forward.

Just as Kaze was completing the knot securing Niiya, he sensed a presence behind him. Grabbing his sword, which he had laid on the ground next to him, Kaze spun halfway around while still kneeling, just in time to block a cut to his head by the man who had been holding the horses. He had come to investigate when his two companions didn't come to the horses to make their escape right after the shot was fired.

At a disadvantage because he was still in a kneeling position, Kaze blocked a second cut without having an opportunity to go on the offensive. The man was smart enough not to let up, and he drew back for a third cut before Kaze could regain his feet. A large shadow suddenly blocked out the sun, and Kaze realized that a horse was jumping over the rock, sailing over Kaze and Niiya. The body of the horse blocked Kaze's view of the blow, but as the horse hit the ground, Kaze was able to see the results. The man's head was flying through the air, cleanly taken by the horseman while still in the midst of the jump. As other horses drew up on either side of the rock, Kaze glanced at the first horseman and saw it was Honda. Honda's eyes burned with excitement, and the call to arms had stripped away years from the old warrior's face.

Honda pulled his horse around and trotted back to Kaze.

"What is the meaning of this?" he demanded.

"This is the assassin of Lord Nakamura," Kaze said, pointing to the prone Niiya, who was just beginning to regain his senses.

Honda peered at the bound figure and said, "Nonsense! That's Captain Niiya. He's in Lord Yoshida's service. I know him. It's impossible that he's the assassin." He pointed at Kaze. "Drop your sword!"

Kaze shook his head. "I'm sorry, but I don't want to do that until I have convinced you that this is the assassin."

Niiya, who was still shaky, had recovered enough to say, "He lies. He's the assassin."

Honda scowled. "Drop your sword," he growled.

"No."

"Then, by the Gods, I'll make you drop your sword or kill you in the process!"

"That wouldn't be wise."

Honda looked up. Ieyasu rode up to the tableau in time to offer advice. "I saw you take that man's head as you cleared the rock, Honda-san, so I know you've lost none of your skills, but it's foolish to fight with this man when you have six other samurai with you, especially since this is the man who won Hideyoshi's sword-fighting tournament."

Honda gave a start, and said, "I knew you were lying! You are the assassin!"

Ieyasu shook his head. "Look at the evidence before you, Honda-san. Do you see a bullet pouch on the ronin? Do you see a powder container? He's not equipped as a musketeer. More important, his weapon is the sword. I was never convinced he would suddenly change to a musket to assassinate me. Now look at Niiya. The ronin has taken off his sash to bind him, but you can clearly see the bullet pouch and powder containers lying next to him.

They were tucked into his sash. Niiya is known to be an expert with a musket. Obviously, he is the assassin."

At Ieyasu's words, Kaze returned his sword to its scabbard.

"This doesn't make sense," Honda spluttered.

"Nevertheless, it appears to be true," Ieyasu said.

"You and your master are the worst kind of traitor," Honda said to Niiya. "Trying to assassinate the Shogun is the worst crime imaginable."

Niiya said nothing, his face a stoic mask.

"With all respect, Honda-san, I think you're wrong," Kaze said.

"What are you talking about? You caught him in the very act of trying to kill Ieyasu-sama."

"No. I think he was trying to kill you."

"Me!" Honda exclaimed. "What possible reason would he have for wanting to kill me?"

"The same reason he had for killing Nakamura-san," Kaze said.

"This is ridiculous," Honda replied. He looked at Ieyasu. "This man must have gone mad."

Ieyasu said nothing, studying Kaze intently.

Kaze thought he was being dissected by those eyes. Every portion of his character was being divided into manageable parts, examined, and then put back together so Ieyasu could have a complete catalog of his soul. Ieyasu's ability to read and manipulate people was the foundation of success for what was otherwise a very ordinary man.

"I know what you're saying," Ieyasu said. "But how can such a thing be proved?"

"Niiya is the finest shot in Japan. I was being chased across the roofs of Edo, and he took a shot at me. He hit my kimono sleeve when no one else could possibly do so. I asked who was in charge of the party pursuing me when that shot was taken. I knew that shot was made by the man in charge, and that man could hit whatever he wanted to. Once the thought occurred to me that you were not the actual target, Ieyasu-sama, I realized that it was the marksman, not the gun, who was the link to the real assassins. At that distance, any man could miss you and hit Nakamura-san by mistake. It would require an extraordinary marksman to ensure he would not hit you, but still kill Nakamura-san, who was standing next to you," Kaze said. "Niiya is that man. If you'll allow me to do a demonstration with him, I can prove it."

"Demonstration! What kind of demonstration?" Honda demanded. "You surely don't intend to give this man his musket?"

Kaze said nothing, looking to Ieyasu to await his decision.

Finally, Ieyasu said, "Go ahead. If it is true that they are not trying to kill me, then I may be more merciful to Yoshida's clan. Otherwise, I'll kill them all—men, women, children, and babies. They'll all die."

Kaze looked at Niiya. "Your master tried to reach for the stars. He has failed. Regardless of the result of our demonstration, he will go to the great void and so will you. But with your skill, you have an opportunity to save the lives of the others in your clan. Perhaps your own family. This is your one chance."

Niiya remained impassive. Kaze untied Niiya's hands. Then he grabbed the pouch with the musket balls from the ground. He reached in the pouch and took out one musket ball. He held it up to Niiya. After a second, Niiya reached out and took the ball, then picked up the gunpowder container.

"Good," Kaze said. Kaze went to retrieve Niiya's musket. From the workmanship, he immediately recognized it as an Inatomi musket. As he handed it back to Niiya, he said, "Do you have a flint and steel to start the fuse burning? It's gone out."

Niiya nodded.

Kaze started walking away from Niiya, pacing off 140 paces, the approximate distance of Niiya's first shot at the castle wall. When he had reached the required distance, he looked around and saw a wild persimmon tree, its fruit past its prime but still a fiery orange. He walked over and picked one, then returned to his position.

Ieyasu, Honda, and the rest had dismounted to watch the exhibition. Kaze could see that Niiya had already used his flint and steel to get the fuse burning on the matchlock. Then Niiya loaded the matchlock with gunpowder and the musket ball given to him.

"I think Honda-san should stand away from Niiya-san, just in case Niiya-san decides that he'd rather finish his mission than exhibit his skills," Kaze shouted.

"This is ridiculous," Honda said. "I won't stand aside."

"Ieyasu-sama, please order him," Kaze shouted, when he saw that Honda was going to be stubborn.

"Stand aside," Ieyasu said. He did not raise his voice, but the tone of command was clear and overwhelming.

Honda gave a short bow and stepped to the side of Niiya, so Niiya couldn't train his gun on him unless he made a complete turn. Kaze took the persimmon and held it up in the palm of his hand, just a hand-span away from his head. Niiya looked at Kaze and then raised the musket up to his shoulder, taking careful aim. Kaze saw the barrel of the gun move almost imperceptibly toward him.

"This is the only chance you have to exhibit your skills in front of Ieyasu-sama," Kaze shouted to Niiya. "I can understand the urge for revenge, but surely you want Ieyasu-sama to know what a fantastic marksman you are. More important, by killing me, you will be killing the rest of your clan."

Niiya put the gun down and wiped his palm on the side of his kimono; then he touched the side of his face where the rock had hit. Then he put the gun back up to his shoulder and in one smooth motion, trained the gun, took aim, and fired. The crack of the musket filled the quiet forest air. Three birds flew out of a tree at the report of the gun. Kaze felt the persimmon in his palm explode as the lead ball hit it.

Involuntarily, Honda exclaimed, "Incredible! That's the finest shot I've ever seen." Kaze shook the persimmon pulp from his hand, and simply said, "Messy."

Niiya showed no pleasure or satisfaction at his accomplishment. He simply put his musket down and waited as Kaze walked back to the group.

Niiya turned to Ieyasu and dropped to both knees. "Would you accept my gun, Ieyasu-sama? It is a superb weapon, one of the last that Inatomi-sensei made, and one of his finest. I am sorry that I had to kill Inatomi-sensei and his household. The men that Matsuyama-san and Honda-san killed were the ones who helped me. Yoshida-san sent us ahead of him, before he arrived with the official party, to eliminate any possible link between Inatomi-sensei and us. That killing is the one thing I regret about this affair, but that regret doesn't diminish the craftsmanship of this musket. I would not like to think of it falling into hands that would not appreciate it."

Ieyasu nodded and signaled for one of his guards to step forward and take the gun out of Niiya's hands.

Honda said, "I don't understand this. What is going on? What was that demonstration supposed to prove?"

"It proves, Honda-san," Ieyasu said quietly, "that I was not the target for the first assassination attempt. It was not the case of the assassin missing me and hitting Nakamura-san by mistake. This man hit exactly whom he intended to hit, just as he would have killed you, if the ronin had not interfered."

"Why would Yoshida-san want to kill Nakamura-san and me?" Honda said. "I don't understand it."

"Because Yoshida-san understood he could not become Shogun, at least right now, even if I died. With you gone and Nakamura-san gone, there would be no other rivals for the top spot in my government. Yoshida-san would be in a position of trust, a position that would allow him to gather power over the years. When it was my time to pass into another existence, he might be strong enough to depose my son Hidetada and become the next Shogun. Even if he couldn't do that, he would have a secure and respected position in the government and would surely prosper from it in the years to come. It's a time-honored tactic for the number-two man to try and become number one when the opportunity presents itself."

Kaze looked at Ieyasu and thought, That's exactly what Ieyasu did when Hideyoshi died.

Ieyasu turned to Kaze. "What is it you call yourself now?" he asked.

"Matsuyama Kaze."

"Well, Matsuyama-san, I owe you a debt. I can only imagine what you must have suffered. But I will restore your name and family, and also restore to you the fief that once was your Lord's. Okubo-san is administering it now, but that's only because he was able to conquer it, not because it was awarded to him. I need men like you to help create a new Japan. Perhaps there will also be a place for you in my new government."

Kaze bowed to show that he was grateful for Ieyasu's offer. "I'm sorry, Ieyasu-sama," Kaze said. "That's not the reward I want."

Okubo arrived with a small escort, galloping across the field to the edge of the woods where Ieyasu and his party were waiting. The sudden summons to meet with Ieyasu had come as a surprise to Okubo, and he had no idea why the new Shogun wanted to see him.

Despite his injured leg, Okubo was able to jump out of his saddle in smart fashion, limping forward to the Shogun and dropping to one knee. "You asked for me, Ieyasu-sama?" he asked.

"Good. Did you bring your weapon?" Ieyasu asked.

"Yes, Ieyasu-sama. My daito is strapped to my horse."

"But no armor?"

Okubo struck his chest, to show he had no chain mail under his kimono. "None, Ieyasu-sama."

"I know this was an unusual request," Ieyasu said.

"I live to obey," Okubo responded.

Ieyasu looked at the daimyo impassively, then said, "Take your weapon and go into those woods. In a short distance, you will find a meadow. In the meadow is an old acquaintance."

Okubo looked up in surprise. "Could you tell me what this is about, Ieyasu-sama? Who is this acquaintance you mentioned?"

"All will be explained when you get to the meadow."

Puzzled, Okubo got up and walked to his horse. He drew the long sword, the daito, from its scabbard. Holding the weapon at the ready, he started walking toward the woods, with his escort following.

"Have your samurai wait here," Ieyasu ordered.

Okubo licked his lips, disquieted by the Shogun's strange orders, but he motioned with his hand for his escort to wait. Okubo's samurai looked at each other, perhaps thinking they should disobey the order and not allow their Lord to go unescorted into the woods. They had seen many examples of Okubo's wrath at not being obeyed, however, and so the samurai stood around, looking alternately at the impassive Shogun and the back of their Lord, retreating into the woods.

Okubo made his way between the trees gingerly. His damaged leg was a hindrance, but he had worked hard at compensating for it through the use of the especially long daito, so he was confident that he was able to handle anyone, or anything, that was waiting for him.

In a few minutes, he found the meadow Ieyasu had mentioned, but found it empty. The sun was high in the sky, and it turned the grass of the meadow a soft golden-green. Okubo walked into the meadow a few feet, then stopped to look around.

"I'm here," a voice said softly from behind him.

Okubo spun around and looked up. He saw a man sitting on a tree limb above his head. He was sitting in the lotus position, an unsheathed sword lying across his knees.

"You!" Okubo's face changed from surprise to hate with the quickness of a summer storm. "I've waited a long time for this!"

"As have I," Kaze said. "And this time your chamberlain isn't here to try to bribe me."

"What do you mean?"

"You don't know?"

Okubo smiled. "Why don't you tell me?"

"The night before the final match of Hideyoshi-sama's sword tournament, the chamberlain of your clan visited me. He promised me that the valley between our two clans, the one your father was always fighting over, would be ceded to our clan if I let you win. It was a devil of an offer, because your chamberlain knew that an offer to enrich me would have no meaning, but an offer to help my clan would tear at my loyalties. Later my Lord came to wish me luck, and he saw I was troubled. When he heard your clan's chamberlain visited me, he didn't ask me the details, he just said to follow the path of honor."

"Honor! You should have taken the offer. It's the way of the world to take the path of advantage. You're a bigger fool than I thought. No matter. I've been training for this moment for years. I expected to meet you under different circumstances, but I will defeat you this time. I'm astounded that Ieyasu-sama arranged this."

"If it makes you feel any better, Ieyasu-sama has a little incentive for you if you're the one who walks out of these woods alive."

At Okubo's puzzled face, Kaze continued. "Ieyasu-sama will give you my old Lord's domains permanently if you are victorious. Currently you only manage them, until Ieyasu-sama decides what to do with them. If you live, he will make them part of your hereditary possessions. I heard him tell Honda-san that to placate him, when Honda-san raised a fuss about letting me have this confrontation with you as a reward."

"Then I'll have a double pleasure at killing you," Okubo said. "My leg is a constant reminder of my hatred of you, and being able to permanently treat your clan the way I want will make things all the sweeter."

Suddenly, Okubo stepped forward and took a vicious overhead cut at Kaze, sitting on the branch. Kaze rolled backward on the limb, grabbing his sword and flipping over in the air, landing on his feet with his sword at the ready as Okubo's daito sliced completely through the limb he was sitting on.

Kaze moved forward to the attack, but Okubo's daito was already in the aimed-at-the-eye position, the extreme length of the blade keeping Kaze at bay. Okubo retreated into the meadow, where he would have free room to maneuver his long sword. As he moved, Okubo talked.

"Have you visited your old home lately?" he asked. "As you know, I am renowned for my strictness as a leader. Your previous lord was such a weakling, he didn't even have pots for boiling criminals in his domain. I've certainly fixed that, and in the few years I've been controlling your old home, I have used them frequently. In fact, your old clansmen have a new saying. They say the fires of their miserable life are hotter than the fires of hell. I hear they call me *Oni Okubo*, the Devil Okubo. That's quite a compliment, don't you think?"

Kaze's face flushed from anger. "You were always good at cruelty," he replied. "It's not something that most men would be proud of."

"On the contrary. I have always been good at pleasure. At least at the things that give me pleasure. Do you know that I had both your Lady and her daughter? I was the first man to enjoy the Lady's pleasures besides her husband, although I did let several of my officers indulge themselves with her after I was done. I also took the virginity of her daughter. I think she was six or seven at the time and raised an awful fuss until I beat her quite senseless. I can't say which I enjoyed more, the mother or the daughter. They each had their special charms."

Making a low cry from his gut, Kaze attacked Okubo, slashing furiously at him. Okubo easily parried Kaze's blows with his long sword. Then, almost as if he was playing with Kaze, he stepped forward into a quick counterattack that drove Kaze back. Kaze parried the blows from the long sword. He was intent on pressing his attack to kill Okubo, but his anger confused his sword sense, making his parries seem mechanical and ponderously slow.

A bad block to one of Okubo's cuts left a deep gash on his forearm, sending a tingling sensation up his arm that spelled a weakening of his use of the arm. For some reason, the skills of a lifetime seemed to desert him when he wanted them most.

"Ah, first blood," Okubo said. "This is a Masamune blade. They're forbidden by Ieyasu-sama, but I don't know why. This one has a special thirst for blood, and seems to seek it every time I draw it. I intend to sate it today, feasting on your blood. You know, you're not really as strong a swordsman as I remembered you. I think in the ten years since we met my skills have increased and yours have declined. In a way, giving me this limp was almost a blessing. It forced me to take up the daito." He made a quick slash with the long sword, creating a vicious *swoosh* as the blade cut through the air at high speed. "With this blade I control twice the area that you can with your katana. It's easy when I can keep a safe distance from you while still threatening you with my blade."

Okubo illustrated his point by stepping forward to attack again. Kaze was driven back. Okubo laughed. "See! Your puny sword is no match for my daito."

Kaze looked down and saw the blood dripping off his arm. He

then looked at the long expanse of Okubo's sword blade, twice as long as his own katana. The daito was gleaming dully and malevolently, even in the bright sunshine; truly a Masamune blade. Kaze's own blade shone brightly and cleanly, but it was far from being close enough to deliver a cut, much less a mortal blow, to Okubo.

Until you defeat yourself, you cannot defeat others.

The words of Kaze's Sensei came to him. It was true that Okubo's long sword gave him superior reach, but, digging deep into his spirit, Kaze knew the reason he was being defeated was not because of superior weaponry. Kaze was being defeated because of a lack of character.

He was attacking Okubo with rage and hate in his heart; two emotions that inevitably destroy the man who holds them. He was letting his anger control his blade and he was letting his hatred control his ability to fight. The result was that he was not using his skills the way he was taught. He could use those skills as an instrument of rage and hatred, or he could use them as an instrument of justice.

For all the wrongs that Okubo had inflicted upon the Lady, the Lady's child, Kaze, Kaze's clan, his own clan, and numerous other victims, Okubo deserved the harsh hand of justice. Okubo was evil. Undoubtedly, the greatest evil embodied in a single man that Kaze had ever come across. But to destroy him, Kaze had to use his sense of righteousness and skills as a swordsman, instead of his rage and anger as one of Okubo's victims.

He stepped back two or three paces, watching Okubo carefully, but lowering his sword to the aimed-at-the-knee position. He took a deep breath and slowly let it exhale, trying to vent the rage within his body with the escaping air. "I am the sword of righteousness. I am the blade of justice," Kaze said in a low voice.

"What are you saying, fool?" Okubo asked, unable to hear Kaze's words. "Don't think that you're going to escape. I've been waiting for this for a long time. For all the hours in the dojo that I trained, I motivated myself by always having your face before me. That's why my skills with the long sword have grown so magnificently. I had a good motivator. My hatred for you. Now, by the gift of the Gods and the machinations of Ieyasu, I will finally be able to satisfy this hatred and kill you. I only pray that I don't have to kill you all at once. That I can cut at you, just as I've damaged your arm, and slowly slice you into pieces, savoring each moment.

"I'm going to tell you something," Okubo said. "I will have a great victory banquet that will celebrate the complete and final destruction of you, your clan, your Lord, your Lady, and all the people that I hate. Your head, pickled in salt, will be the centerpiece for that banquet. I'll invite all my samurai, each in turn, to relieve themselves on your face, to show the contempt I have for you. And I won't forget Ieyasu, either," Okubo said with a small smile. "As my destruction of you and your clan has shown, I'm a patient man when I need to be. I will eventually take my revenge on Ieyasu. I had hoped to work with Ieyasu and improve my position. I'll still do that. I'll also wait for any opportunity to destroy Ieyasu and his entire household."

Kaze was surprised that Okubo revealed so much of himself, but he realized that Okubo felt free to display his inner thoughts because he knew that only one of them would be alive at the end of the duel.

Kaze knew the same thing.

Unlike Okubo, however, Kaze felt no need to provoke or taunt. In fact, he was trying to do the opposite; to withdraw emotionally from the duel, to swallow his rage and achieve a state of non-mindedness, to defeat himself before he tried to defeat another. He realized that the more he wanted Okubo dead, the less likely it was that he would achieve his goal. The more he tried to control the bout, the less he was in control of himself.

Okubo stepped forward to attack once again. Kaze planted his feet, feeling the strength flow into him from the earth. Automatically, Kaze's blade flew to the right position to block Okubo's daito, the slim sliver of steel moving almost of its own accord, without Kaze having to consciously direct it.

When Kaze didn't give ground, Okubo stepped back. He had a look of concern on his face, wondering what sudden change had occurred so that the techniques and tactics he had used successfully just moments before were now neutralized.

"I am the sword of righteousness. I am the blade of justice," Kaze said to himself. Over and over like a mantra. The sword of righteousness and the blade of justice.

With his blade at the aimed-at-the-knee position, Kaze twisted his sword until the shiny surface caught the sun's rays, bouncing a shaft of light upward and into Okubo's face. Okubo blinked at the flash of light hitting his eyes, and Kaze stepped forward, putting himself inside the arc of Okubo's blade. He was putting himself into the reach of death, but it was the only way to get close enough to deliver a cut at Okubo.

Okubo slashed downward at Kaze, intending to cleave him in two. With Okubo slightly off balance from the blinding light, Kaze was able to move to one side. He felt Okubo's blade swing past his face and come close to his shoulder. The deadly edge of the blade slightly brushed the cloth of his kimono, and he actually felt the wind generated by the moving sword slide down his arm.

Once Kaze was safely inside the arc of Okubo's blade, the long sword turned from an asset into a liability. Although it had greater reach, it was not as nimble as a standard katana. Without Kaze's thinking, without his planning the blow, his blade came across horizontally and transversely sliced Okubo's stomach, just like the cut made during seppuku. Okubo gave a cry of pain and looked down to see his entrails bursting forth from the wound. He gave a moan and reached out with one hand to hold his guts in.

Holding his long sword with the other hand, he took an inef-fectual slice at Kaze, one Kaze easily blocked. Kaze stood back and assured himself that the cut he delivered was mortal. He looked at Okubo's face and saw pain and fear painted across it. He should have stepped forward to deliver a blow to Okubo's neck, taking his head and putting Okubo out of his misery. Instead, Kaze turned on his heel and started walking out of the grove. Behind him, he heard Okubo give a gasp of pain. Kaze looked over his shoulder and saw Okubo take two staggering steps, and then crumple to the ground, like a rotting leaf falling off a branch. Lying on the ground, Okubo looked up and his tearful eyes caught Kaze's for a brief instant.

"I'll see you at the gates of hell," Okubo said, before the pain caused him to suck in his breath sharply and say no more.

"Perhaps," Kaze answered. "I've killed too many men not to make hell a possibility. But everyone I've killed had an equal chance of killing me. More important, most that I've killed have made the world a better place by leaving it. You, on the other hand, have always sought out the weak and helpless to kill. You relished making their death as slow and painful as possible. You're one of those twisted men who take pleasure in the pain of others. If I were a truly good man, I'd come over there and take your head, putting an end to your suffering as you spill your life and guts on the ground. But, unfortunately, Okubo, I am not that good. For what you've done, it would take a Buddha to want to ease your passage into the void. For the deaths I've caused and the suffering I'm putting you through, my karma may lead me to hell. But you'll be going before me."

Kaze left the grove, leaving his enemy to die a slow and ago-nizing death. When he approached Ieyasu, the Shogun knew how the duel had gone.

"It's a pity," Ieyasu said.

Kaze wasn't quite sure what Ieyasu meant by that. Maybe he

thought it was a pity that a ronin killed a daimyo. Perhaps he thought it was a pity that it was the human condition to fight. Maybe he just thought Kaze was a fool for taking Okubo instead of the other rewards offered him.

Ieyasu didn't elaborate, and instead, seeing the wound on Kaze's arm, he ordered a retainer to bring Kaze a bandage. As the bandage was being tied, Ieyasu said conversationally, "I saw you the last time you fought Okubo at Hideyoshi's great sword exhibition. I enjoyed that. I would have liked seeing you this time, too, to see if your skills have diminished."

"You would have seen a poor exhibition," Kaze said frankly. "I let anger control my sword, not righteousness. Until righteousness controlled my sword, I was losing."

Ieyasu nodded. "Anger is an enemy."

When the bandage was tied tight, Kaze stood and gave a stiff, formal bow to the Shogun.

"Thank you for having my wound bandaged, Ieyasu-sama."

"Are you sure you won't reconsider joining me?" Ieyasu asked. "Yagyu is my fencing master, but I can always use a sharp blade like yours."

"Perhaps my blade is too sharp, Ieyasu-sama, for I find I must balance on it as best I can. I mean no disrespect, Ieyasu-sama, but if I should change my loyalty so easily, then I would surely fall off that blade, tumbling to one side or the other, and never able to get back to a state of equilibrium."

Ieyasu looked at the ronin. Matsuyama was tired from his recent bout with Okubo, but he showed modesty, restraint, and a lack of exaltation in his victory over his enemy. Ieyasu was a patient man. He would not have obtained the Shogunate if he were not. He stored away this man's face and his new name of Matsuyama Kaze, feeling that, if he remained patient, somehow in the future he might get this remarkable swordsman to serve him.

Expressing none of this, Ieyasu walked to his horse and, despite his potbelly, swung up to his saddle with the ease brought by over fifty years of riding.

"I'll take your name off the list of wanted men," Ieyasu said to Kaze. He glanced at Okubo's retainers, who were still confused about what was happening. "I can't promise that Okubo's clan or that Yoshida's clan will not want revenge for what has happened today, but I won't allow them to register an official vendetta against you." He gave a curt nod of his head and galloped off, his surprised retainers scrambling to gain their own saddles and catch up with the man who was the ruler of Japan.

CHAPTER 22

One path is finished.
Another path looms ahead.
The cycle of life.

That night Ieyasu had a Noh performance to celebrate the smashing of the assassination plot. He ate rice gruel and vegetables, as was his preference. Honda joined his master in the simple fare with relish, but Ieyasu noticed that others didn't appreciate culinary simplicity. Toyama especially curled his lip at the food served and seemed to force himself to eat it. Ieyasu had already decided that Toyama, although from an ancient family, was a fool; too much of a fool to leave in charge of such a lucrative fief. Toyama would be invited to trade his current fief for one a tenth its size on the island of Shikoku. If he didn't accept this invitation, he would then be invited to slit his belly, and acceptance of this second invitation would be mandatory. Either way, that would remove Toyama from both the capital and national life.

After several flasks of sakè, Ieyasu was in a sufficiently good mood that he decided to take a part in the *kyogen* that added buffoonish comic relief between acts of the Noh drama.

Ieyasu chose *Kane no kane,* a kyogen that revolved around the Japanese love of puns. A Lord wants to check the price of silver in the city, so he asks his bailiff to go into the city to check on the price of money *(kane)*. The bailiff confuses the Lord's desire with a curiosity about the bells *(kane)* of the city. The humor is generated as the Lord and the bailiff discuss the trip, with the resulting confusion as one is talking about money and the other is talking about bells.

Ieyasu played the part of the bailiff. As with many kyogen, this one was a bit subversive about authority, and the pompous Lord was the butt of most of the jokes, so Ieyasu selected the role that allowed him to generate most of the laughter. He was astounded when Honda offered to play the part of the Lord. Despite their decades of association, Ieyasu had never seen Honda take a part in Noh.

"This is a new talent, Honda," Ieyasu remarked.

The old warrior glowered, then almost blushed. "I've been taking lessons," he said gruffly.

"That is a surprise."

Honda, a warrior who had faced charging hordes of enemy samurai and literally laughed, actually looked at the ground in embarrassment. "I've been taking the lessons in secret," he admitted. "We're at peace. We have one big problem still to fix," he said, clearly making reference to Hideyoshi's heir, still strongly ensconced in Osaka Castle, "but until you finally decide to remove that threat, even an old warrior like me has to figure out how to fit into this new society you're building. I thought I'd start with Noh."

Ieyasu motioned Honda to join him in the kyogen. Unlike Noh, kyogen didn't use masks or elaborate costumes, so the two men just stood and took their places in the torch-lit square that formed the Noh stage. Although Honda stumbled through his lines and stage movements, Ieyasu, who was an experienced performer, still managed to evoke laughter with his antics as the bailiff.

After the kyogen was finished, the Noh proceeded. Ieyasu could have taken a role in the formal Noh, but decided he would rather pour drinks for Honda, proud that an old warhorse was willing to adapt to the new order.

On the Noh stage, the pageantry of motion was framed by the accompanying music and the sumptuous costumes, masks, and fans used by the actors. When the formal performance was over, Ieyasu decided it was time to view the heads.

Samurai brought two spike boards out and took them to Ieyasu. These were finely lacquered boards with a metal spike projecting from the center. The spike was shoved into the neck of a severed head. The samurai carried the heads with a *himogatana*, a one-piece dirk that was stuck through the topknot of the severed head, forming a convenient handle.

The heads were placed before Ieyasu, who studied them one after the other.

"This was Niiya," Ieyasu remarked. "It's interesting that his eyes are open. He was a superb shot, so I suppose it's only natural that he would want to use his keen eyes to guide him into the next life. How did he die?" Ieyasu asked the samurai who brought this head. Ieyasu knew that Niiya had been allowed to commit seppuku, so he wasn't inquiring as to the cause of Niiya's death, but Niiya's composure during the suicide.

"Very well, Ieyasu-sama. Niiya-san made two full cuts across his belly before he would allow me to cut off his head. It was a fine and courageous death."

"Such a fine shot. It's a shame he had to die." Ieyasu then turned his attention to the second head.

Yoshida's severed head looked ashen, but a smoky, sweet odor came from it.

"Did Yoshida-san waft incense smoke into his hair?" Ieyasu asked, puzzled.

"Not while we were there, Ieyasu-sama. Once he read your order to commit seppuku, he proceeded with dispatch to fulfill it."

Ieyasu nodded and remarked to the others at the banquet, "Most efficient. Here was a man whose ambition was too great, but whose skills were great, too. He conceived a very clever plot and implemented it with initial success. It's fortunate for me that Yoshida's karma was to cross that of the ronin Matsuyama Kaze. Still, Yoshida shows his foresight and efficiency, even in death. When Niiya went to assassinate Honda-san, Yoshida knew there was a possibility of failure and the disclosure of his plot. Because of that, he scented his hair with incense smoke before he knew of its failure, on the chance that this very fate would befall him. Now his head is suitably presented, and also perfumed by incense." Ieyasu looked at the assembled guests at the banquet. "This is an example of efficiency you can all learn from."

At about the time that Ieyasu was viewing the heads, Kaze and Kiku-chan were settling into the straw of a warm barn. Normally, Kaze would sleep outdoors in fair weather, but he realized that traveling with the young girl would force many changes in his lifestyle. Finding shelter at night, whenever possible, was just the first of these changes.

Kaze and the girl had started walking west on the Tokaido Road until they left the outskirts of Edo. Then, because he thought it would help him avoid any of Okubo's or Yoshida's men who might be intent on revenge for the death of their masters, he had taken a side road and walked until late at night, sharing toasted rice balls with the girl as they walked.

Kiku-chan was clearly exhausted, but she made no complaints as they walked. Each step took her farther away from the horrors of the Little Flower.

Kaze could have continued, but he perceived the girl was getting too weary, so he found an accommodating farmer who let him use his barn. Kaze and the girl settled in amid the smell of hay and animals and fell asleep almost immediately.

Kaze didn't know how long he was asleep before the Lady came to him in his dreams. This was the normal way for a Japanese to talk to the dead, so this neither disturbed nor surprised him. His previous encounters with the deceased Lady had been in the form of a faceless obake, a ghost, so this encounter seemed almost normal.

In his dream, the Lady descended from heaven with blue tendrils of clouds trailing after her. She was dressed in her most beautiful kimono, the one with the red-headed cranes flying across a silk field of gray clouds. Their majestic white wings beat the air, causing the clouds to billow about, and Kaze was not sure if the clouds were painted on the kimono or actual clouds that clung to the Lady.

Kaze bowed as the Lady drew near to him. When he straightened out, he was pleased to see that her face was as lovely and serene as he remembered, and that she was actually smiling. She was no longer faceless.

"So you know?" Kaze asked.

She nodded.

"Your daughter is with me. She . . . well, she's had a hard time of it, my Lady. I don't know what kind of life I can arrange for her. I always thought that after I found her, I would find some relative of yours who would take care of her. Perhaps I can still do that. In the meantime, she must stay with me. It is not an easy life. I am wandering constantly and don't know what dangers still wait for me. Okubo was not loved by his clan, but it will be a point of honor for his vassals to hunt me down and kill me. When my role in bringing about the downfall of Yoshida and Niiya is known, their clan will be intent on revenge, too. In addition, Lady, I don't know how to take care of a child, especially a ten-year-old girl. In my former life, I had a wife and servants to take care of children. Now I have neither and, frankly, my Lady, now that your daughter is free, I'm not sure that I am the one she should stay with."

The Lady continued looking at Kaze, a curl of amusement broadening the edges of her smile.

He sighed. "All right. I can see you're determined that the girl should stay with me. I'll do my best, my Lady, but I'm not sure my best will be the best for the girl. *Shikata ga nai.* I guess it can't be helped. But tell me, Lady, are you happy? Can I go to your funeral temple and reclaim my short sword, my wakizashi, the keeper of the samurai's honor? Is my honor mine again?"

The Lady smiled and nodded yes. Continuing to smile, her body ascended back to heaven. Kaze watched her rise into the cloudy skies, growing smaller and smaller until she disappeared entirely.

Kaze was about to drift back into a mindless sleep when suddenly he felt the Lady was next to him again. This time, however, her body was right next to his. Confused, Kaze asked the Lady, "Is there something more?"

The dream figure of the Lady looked at Kaze, but she was not smiling. Kaze didn't understand why her ghost would invade his dreams a second time in one night, and asked, "What is it you want, my Lady?"

The ghost of the Lady reached forward and pressed against Kaze's chest. He was so astounded that he flinched. Then the ghost did something that made Kaze realize he was not dreaming. She slipped her small hand inside his kimono and touched his bare flesh. No matter what feelings Kaze might have for her, the Lady was still the wife of his Lord. Even in death, Kaze could not imagine her taking such an action. His eyes snapped open and he saw that Kiku-chan was snuggled up to him, with her hand placed inside his kimono. She was awake and watching him intently, as if looking for some sign.

"What are you doing?" Kaze said, roughly grabbing her arm and jerking it away from him.

Kiku-chan looked confused and in pain. She cried, "You're hurting my arm!"

Kaze eased the grip on her arm. Kiku-chan was crying, her hot tears falling down on his kimono. Kaze hesitated a moment, then instead of shoving her away, he drew her next to him, placing his arms around her and comforting her.

"Don't cry, Kiku-chan," he said soothingly. "I know you've come from a place where you were taught to do things to please men, but those are not things I want you doing to me. There is nothing wrong with those things when they're done by men and women, but they are wrong when an adult takes advantage of a child.

"The past few years must have been like a nightmare for you. There is nothing I can do to erase those years. There is also nothing I can do to restore your former life, when you were happy with your mother and father, and living in their castle. I can only deal with here and now, and even then the present is uncertain. I don't know what the future will bring, but it's likely to involve wandering and hardship and perhaps even danger. That is our karma. But from this moment, our karmas are linked, and I will do my best to make sure you are protected and safe.

"Your mother sent me to find you. It took almost three years, and I'm sorry for every second of those years, because you had to endure many hardships. I know that. But you have to know that I will cherish and protect you, no matter what. Do you understand that? You have my sacred word on it. You do not have to do things to please me as you were taught to do in that place. Do you understand, Kiku-chan? I am here to protect you, no matter what. Your mother wanted that, and so do I."

The child looked up at Kaze. In the dim light of the barn, illuminated by moonlight filtering in through cracks in the board walls, Kaze saw confusion, uncertainty, and apprehension in the child's face. But he also saw hope.

This book is the third volume in the Samurai Mystery Trilogy. Like the other books, it can be read as a stand-alone mystery. It was my goal, however, to have these three books meld into a single narrative, if anyone should choose to read all the books in the trilogy. The action in all three books spans a relatively short period, from late summer to early fall in 1603.

Like the other volumes in the trilogy, this book sprang from an experience of mine in Japan. The first time I went to Tokyo, in the winter of 1975, the streets were teeming with *monouri*, street vendors, every evening. Alas, they seem to be disappearing now, but there are still a few hardy souls who make a living in the same way street vendors did in the Tokugawa period. I've read that there are even records of street vendors going back to the Heian period (794–1185 of the modern era).

The vendors sold all sorts of food and provided entertainment. My favorite was the roasted-sweet-potato man. I never did get the hang of eating the steaming flesh of the potato without burning myself, but it was still a great treat on a cold winter's night. Another favorite was the maker of fancy candy. He would take hot lumps of colored sugar and fashion them into dragons and unicorns. It was more show than confection, because the creations were too pretty to eat. I once even saw a kami-shibai, a paper-puppet storyteller.

During my early trips to Tokyo, the street vendors were so ubiquitous that they almost disappeared into the background. It occurred to me that a street vendor could wander the city and yet be relatively invisible. In this book, I have Kaze using that to his advantage.

In this book, I also write about Tokugawa Ieyasu. He's by far the most important figure in Japanese history, although, in my opinion, not the most fascinating. Hideyoshi, Nobunaga, Takeda Shingen, and a host of others seem more colorful than Ieyasu to me, but because they were so colorful, their dynasties either didn't last or didn't triumph. Perhaps the tortoise does beat the hare, at least when it comes to establishing governments. The Tokugawa Shogunate lasted over 250 years!

Some readers may be surprised that this book contains no reference to Yoshiwara, the famous brothel section of ancient Edo. Yoshiwara was actually established decades after 1603, and at the time of this book it was a marshy swamp. Other readers may also be surprised at the references to tobacco in the book, because Edo Japanese were (and modern Japanese still are) heavy smokers. Ieyasu hated tobacco, and like King James I of England, he tried to ban it in the first years of his reign. Also like James I, he was utterly unsuccessful.

As always, I've tried to be as accurate as my research and talents allow me to be, but my intention with this series is to entertain. I apologize to the true experts on the Edo period for any liberties I've taken to tell my story and for any inadvertent errors.

—DALE FURUTANI

Ieyasu - deep, leader
Honda - gruff, Mifune
Nakamura - calm, snake
Okubo - tall, thin voice
Nobu - big dumb wrestler
Goro - blustery, big
Hanzo - higher, simple
Yoshida - Tommy Lee Jones in Fugitive
Akinari - low, quiet, threatening